THE VILLAIN

THE VILLAIN DUOLOGY BOOK 1

VICTORIA VALE

1

Scotland, 1819

L ady Daphne Fairchild lowered her head against the rain and
spurred her mount toward her destination. Looming against
a backdrop of angry, storm-cloud-riddled sky, a huge black
shape thrust up from the summit of a steep cliff. A flash of lightning
illuminated it briefly, a menacing roar of thunder seeming to warn
her away.

Turn back, it cautioned.

I cannot, she replied.

Not after she had hastily fled London in the dead of night, with
only the clothes on her back and the meager provisions she could
carry. She'd braved ruin and scandal to come here—and now that
winds and torrential rain had lent themselves to the frigid cold, she
also risked catching her death.

Yet, nothing would stop her from reaching the summit, from
striding right up to the front door of the imposing Scottish castle and
demanding an audience with its owner. Even if it was the middle of
the night, when no decent young woman would dare pay a call upon
an unattached man. Even if she felt more than certain he would

throw her out upon her arse the moment she opened her mouth to proclaim herself a Fairchild. Even if she had risked everything, with no certainty that she would find what she'd come for.

Squinting to see through the unrelenting sheet of rain seeming to actively fight her horse's every step, she spotted the only path leading up the steep escarpment. Winding up what might be a grassy slope in the light of day, it would lead her straight into the maw of the very devil.

"Courage, Daphne," she whispered to herself as she approached the lane. "Have courage."

She craned her neck to better see her destination, but could make out no more than the enormous black silhouettes making up the famed Scottish keep.

Lightning flickered again—once, twice—followed by a roar of thunder. In the brief moment that the sky had crackled with jagged light, the devil's lair had revealed itself.

A jumbled collection of outbuildings sitting behind a stone curtain wall, and, somewhere outside her view, the palace itself.

Castle Dunnottar.

Once a well-fortified place of defense and center of political intrigue; now a legendary relic, restored to become the home of a man who lived like a king. However, the ruler of this castle was no monarch. Nor could he be likened to some gothic novel hero—despite residing in a place that would serve as the perfect backdrop for such a story.

No, this man was the thing nightmares were made of. The whisper of his name caused her heart to pound and tears to well up in her eyes.

He was a rogue. A thief. A blight upon the Earth.

A villain.

Rounding a bend in the path, she approached the curtain wall and the looming gatehouse built into it. An old iron portcullis barred anyone from entering, but as she drew near, she spied a lone man just within the stone structure.

Dismounting and grasping the reigns of her horse, she peered through the metal bars. A wooden door stood open to the gatehouse, revealing a man seated near a glowing hearth inside. She envied him the warmth of even so small a fire while her fingers had grown so stiff from the cold, she feared they would break away from her hands.

"Pardon me," she called out to be heard over the rain.

Lifting his head, the gate keeper spotted her, his eyes going wide. Daphne clung to the bars of the portcullis, tightening her grip to still her shaking hands.

"What on Earth are ya doin' out here in the dead 'o night—and in a storm, no less?" he bellowed in a rough, Scottish burr as he approached the gate.

"I've come to see Lord Hartmoor," she replied, doing her best to deepen her voice.

With her disguise of breeches, boots, and a man's coat, she hoped to pass as a male until she could obtain an audience with the master of the house.

The man wrinkled his brow, looking at her as if he thought her an escapee from Bedlam. Not altogether impossible, as only madness could have prompted her to do such a foolhardy thing. Now, here she stood with no intention of leaving until she'd gotten what she'd come for.

"Are ye daft?" he exclaimed. "'Tis the middle o' the night, and the master cannae be expectin' ye!"

"I have traveled all the way from London on horseback in this ghastly weather," she argued. "I will not be turned back now. Please … my business with the earl is most urgent."

With a shake of his head, the man waved her off as if she were some bothersome fly buzzing about his head. "Your urgent business can wait 'til tomorrow. Back down the mountain with ye."

Desperation clogged her throat as he turned away, heading back toward his little nook in the gatehouse. That was it? After she'd come all this way, some stodgy old gatekeeper would turn her away at the gate?

No … she could *not* be turned away.

"Tell him Fairchild wishes a word with him!" she cried out, not bothering to deepen her voice as she attempted to be heard over the rain.

He paused, his shoulders going rigid. Turning back to the gate, he watched her with a pensive intensity that left her shivering. As if her name had angered him somehow ... and yet, he did not shoo her away as he had before. Inclining his head, he narrowed his eyes at her.

"Fairchild, ye say?" he muttered.

Raising her chin and squaring her shoulders, she nodded. "That is correct."

Rubbing his bearded chin, the old man nodded. Without another word, he backed away from her and toward the crank that operated the portcullis. The ancient gate creaked and groaned as the chain pulled it up its shaft.

"Oh, thank you," she said as she dashed into the courtyard, pulling her mount along behind her. "Thank you so much."

"Present yerself at the front door o' the palace," he grumbled, jerking his thumb toward the large, dark building looming in the back corner of the curtain wall. "Be sure you tell 'em ye're Fairchild *afore* ye ask for your audience. You'll be taken right to him."

Daphne gave him a quizzical glance, a question burning on the tip of her tongue. Had Lord Hartmoor been expecting her? No, of course he could not have been. Perhaps he anticipated her brother, Bertram. It had been smart, then, using only her surname.

Reaching out to take her reins, the gatekeeper inclined his head toward one of the outbuildings—a stable, Daphne realized.

"I'll tend yer horse," he said.

She nodded her thanks and followed the wide path winding through the small buildings spotting the massive courtyard, her head tipped back so she could stare at the dwelling known simply as the 'palace' of Dunnottar. With rain sluicing down her face and her hands clenched into fists at her sides, she approached with sure strides, determination clenching her teeth.

A set of smooth stone steps led up to carved wooden doors which loomed up several feet taller than her. Taking them two at a time, she approached the door with her fist raised, pounding on it as hard as she could. The impact rattled along her arm, stinging her frozen, stiff hands. Yet, she persisted, pounding and pounding until, at last, one of the heavy doors swung open.

She was met by a man as large and imposing as the palace; who, despite his obvious status as the butler, appeared to have been born for a less refined position. A jagged scar ran the length of one side of his face, the rough planes as terrifying as his cold, dark eyes. His bulky body strained the seams of his black coat, and his cravat could hardly contain his thick neck.

"Whadye want?" he grumbled in a Scottish burr as thick as the gatekeeper's.

Daphne's mouth fell open, shock momentarily robbing her of words. Such an unconventional butler, this man; yet, she remained aware of the oddness of this entire situation. When he raised his eyebrows and stared at her as if she were mad, she cleared her throat.

Affecting her deep voice, she squared her shoulders. "Fairchild, here to see Lord Hartmoor."

The butler's expression morphed from one of disinterest and apathy to one of disgust. "Fairchild, is it?"

She flinched at the way he said her surname, as if uttering a foul epithet. "Yes. I must speak with His Lordship at once."

Raking her from head to toe with his hawkish gaze, he gave a curt nod and stepped aside to clear the path through the doorway. He said nothing, but she accepted the silent invitation and swept through the entrance.

The door scraped close behind her, the audible echo of it slamming into the frame resounding through her with an odd sort of finality. Her blood ran cold as she gazed about the large main hall— the stone walls hung with rich tapestries, iron candelabras holding dripping tapers, thick rugs guiding a path forward.

Here she stood, poised just within the jaws of the beast, the keep known as Dunnottar and the monster who lived in its depths. One more step, and she might find herself devoured whole, swallowed into its belly and left to languish until it had digested her with excruciating slowness. But she'd come here willingly and could only pray that she'd emerge as whole as she'd entered.

"Follow me," the butler said, his tone clipped as he breezed past her and through the main hall.

Daphne struggled to keep up with his long strides as he led her down an endless corridor with no thought to her shorter legs. Her gaze barely registered her surroundings as she followed him, her feet falling silently on the thick runners carpeting the hallway, the flicking flames of candles in sconces making shadows dance across pieces of art in gilded frames. The evidence of Hartmoor's wealth made itself apparent in every object her gaze fell upon—the expensive Aubusson rugs, the paintings commissioned by well-known artists, the wood paneling covering walls that had once been made of stone. The elements of the old medieval keep that had been allowed to remain melded well with the new, creating an intriguing medley of past and present.

Despite the urgency of her mission and the anger simmering in her belly at the man who owned it all, she could not help but grudgingly admit the parts of Dunnottar she'd seen left her intrigued. Laid out in a quadrangle, the palace boasted large wings filled with rooms, the contents of which she could only guess at. Rumors of secret passages and underground tunnels always came with stories of the place where battles had been fought and monarchs had hidden in the midst of rebellion. Were it not for her urgent business, she might allow herself to imagine what she would find if allowed to wander at will.

"Wait here," the butler said abruptly, coming to a stop before one of many doors.

Opening it, he allowed her only a brief glimpse of what appeared to be a study before slamming the panel unceremoniously in her face. The low rumble of male voices filtered into the corridor beneath the crack in the door, but she could not distinguish one from the other. She stood staring at the heavy wood for what felt like an eternity before it opened again, and the butler reappeared, filling the entire frame with his bulk.

"The Master will see you now," he rumbled in his ominous voice.

The Master. Not 'His Lordship,' or 'Lord Hartmoor,' but 'The Master.' Yes, she could imagine that a man who owned one of the country's most treasured castles would wish to be referred to as the master of said domain. And in Scotland, she did believe that lords were often referred to in this way. Still, the reference sent another shiver through her. Lord Hartmoor was the master of this palace, of everything within the stone curtain wall she'd just passed through, and of everyone who lived within these premises. Now that she had passed through that portcullis and entered the jaws of the palace, did that make him her master, too?

Brushing past her, the butler jolted her out of her thoughts, retreating back the way they'd come, the dark shadows of the corridor eventually swallowing him out of sight.

Daphne stared through the open doorway, finding more thick rugs laid upon the floor and the flicker of flames cast against the walls. The crackling of a fire invited her inside with the promise of warmth; yet, fear kept her poised in the corridor. She remained standing in the open doorway for what felt like hours, and still, no one appeared within her field of vision, and no voice called out to beckon her inside.

"Courage, Daphne," she whispered, repeating the words she'd been saying to herself throughout the long journey. "Have courage."

She had come this far and could not turn back now. The fate of her family depended upon her walking into that study to confront the man who had ruined them. Cruelly. Methodically. Purposely.

The first step proved the hardest. Once she'd crossed the threshold, she could move more easily, taking slow steps to enter the study. Turning left, she discovered a long room stretching away from her, lit and warmed by two large, yawning hearths cut in the left and right walls. The space was bare of any furniture except for a large mahogany desk before which stood a man who looked as large as the butler. Turned away from her, hands clasped behind his back, he seemed not to realize she had entered the room. Broad shoulders stretched the fabric of a white linen shirt, and he went without a coat or waistcoat. Fawn breeches clung to his lower body, showcasing powerful legs. Gleaming black boots adhered lovingly to his calves, the muscled limbs filling out the supple leather in a way most London men would envy.

Long, waving strands of dark brown hair fell past his shoulder blades in wild disarray. The deep sable hue of those locks was interrupted by haphazard strands of gold, which caught the light of the fire here and there.

Pausing halfway into the room, she swallowed past the lump in her throat while the warmth of the two fires sank through her soaked clothes and offered a bit of relief. What she wouldn't give for a hot cup of tea and her warm bed.

The man before her suddenly moved, turning slowly to face her, as if possessing all the time in the world. As if he bent time to his will instead of the other way around.

Her mouth fell open, shock rippling through her as she was confronted with the rest of him. The rough-hewn muscles of his form became even more imposing, the evidence of strength in the bulges of his arms showing through the fabric of his shirt, along with the swell of his wide chest. Her mouth went dry when her gaze fell to the patch of skin revealed by his loose buttons, a peppering of dark hair showing in the gap.

She paused there, terrified to look any further, for reasons she did not comprehend. But she sensed his gaze on her, and even without meeting that stare, could feel him studying her, assessing her, stripping the clothes from her body and the flesh from her bones.

Finally, she forced herself to continue, lifting her eyes and taking in the thick cylinder of his neck, and up, up toward a face that looked as if it had been carved from granite. Harsh lines and planes mingled with solid angles, a square jaw set off by a slightly crooked nose that appeared as if it might have once been broken. A mouth that might have been full and lush set in a firm line, pulled tight at the corners. The rough stubble of whiskers sprouted along his jaw, as if he hadn't taken a razor to it in days.

At last, her gaze clashed with his, and the dread in her belly solidified into a solid, frigid mass of outright terror. In the light of the fire, they appeared golden in color, with a rim of dark brown along the outer edges. The longer Daphne stared into them, she began to detect flecks of green near the irises—creating a convoluted jumble of colors that likely transformed depending on the lighting of a room or position of the sun. That long, wild hair framed his face, though it did nothing to soften the features. She imagined the effect would be twice as intimidating with it pulled back.

He began to move toward her, and the urge to backpedal as fast as her legs would carry her caused the hairs on the nape of her neck to stand on end. Yet, she held her ground, remaining rooted to the spot as he advanced on her with an almost feline sort of grace, the muscles that once appeared hard now liquid with fluidity, rippling and rolling beneath his clothes.

He paused when they stood but a few inches apart, and his scent reached out to her, striking her as decidedly masculine. Cedar, the smoke of a cigar, brandy, and ... and something else. Some primitive scent she could only describe as 'male.' His eyes gave not a hint of what he thought as he searched out her features beneath her hat. It hid her hair, the long, auburn braid tucked into the collar of her jacket while only a few wispy strands fell around her face.

"You are not Bertram Fairchild," he said, his voice hard and clipped.

The low, rumbling tones reminded her of a cat's purr—a very *large* cat. A lion. She had never heard or seen one, but she imagined his rough-sounding voice and its underlying purr would be exactly what the big cat would sound like. His cultured tones held a slight Scottish burr—though not as strong as that of his butler and gatekeeper.

Removing her hat, she lifted her chin and revealed herself. "No, my lord, I am not. But your staff would not have allowed me entrance had I not used his name."

"Lady Daphne, I presume," he stated.

Not a question, but a mere statement of fact.

Of course he knew who she was. Considering the way he'd gone about tearing apart everything even remotely connected to the Fairchild name, it stood to reason that he would know quite a bit about their family.

"You know who I am," she said with a resolute nod. "Good. Then we may dispense with pleasantries."

He quirked one eyebrow up at her, his expression clearly stating he hadn't been inclined to offer any. "You braved the journey from London and the wilds of Scotland alone to come here. Why?"

Folding her arms across her chest, she narrowed her eyes at him. "You, Lord Hartmoor, are a despicable lecher ... a villain of the worst order."

He grinned, the blinding flash of white teeth startling her momentarily. God in Heaven, even when the man smiled, he looked like some wild beast ready to devour its prey. The smile was mocking and lacked humor, causing annoyance to ripple along her spine.

"You came all the way here just to tell me that?"

She clenched her jaw so tight, her teeth began to ache. "I have come to demand an explanation for your vendetta against my family. You have relentlessly pursued our downfall, and I wish to know why. Do not do me the disservice of thinking me daft—I know it was you manipulating events so they would ruin my father, my brother, and my uncle. We are now destitute, my father's title and lands meaningless without the clout to back them, my brother's engagement ruined with but a word from your lips, my uncle ..."

Her throat constricted as she thought of Uncle William.

"A sad state of affairs when a man is driven to put his own pistol in his mouth and pull the trigger," Lord Hartmoor replied drolly.

Daphne gasped at the callous way the words fell from his mouth, lashing against her like the crack of a whip. "Have you no couth? No sense of decency? You drove a man to murder himself without cause!"

That eyebrow of his twitched, lifting upward as he pursed his lips at her. "Who says I did not have cause?"

Determined not to be swayed by his avoidance, she braced her hands upon her hips and took another step toward him, feigning a boldness she did not feel. "We have nothing, and my father and brother have become shells of the men they once were. I demand to know why. What on Earth have the Fairchilds ever done to you to deserve such cruelty?"

Folding his arms across his chest, he inclined his head. "What, indeed?"

Vexation finally overcame the fear he'd inspired in her, and she reached out to jab him in the chest with her index finger. "Now, see here! I did not brave ruin and illness in this horrific weather to come here and be mocked. I am owed an explanation, and I will have it, my lord ... the sooner, the better so I might take my leave."

Turning his back on her, he rounded the desk toward the large seat behind it. He seemed content to take his time sitting—pulling the chair out and lowering himself into it. Then, tipping it back on two legs, he lifted first one foot, then the other, carefully balancing them on the desk. He seemed completely at ease in the precarious position, only frustrating her further. The urge to rush the desk and push him over seized her hard and fast. However, she was angry, not suicidal.

"I warn you now, my lady ... your queries will not bring you peace," he said, avoiding her gaze and staring off somewhere across the study. "Young ladies like you are sheltered for a reason—going straight from the schoolroom and out to secure a husband who will pamper and cosset you just as your father has. You, with your lily-white skin protected by bonnets and parasols, your hands as soft as the day you were born ... like a little dove in a cage to be admired by the men who protect you."

She opened her mouth to deny his claims, to insist he was wrong about her. However, his words struck her as being annoyingly *true*, and the words died on her tongue. Like any other young, unwed lady, she had been sheltered and protected, kept from seeing any of the world's ugliness. However, the destruction of everything her family held dear had prompted her to seek the truth—to purposely unearth the things that had been hidden from her.

It had frustrated her to no end the way her father and brother had passively accepted the blows this man had dealt them ... refusing to fight back, to do anything to stop him. Her mother had never been a strong woman, seeming content to follow her husband's dictates always.

That left her, the only person who had possessed the courage to confront the person responsible for their ruin. She would not be put off.

Drawing herself up to her full height, she took a deep breath and tried again.

"I am no schoolroom chit," she insisted. "I am four and twenty years of age, and know far more about the world than you might think. For instance, I know there are men like you who delight in hurting others, in taking what does not belong to you, pilfering things like some great dragon gathering treasure in his dark cave."

He smirked at that, bringing the thumb of his left hand against his fingers. Rubbing the thumb against the pad of each digit, he eyed her boldly, assessing. The motion repeating over and over, he issued a silent challenge. She tore her gaze from his, only to find it falling to that hand, to the thumb caressing each finger in what felt like a calculated gesture.

"I would pilfer *you*, little dove. I'd drag your cage into my lair and hang you from the ceiling, admiring you whenever I wish. Is that why you've come?"

A bitter taste filled her mouth at his insinuation, her face heating at what his words implied. "How dare you—"

"No, my lady, how dare *you*," he snapped, suddenly straightening and allowing his feet to fall to the floor, the boots echoing with a loud thud. "You come here—in the middle of the night, no less—and demand answers of me. Answers to questions which you are not ready for, may never be fully prepared to hear. I warn you again to turn around and walk back through that door. Leave this place, now, and take the last shred of your dignity with you. This is the last time I will make such an offer."

The weight of his words hung heavy on the air between them, the threat in them clear. What would he do if she refused to leave? Would he hurt her physically? Tear her down with cruel words? Perhaps he spoke true—turning around and leaving now might be best. If she rode hard and fast, she could be back in London before any lasting damage had been done to her reputation. Her family would cover her disappearance as well as they were able until she returned. It was not too late to go back.

But no ... she could not go back. Not now. Not when she'd already lost so much.

"I would have the answers to my questions, and damn your notions of what I can or cannot handle!" she cried, her voice quivering with the force of her frustration.

She'd asked her brother why such bad blood existed between them and Lord Hartmoor, but Bertram had simply shrugged and given her a baffled look.

"I haven't the foggiest idea, Daff," he had replied. "I'd never met the man in my life before he set about ruining me."

Which could only mean Hartmoor had his own motives—something driving him that she must uncover if she had any hope of making things right.

Not that she possessed any idea how to go about doing so.

Slowly rising from his chair, he curled his hands into fists and braced them upon the surface of the desk. He leaned forward a bit, the powerful muscles in his shoulders bunching beneath his shirt. He stared up at her, and the firelight turned his eyes to liquid gold.

"Very well," he said, his voice ominously low. "Have it your way. I shall reveal the reason behind my actions to you ... over the span of thirty days, and thirty nights."

Daphne frowned, bemused. "I do not understand."

"No," he murmured, coming upright and circling the desk to approach her again. "But I will explain. I am aware of your family's ... desperate situation."

"Naturally," she growled from between clenched teeth. "You caused it."

He shrugged as if they were discussing the weather and continued. "I am prepared to write you a bank draft for thirty thousand pounds."

Her eyes widened at the absurd sum. It was three times the amount of her dowry, which her father had used to pay his debts. And even then, it hadn't been enough. The debts had continued to pile up, threatening their livelihood more and more by the day.

Thirty thousand pounds ... it would be enough to set everything right, though it might never repair Bertram's broken engagement. No matter. Her brother was a handsome man, sharing her auburn hair and blue eyes—Fairchild traits passed down through the generations. He was known among the members of the *ton* for his quick smile and easy charm. There would be other women, other chances for Bertram to make a good match.

But, the money ... there would never be another opportunity like this one. A chance to earn enough to pull the Fairchilds back from the brink of poverty.

"And in return?" she prodded, certain this man—this *monster*— would not simply offer her the money for nothing.

"In return, you will remain here at Dunnottar for thirty days and nights, with me," he murmured, reaching up to grasp the plait running down into the collar of her jacket. He yanked it free—not gently—and fisted it in his massive hand, studying it as if it fascinated him to no end.

She stiffened, offended at what he suggested. "I am a lady, not a whore."

He glanced up to meet her gaze once more and smiled, a slow, lazy curving of lips and flash of teeth. Was it her imagination, or were his canines a bit longer than any she'd ever seen?

Dear God, she was going mad.

"You will be one when I'm done with you, Daphne," he stated, running her braid through his fingers and releasing it once he'd reached its end. "Give yourself to me for thirty days, and not only will I reveal to you—in my own time—the answers you seek, but I will restore what I took from your family by giving you the funds to set things right."

Her neck heated as he perused her body from head to toe with an undoubtedly lascivious glance. Despite the heavy, damp wool coat concealing her form, she remained aware of how indecent her attire was; breeches clinging to her hips and legs, and a man's shirt with nothing underneath. It left her feeling disarmed, when she usually had her corset and petticoats to don beneath her gowns like a form of armor.

She opened her mouth to rebuke him, but one heavy, blunt finger fell against her lips, silencing her.

"Before you take me to task for being indecent, allow me to enlighten you," he said, his eyes appearing darker when he stood so close—like polished brass. "I do not care for your maidenly sensibilities. I know you are a virgin like most unwed chits, and I do not care. I will take your maidenhead with relish, with no concern to what state you go to your future husband in. I will debase you and own you for every single one of the thirty days and nights I require. You will submit to my will and obey, or there will be consequences. If you are strong enough to endure, in the end, you shall have your reward—the truth you seek, plus the grand sum of thirty thousand pounds."

A stinging retort died on her lips. His promises of debasement and the loss of her virtue should have frightened her. They should have sent her running through that door and back out into the stormy night. However, her mind chose to latch on to the only words he could have said to make her consider going through with it.

If you are strong enough to endure ...

Her spine straightened, and her nostrils flared as a rebelliousness her mother had been trying to squelch her entire life rose to the surface. If Lady Fairchild were here, she might warn her against impulsiveness, a trait that had gotten her into trouble on more than one occasion. *A cautious woman is a safe one,* she had said before Daphne's first Season, hoping to keep her from putting herself in a situation that might lead to public ruination.

Her father would scoff and insist that her mother might as well give her warning to a wall made of stone, as rising to a dare seemed to be part of Daphne's very nature. Bertram would simply laugh and remind them how many times he himself had gotten a rise out of her by insisting she could not do something as well as him.

She could not stand for anyone to tell her she could not do something, and she'd had enough being coddled.

As much as she loathed this man, she could not deny the truth of
his earlier words comparing her to a dove. White, pristine, unsullied.
Protected, indulged, sheltered.

Look away, Daphne, her mother would say to keep her from
witnessing anything that might upset her.

It is no concern of a gently bred lady, her father would say whenever
she pried into matters of import.

*Someday, your husband will teach you about what goes on in the
marriage bed,* every married lady she knew would tell her, as if
revealing the coveted secrets of the bedchamber would cause her to
swoon in a dead faint.

She was tired of being sheltered, of being told that matters
concerning her well-being were 'none of her affair.' Of allowing her
parents to rule her life, passively accepting their every decision. In
the past five years, they'd sunk deeper and deeper into destitution,
and neither of them had been able to set matters right.

But, she could.

And all it would cost was her maidenhead and a short time
allowing him access to her body.

No, she realized as she met his challenging gaze. If this man had
his way, it would cost her soul. He had destroyed her family and way
of life ... what guarantee did she have that he wouldn't destroy
her, too?

"Would I have your promise not to ... to ill-treat me?" she stammered, lowering her eyes.

Embarrassment filled her as she was reminded just how out of
her depth she swam. How was she to know what to do in such situa-
tions? Nevertheless, this was her body they were negotiating over—
she could not afford to put it on the line without certain assurances.

He chuckled, the sound making her belly grow warm. That heat
suffused out through her, leaving behind an odd sensation she did
not understand.

"How naive you are, little dove," he teased, reaching out to grasp her face with one large hand. His hold did not hurt, but neither would it allow her to move or pull away. His thumb caressed her lower lip, causing her mouth to fall open. "It will hurt, and not just the first time. There will be times when I will *make* it hurt. But, Daphne ... you will like it. Not only can I promise you will like it—by the end, you'll be begging me for it."

She wanted to scoff and tell him it wasn't bloody likely. She wanted to slap his arrogant face and tell him to sod off; she wasn't some Haymarket strumpet, and her body was not for sale. Yet, the promise veiled as a threat did not frighten her the way he'd likely thought it would.

If you are strong enough to endure ...

There was nothing she hated more than being baited ... except, perhaps being taunted by the person doing the baiting.

Lifting her chin, she met his gaze, refusing to flinch away as he traced the inside of her lower lip with his thumb. "I want the bank draft written out in advance. I want to see you sign it, and I want to be assured that it will be placed in my hand in thirty days."

He inclined his head, but gave no indication of whether her acquiescence surprised him. "Am I to believe you are accepting my offer?"

"First I see the bank draft," she said. "Then, I shall accept."

With a smile, he nodded, lowering his hand until it circled her throat. Her eyes went wide, fear creeping back in as the threat of his thumb pressing against her pulse made her want to flee. But she held still, sucking in deep breaths as he caressed the throbbing vein in her throat in a slow circle.

"I am so going to enjoy this," he said before releasing her and moving back behind his desk.

Unlocking a drawer, he retrieved a stack of bank drafts, pulling one free and laying it flat upon the desk. He glanced up at her as he retrieved a pen and unplugged his inkwell. Then, lowering his head, he filled in the draft. Straightening, he lifted the paper and blew upon it to dry the ink before extending it to her. She could not reach it from where she stood, and he seemed content to wait for her to come to him.

She edged toward him slowly, watching for any sign of duplicity or ill-intent. Once she stood within arm's reach, would he maul her— drag her into a dark corner of the study and deliver the pain he'd promised?

No, she decided. He was simply trying to frighten her. Yes, Lord Hartmoor had ruined her family; yet, he had never done them physical harm. This was why Daphne had come on this errand alone, knowing no court in England would find him guilty. He had simply manipulated circumstances until reaching his desired outcome. While he might have maneuvered her into this agreement, she saw this as the opportunity it was. She would protect herself from this man—giving him only her body while protecting her heart and soul.

He had destroyed the Fairchild men, but she had always believed women to be made of sterner stuff than their male counterparts. After all, what man could boast surviving the horrors of childbirth again and again? Or suffer the monthly ailments of a woman without languishing until death? Bertram became an infant when attacked by something as minor as a cold.

She could do this.

She *would* do this.

Approaching the desk, she glanced down at the bank draft. Sure enough, in his precise, neat scrawl, the promised thirty-thousand pounds was written in, along with his signature. She had never known his given name, but saw it now upon the draft.

Lord Adam Callahan.

"My family ..." she began.

"I care not for your family," he stated.

"They do not know where I have gone," she insisted. "I should send word—"

"I will see to it they are informed of your well-being," he said with a casual wave of his hand. "You will remain the entire thirty days, or receive nothing. Nor will you learn the entire truth of my vendetta against the men of your family. Do we have an agreement?"

She stared down at the draft and the promise it offered. The possibility of financial security, and of eventually learning the truth. What was the nuisance of her maidenhead in comparison to that? No man would wed her if word spread that she'd dashed off to Scotland alone—not that her family's troubles hadn't already left a stain upon her, branding her as *desperate* and not quite the diamond of the first water she'd been in her initial Season.

Inclining her head, she met his stare without wavering. And with a handful of words, poised herself within the jaws of the beast.

"We have an agreement ... Adam."

2

After agreeing to Lord Hartmoor's indecent proposal, Daphne was ushered from the study by the frightening butler—who silently led her back down the winding corridor and along a maze of nearly identical hallways until they had come to a different wing of the palace altogether. Just as she began to wonder just where he was taking her, he paused before one of many carved oak doors and pushed it open.

"Ye'll sleep here," he'd said simply, before turning to walk away, leaving her standing in the open doorway.

She had scowled at his back, baffled by this man who must be the most unconventional butler she'd ever encountered. A London servant would have seen to her comfort—offered her something to eat, inquired if she needed someone to fetch the supplies she'd left on the back of her horse. She had decided then to have a word with Adam concerning the hospitality of his house—if he expected her to remain and ... service him, then she would expect to be treated with common decency.

Though, as far as she knew, the thirty-thousand-pound bank draft he'd written right in front of her might be the extent of the consideration she'd receive for her sacrifice.

Those thoughts died the moment she stepped into the room and found both a crackling fire and steaming bathtub waiting for her. Beside it stood a young woman in the plain attire of a maid. She had seemed out of place in the dark, imposing castle where a savage lord insisted on being referred to as 'The Master,' and large butlers with scarred faces treated guests as if they bothered them by simply existing. With a friendly smile, ruddy cheeks, and blonde hair arranged in a soft chignon, she appeared like a wildflower in the midst of a cracked desert.

"Good evening, my lady," she said with a curtsy. "The Master has chosen me to act as your lady's maid during your time here. Would you care for a bath?"

The girl's accent struck her as distinctively English, a bit more polished than the average servant's, but still not quite cultured. How did this girl know to curtsy to her and refer to her as 'lady'? For that matter, how had a room and bath been prepared for her so quickly, when Adam could not have known she would accept his offer? When he'd rung for the butler, he had issued no instructions beyond "escort Lady Daphne to her guest chamber."

Then, she recalled the murmured conversation she'd heard between the master and butler as she'd stood outside the study. Perhaps the instructions had been given before the conversation had even taken place—which meant he'd known all along that Bertram had not arrived on his doorstep demanding an audience. He'd figured out who she was before he'd even turned to greet her—had assumed with the typical arrogance of men of power than she would accept.

For now, fatigue overwhelmed her, and she did not have it in her to question or argue.

"A bath would be splendid, thank you," she said to the girl. "What is your name?"

"I am Maeve, my lady," the maid replied as she approached and began helping Daphne undress. "You poor thing ... you must be chilled to the bone. Let's get you out of these wet clothes."

The heavy clothes fell in a wet heap on the floor, and Maeve helped her into the bathtub, where she sank into the steaming water with a sigh. She allowed the maid to tend to her, lying against the back of the tub while Maeve took up a sponge and scrubbed her arms, neck, and chest with a sweet-smelling soap. Seeming to disconnect from her body, she let the maid manipulate her like a rag doll, shifting her about to reach different areas of her body.

I've just sold my body to a monster.

The thought resounded through her mind, echoing as ominously as Adam's voice had through his cavernous study. It caused her to grow numb, her limbs hanging uselessly from her body and her eyes growing unfocused. Perhaps it was not too late to renege on their agreement. After all, her virginity remained intact. However, returning to London would feel too much like failure without the answers she sought—without the money that could save her family.

I've just sold my body to a monster. But I did not sell my soul.

Resolved, she left the tub and pushed Maeve's fussy hands away. Dismissing the maid and assuring her she'd do all right on her own, Daphne dried herself and slipped into the nightgown she'd been offered. The thing was prim and trimmed in lace; a bit at odds with the role she was to play, but she would not question it. The gown proved warm and comfortable against her freshly scrubbed skin, and the turned-down bedclothes appeared inviting.

Tomorrow, she would steel herself to come face to face with Lord Adam Callahan again. Tonight, she would rest so she'd have the strength to fight.

For fight, she must.

To guard her soul from the beast, to save her mind from the ruin his sharp words and foul deeds could cause. A body could heal ... a broken spirit would never be the same.

As she climbed into the large four-poster bed in the center of the room, Daphne wondered where in the castle Lord Hartmoor slept in relation to her. Did he undress for bed down the hall, or even just next door? Or had he banished her to some far-flung wing, where she was to remain until he came to claim what she'd promised him— what belonged to him by way of their agreement?

Despite the anxiety caused by imagining waking up with him on top of her, she could not keep her eyes opened once she'd slipped beneath the bedclothes. No ... Adam would never be so duplicitous. A man who so clearly stated his intentions would not skulk about in the dark and take what he wanted with the tapers snuffed out. He would come to her with every candle in the room blazing, so she would be forced to look upon him as he claimed her, defiled her, treated her like the whore he'd promised she would become.

She would need her wits about her when she faced him again, and that knowledge allowed her to slip into a sound slumber.

WHEN MAEVE ENTERED her room the next morning, Daphne had already awakened. Having found a dressing gown draped across the foot of the bed, she'd pulled it on over her nightgown. Smoothing a hand over the heavy, rich fabric, she'd wondered who it had belonged to before her. The thought of some other young, unsuspecting chit in this room, wearing this same robe as she waited for Adam to come despoil her, had made her shudder. However, the frigid chill lingering in her room had kept her wrapped in the warm garment while she'd padded barefoot across the room to spark a fire in the hearth.

Once she had coaxed the flames to life, she had remained before the large fireplace, her back turned to soak up the warmth of the blaze. She'd studied her surroundings with curious eyes, grudgingly forced to admit she had been given a room fit for a princess. As prison cells went, one truly could not ask for better.

The large bed sat elevated on a platform in the center of the room, draped with blue damask curtains tied back to the posts with tasseled ropes. Thick rugs matching the curtains covered stone floors, and the lower half of the walls had been paneled in rich, dark wood. The upper half boasted blue wallpaper printed with a silvery filigree. She'd approached the wall to touch the paper for herself, marveling at its rich texture. No expense had been spared to refurnish and remodel this room, and she supposed it must be the same for the rest of the ancient castle. She had not been certain what to expect when setting out for Dunnottar, but it certainly hadn't been paneled walls and brass sconces.

This was how Maeve found her, stroking the wallpaper. Pausing near the door, she smiled and curtsied as if she had been chosen to serve the queen instead of a woman contracted to act as Lord Hartmoor's plaything.

"Good morning, my lady," she chirped happily, moving to the large, ornate armoire located in the corner of the chamber. "The Master has requested your presence in the adjoining drawing room, where breakfast will be served."

So, it would begin. Squaring her shoulders, Daphne nodded as the maid faced her with a gown draped over one arm.

"Very well," she replied. "Might I ask whose clothing I will be borrowing during my stay here?

Allowing Maeve to help her out of the dressing gown, she studied the maid closely. The girl avoided her gaze.

"These are the only loaned items you'll need to wear while you are here," she replied as she unbuttoned Daphne's nightgown. "The Master will have your measurements taken and garments purchased for you."

Daphne scowled as the nightgown fell away from her body. Why extend such a courtesy, when his motives toward her proved the unsavory sort? Would it amuse him to dress her in rich garments only to rip them from her back before plundering her body?

"That is entirely unnecessary," she protested while Maeve helped her into a pair of stockings and garters. "My stay here will be a short one, and a few borrowed garments will suffice."

"Master's orders, my lady," the maid replied, her cheery tone never faltering. "You will find it easier to simply acquiesce to his wishes, and all will be well."

Anger burned like a lump of hot coal in her throat, rebellion rising from her gut to fill her chest. Yet another person who expected her simply accept the dictates of the man controlling her fate. If she'd had enough of that from her brother and father, then she certainly would not tolerate such from him.

"Perhaps you do, but I do not," she argued. "I shall address the issue with him myself over breakfast."

Amusement pulled at the corner of Maeve's mouth as she approached Daphne with the gown. The expression mocked her, seeming to warn that she might broach the subject with Adam, but should not expect him to bend. Well, the maid and her so-called 'Master' had another thought coming. Just because he had purchased the right to use her body for thirty days and nights did not mean she could not stand her ground on matters such as these.

Glancing down, she gasped, realizing that while her thoughts had wandered, Maeve had begun dressing her in the gown ... with no undergarments beneath them.

"Is there at least a chemise I might wear beneath this?" she asked, feeling completely naked without the layers of her petticoats, corset, and drawers.

At last, Maeve's demeanor faltered, her cheeks flushing crimson as she seemed to fumble for words. Finally, she managed to mutter something about "Master's orders" and "no undergarments." Daphne's face heated as the maid finished the row of buttons running down her back, her ire at Adam rising even more.

"Another matter I shall have to address with Lord Hartmoor," she declared.

Maeve's smirk returned as she urged Daphne to sit at the vanity to have her hair brushed.

"Of course, my lady," she murmured.

Suffering through the rest of her toilette in silence, she remained still while Maeve loosened her braid and brushed her hair, leaving it hanging free down her back. Then, in an act that sent bile rising up in the back of her mouth, Maeve tied a length of ribbon around her neck in a makeshift choker, creating a saucy bow against her collarbone.

As if she were a cat to be adorned before presentation to her master.

The maid turned her to face an ornate mirror, standing behind her and beaming as if proud of her handiwork. The previous owner of the navy velvet gown she wore must have possessed a petite frame, for it fell a few inches short and hugged her body a bit too tightly. She supposed she ought to be grateful not to have a corset on, as the dress cinched in her waist quite a bit on its own, the neckline biting into her breasts. The plump flesh spilled from the bodice, and despite trying to pull the fabric up to cover herself, Daphne eventually gave up. The frock was too small, and no amount of tugging could change that.

She had to admit the choker Maeve had fashioned out of ribbon enhanced her neck, causing it to appear longer and slenderer. Its navy color—a match for her gown—caused the blue of her eyes to appear brighter and more vibrant.

"Perhaps a chignon," she suggested, running a strand of hair between her fingers.

Maeve inclined her head. "The Master—"

"Has ordered that I wear it unbound," Daphne finished for her with a sigh.

"Now you're catching on, my lady," Maeve replied with a giggle. "You will find him through that door, there."

Following the maid's pointing finger, Daphne spotted a door she had not noticed before—the wooden panel apparently leading to the aforementioned sitting room.

Turning to tidy up the bed, Maeve seemed content to pretend she was no longer in the room.

Daphne took a deep breath, squared her shoulders, and marched toward the door with resolute intent. Never one to cower or hide, she would face him and show no fear. He might have broken the men of her family, but Adam Callahan would not break her.

She opened the door to find herself in a drawing room with decor matching her bedroom. The same blue and silver paper covered the walls while oversized furniture in matching shades sat positioned to face the hearth. Across the room from her rested a table covered in a white cloth, adorned by silver candelabras and tapers dripping wax, laden with several platters of food.

It was here she found Adam, seated in one of the two chairs, his long legs crossed and angled so they did not hide beneath the table. A white linen napkin lay draped over his thigh, and he sipped tea from a china cup that appeared no larger than a thimble in his massive hand.

Her mouth went dry, and she faltered halfway across the room at the sight of him. Heavens, she had forgotten how large he was—his shoulders and arms bulging against the fabric of his coat, skintight breeches clinging to powerful thighs.

Clenching her hands and swallowing past the knot of anxiety in her throat, she raised her chin, refusing to be intimidated.

"Good morning," he said without turning his head to look at her. "Come. Eat."

His words fell on her like the curt commands they were, causing her to stiffen. Yet, she did as he said, having no intention of shunning a meal after having ridden through the night without dinner.

As she neared the table, a dark shadow peeled itself away from the corner and converged upon her. A strangled cry died in her throat as she recognized the butler—still shrouded in unrelenting black, still wearing an expression of disdain at the sight of her.

He remained silent and stone-faced as he approached the table, pulling out the empty chair for her. Nodding her thanks, she sank into it and studied the platters spread out before her. For a moment, she simply stared at the various foods presented, overwhelmed by the choices.

After pouring a cup of tea for her from the silver tea service placed at the center of the table, the butler returned to his place in the corner.

"Help yourself to whatever you wish," Adam said. "I certainly hope you are not one of those chits who insists upon pretending to have the appetite of a bird."

Reaching for the dish of coddled eggs, she raised an eyebrow at him. "Many ladies eat that way in public because of the way our undergarments restrict our bellies. Though, during my time here, I suppose I shall not have that problem."

He paused in buttering his toast and glanced up at her, humor dancing in his eyes, though his mouth remained a hard, unmoving line. She smirked, certain he had understood her subtle jibe. Good. She would ensure he knew how displeased she was at being forced to prance about without proper undergarments.

Returning to his breakfast, he declined to answer her. Her stomach had begun to ache from hunger, so she filled her plate with slices of ham and toast, then laced her tea with sugar and milk. As she ate, she snuck glances at the man seated across from her—the fiend who had savagely destroyed her family.

He had the sort of Corinthian frame the men of London used padding beneath their clothes to achieve and the ladies giggled over behind their fans. His clothing proved plain and unadorned, nor were they latest fashion, but they had been tailored to fit him perfectly and appeared to be of high quality.

Still hanging loose around his face, his dark brown locks gleamed with golden highlights in the glow of the candles. This morning, his eyes appeared dark brown, the golden and green flecks practically invisible. His expression offered no hint of his thoughts or mood, which Daphne found disconcerting. It made this man dangerous, more so than she had imagined before coming here.

Once she'd eaten enough to ease the hollow sensation yawning in her stomach, she took a sip of her tea and glanced up to find him watching her. He'd cleaned his plate and now leaned back in his chair, staring at her in a way that left her feeling like a mouse being stalked by a cat.

Prey. That was how he made her feel ... like game to be devoured by a predator.

"Is there something on your mind, little dove?" he murmured, inclining his head.

His pet name for her rankled, reminding her of the insults he'd hurled at her the night before. He thought her weak, a simpering chit cowering in a gilded cage, preening for those who admired and protected her.

Her nostrils flared as she took in a deep breath, determined not to allow him to ruffle her. "I would like to have a word with you, Adam."

The only response to her use of his Christian name came with the slight lift of his eyebrows.

Waving a hand, he shrugged. "Speak your mind freely ... *Daphne.*"

He'd purposely emphasized her name, the underlying growl in his deep voice rumbling through the syllables like a purr. The sound did strange things to her belly.

Inclining her head to the large butler lurking in the corner, she cleared her throat. "Alone."

Adam smiled, the flash of teeth both sudden and startling. The motion lacked all humor, though, more akin to a lion baring its teeth.

"Niall, Daphne is uncomfortable with your presence," he declared, glancing over her shoulder at the silent butler. "You've frightened the girl half out of her wits. Would it kill you to crack a smile from time to time?"

Her eyes widened, and she glanced over her shoulder at the butler—who was apparently named Niall. Her face burned with embarrassment, but he hardly seemed ruffled.

"Of course I'm not afraid," she said, turning back to Adam. "What I wish to discuss is a delicate matter, and—"

"Excellent," he quipped with a dismissive motion of his hand. "Niall loves nothing more than listening to the inane concerns of pampered ladies, don't you, Niall?"

The butler remained where he stood, but did turn his head to meet his lord's gaze. "I've been known to indulge in a wee bit o' gossip, Master."

The mocking tone of both their voices set her teeth on edge.

"My lord, I really must insist—"

Adam's fist came down on the surface of the table, causing the silverware to rattle and tea to slosh from her cup and pool in the saucer. She started, flinching in reaction to the sudden outburst, her heart taking up a rapid cadence. Any humor in his expression fled as he slowly rose to his feet, the golden prisms in his eyes flaring to life as if stoked by some inner fire.

Rounding the table in two quick strides, he took her arm in an iron grip and hauled her to her feet. She struggled against his hold, but he gave her a swift tug and wrapped his other arm around her waist. Her entire body stiffened as it came against his—the hard planes of his chest digging into the soft flesh of her breasts.

Her breath caught and held in her throat while his huffed against her cheek.

"Perhaps I am not making myself clear enough," he whispered, his voice low and ominous as he pressed his mouth against her ear. "This is *my* domain. I am the master of everything and everyone inside it, and for the next thirty days and nights, that includes you. Aside from your lady's maid, you do not possess the authority to order my staff about. This is not London, little dove … you cannot shoo Niall from the room as if he were some bothersome fly. If you do not wish to speak in front of him, then I suggest you keep those pretty lips of yours shut lest I find some other way for you to occupy them."

Short pants made her breasts heave against his chest, the anger and confusion this man made her feel setting the surface of her skin on fire. One second, she was ready to take him to task; the next, he was catching her off guard with his sudden shifts in demeanor. Going slack in his arms, she ceased fighting his ironclad hold and glared at him, refusing to avoid his piercing gaze.

"I was informed you intend to purchase clothing for me," she snapped. "I simply wanted to tell you there is no need to go to such lengths. If there are more where these borrowed clothes came from, I am happy to make do with them. Or, perhaps Maeve might loan me a few simple garments."

He chuckled, the sound vibrating through his entire body—and, by proxy, hers. His teeth flashed again with a sardonic smile, and he kept one arm around her, but released the one he'd been holding, using the now-empty hand to cup her face.

"Isn't that just darling, Niall?" he teased, stroking a thumb along her lower lip. "The little chit would rather wear the rags of a maid than the expensive trappings I could provide her. Could it be because she doesn't want to be pretty for me?"

"I cannae pretend to know, Master," Niall replied dryly.

"It does not matter whether you're dressed in rags, the finest ball gowns, or nothing at all," he continued, stroking her lower lip with slow swipes of his thumb. "You are mine to do with as I please. I am paying good money for access to your ripe, virginal body, and that means I will use you how I wish, when I wish, where I wish. It also means you will wear what I tell you to wear, or you shall wear nothing at all."

As he leered at the generous amount of flesh revealed by her indecently low bodice, a niggling of fear trickled down her spine. Something told her he would make good on his threat to have her traipse about nude.

"Might I at least be allowed a chemise?" she asked, hating that he would reduce her to begging for so basic a dignity as smallclothes.

But, dash it all, she could not let this encounter past without gaining anything—even something so small as a pair of drawers. Not after he'd taunted and humiliated her in front of Niall.

"No," he replied. "I want as few layers between me and you as possible. What fun would this be if you wore a chemise under that gown?"

He emphasized his last words by moving his hand from her face and placing it between her shoulder blades. With a flick of his fingers, the first button loosened from its hole.

She sucked in a sharp breath, thrashing in his hold. No man had ever seen her completely undressed, and her limited experience had not prepared her for this. The soft kisses and tentative caresses she'd been treated to in the past should not be expected here—she had known that. But, when setting out to do battle with him, she had never expected him to disarm her so quickly.

He tightened his arm around her, the hand at her back now moving up to clutch her neck. He stilled her movements and forced her to look at him, his hooded gaze deceptively calm. Beneath the limpid stare, she saw the depravity simmering in the depths—the hunger of a predator prepared to maul and devour its prey.

"Shh," he murmured. "Fighting will not cool my ardor, little dove. In fact, it will only stoke it. Is that what you want?"

Trembling in his hold, she shook her head. Of course he would enjoy the hunt, the chase, and the inevitable surrender. No monster wanted to pursue a victim that lay limp and accepted its fate. Perhaps that would be her salvation—passively accepting his attentions instead of fighting against them. If she could cause him to grow bored with her, she might escape this ordeal unscathed. She certainly was not worldly enough to raise any other sort of defense. Cursing her inexperience, she wished she knew what to do, what to say to gain firmer footing with him.

"I will undress you now, and you will let me," he said, his voice low but his tone firm. "Yes?"

Taking a deep breath, she released it on a shaky exhale. What else could she do but allow it?

"Yes."

Going back to her buttons, he smirked. "Good girl."

She avoided his gaze, staring off across the room as he worked his way down her spine, steadily slipping the buttons free and causing her dress to slacken until it slipped off her shoulders. The warmth of the fire caressed her bare back, but she avoided thinking about it—or about the fact that only his body mashed tightly against hers kept the gown from falling away and baring her completely. She tried to distance herself from him entirely, to become nothing more than a piece of flesh for him to manipulate—not a living, breathing woman who could be hurt on a whim.

Keeping her pressed up against him, he lowered her, allowing her body to drag against his in a slow caress. The fabric of his wool coat rasped her nipples through the velvet of her gown, and his cock brushed against her stomach. Heat flamed in her cheeks at the feel of his masculine organ, hard and pulsating against her.

"You will not try to run or claw my eyes out when I release you, will you?" he teased with a glance at the gown still held up over her breasts.

It would seem he did not intend to *allow* her the distance she needed to survive this encounter. Very well, then. She would do what she'd intended from the moment she'd agreed to this preposterous arrangement ... she would face him, confront him, meet his challenge by showing him that she would not be so easily fazed.

Still avoiding his gaze, she kept her lips pressed together as she took a step away from him—not far enough that he mistook the movement as evasive, but just enough that the gown sagged down to her waist. With her forearms still trapped inside the long sleeves, her breasts and belly now lay bare to his view, the gown resting at her hips.

Only Adam's eyes reacted to her state of half-nudity, the dark pupils dilating and the golden flecks dancing with the green. Goosebumps rippled along her skin as his gaze skimmed her naked breasts and traveled over the plane of her stomach. Reaching out with one hand, he fisted the front of the gown and gave it a rough jerk, leaving it in a pile at her feet. She flinched, but held her ground as he stood back, studying her with an almost clinical sort of detachment.

The mystery of what he might be thinking as he traced the curves of her waist and hips with his scrutiny put her on edge. While she did not care whether she possessed enough womanly appeal to tempt him, she did not want him to become displeased by the simple sight of her. After all, he had paid thirty thousand pounds for every inch of the skin he stared at now.

"Would you look at that?" he murmured, his voice joining his gaze to travel over her in a handless caress. "Niall, isn't she the bonniest thing?"

Gasping, she covered herself—one hand cupping her mons and an arm shielding her breasts. He'd caused her to forget the presence of the butler, who loomed somewhere behind her, silently witnessing this entire encounter. Willingly allowing him to inspect her had been one thing ... being forced to let another man witness it, quite another.

"'Tis hard to say from behind, Master," Niall replied, his tone light, as if the two men were discussing the weather instead of the nude woman standing between them. "Though from here, I can attest she's got a lovely arse."

If she flushed any more, she might go up in flames, her entire body from scalp to toes alight with humiliation.

"Well, don't be shy," Adam prompted, grasping her shoulders. "I'm a bit jealous of Niall's view of your arse, and I know he's keen to see those fine tits of yours."

Before she could blink, he had spun her to face the butler, who remained at his post in the corner of the room. He had an unobstructed view of her as Adam gave her a little push forward. Then, coming up behind her, he grasped her hands and forced them away from her body, revealing every bit of what she'd tried to hide. Keeping a firm hold on her wrists, he lowered them to her sides and pressed his front against her back, his pelvis cradling her arse and giving her another feel of the hard ridge between his legs.

"You enjoy his eyes on you, don't you, Daphne?" he rasped against her ear as across the room, Niall appraised her with eyes that betrayed nothing.

Lifting her chin, she met Niall's gaze defiantly. "No."

Adam nuzzled her neck, inhaling deeply and then releasing his breath on a chuckle. "Liar. You know how bonny you are, don't you? You primp and preen for the young blades of London, priding yourself on remaining chaste while driving them mad with lust for you. Swaying those hips of yours when you walk and batting those long eyelashes for their attention, then retreating to the protection of the men who cosset you. Back into your cage where it's safe, little dove ... they cannot touch you there. And there you remain, pretty, unsullied, and pure."

"Not for long, eh?" Niall mumbled, prompting another laugh from Adam.

"Not for long, indeed," he agreed.

Releasing her, he approached the butler, turning his back to her dismissively as he reached into the breast pocket of his coat. Daphne refused to cover herself, not wanting to give him the satisfaction of knowing how he'd humiliated her. She kept her head held high and her gaze locked on him as he handed an envelope to Niall.

"Have this letter delivered to Fairchild House in London, posthaste," Adam commanded. "We must let Daphne's family know their pampered princess will be safe with us."

Bowing to his lord, Niall then cast her one last cursory glance. "Right away, Master."

As the butler retreated from the room, tucking the envelope into his breast pocket, she breathed a sigh of relief. At least Adam would remain true to his word and ensure her family knew she was safe. At least, as safe as she could be in the company of the man who seemed set on their destruction.

They would be horrified to know where she had gone, but not foolish enough to come after her. Too much hung in the balance, and with Bertram's reputation already in tatters, they would do everything they could to conceal her absence from the *ton*. They would understand that it had to be her—that she was the only Fairchild with anything of value left to barter with.

When she returned home thirty thousand pounds wealthier, she hoped they would be able to forgive her for what she'd had to do. She hoped Bertram would understand she'd done it all for him—her brother; the only man who had ever treated her as if she possessed a mind of her own. The only man to treat her as an equal.

Her virtue in exchange for her family—a price she was more than willing to pay. They might not have always understood her—her parents trying to stifle some of her less than ladylike propensities— but they loved her, and had done what they could to help her fit in with the other ladies of her age, to ensure she had a secure future and could make a good match for marriage. Bertram had accepted her as she was, often giving her the sort of understanding and affection their father had seemed incapable of. When they were finished being hurt that she'd acted without their leave, they would forgive her. Perhaps, they would even thank her.

Once Niall had gone, Adam returned to her, arms folded over his chest. All the humor had fled the room, as if the butler had taken it with him. Adam's gaze upon her felt cold now, as if he assessed how best to effectively dismantle her.

Then, he was moving to the table where they'd shared breakfast, shoving dishes and platters aside. Turning to her, he grasped her waist and lifted her as if she weighed no more than a feather. He deposited her upon the table, grasping her knees and pulling her legs apart as wide as they would go. The swift motion threw her off balance, and she used her hands to brace herself, forcing her back to arch and thrusting her breasts upward. She wanted nothing more than to right herself and close her legs, but he quickly stepped between them, looming over her and bracing his hands on the edges of the table to trap her between his arms.

"The idea of forcing you to run about naked has just become more appealing," he said, his lips brushing against her jaw. "Yes, I can see it now ... you crawling to me on your hands and knees wearing only those stockings."

She turned her head just before his lips could touch hers, narrowing her eyes at him. "I am not a dog, and I will not crawl about on the floor like one."

Leaning even closer, he nuzzled her nose with his, momentarily disarming her with the unexpected gesture. Were he not looking at her as if prepared to rip her to shreds, she might have mistaken it as one of affection.

"No, not a dog," he agreed. "More like a kitten wearing a bonny little ribbon."

Taking the end of the ribbon tied around her throat between his fingers, he caressed it, his sun-kissed skin dark against her porcelain. His knuckles brushed her breast, and when she shuddered in response, he grinned and repeated the motion—dragging his knuckles across her nipple over and over as his thumb and forefinger played with the silk ribbon.

"Will you purr for me when I pet you?" he whispered.

She had just opened her mouth to hurl a stinging retort when he suddenly slammed his lips over hers. The words lodged in her throat, shoved down by the invasion of his tongue as he slipped it into her mouth.

Daphne had been kissed before, and in truth had always found the experience varied depending upon who one happened to be kissing. She would have liked to think her past experiences would prepare her to be kissed by Adam.

As it turned out, nothing could have prepared her for this.

His mouth pressed hard against hers, his lips parting and closing in a languid rhythm that left her drugged, his tongue retreating to trace the seam between them before invading to search for hers again. The velvet rasp of his tongue sent a little thrill through her, causing the tips of her breasts to tighten.

A low sound rumbled between them—a growl vibrating through his chest and echoing between their parted mouths. Her head began to spin as the primal sound echoed around them while he mauled her with his lips and tongue and teeth. She winced when he bit her lower lip, then sighed when his tongue caressed away the sting. Then, as if the first bite had been a prelude, he nipped her again, hard enough to draw a sharp cry from her. He followed the bite with gentler bites, then slowed the tempo of their kiss entirely, languidly brushing his mouth over hers as their racing breaths mingled on the air between them.

Before she could make sense of the mess his assault had made of her faculties, his heavy hand fell onto her belly. Meeting her gaze, he held it as his hand began to slide down toward the mound between her legs. Despite her intentions to remain passive, she couldn't muffle the low whimper of panic that escaped as her thighs clenched, impeded from closing by his body wedged effectively between her knees.

"Shh," he crooned, still steadily brushing his lips over hers. "Let me touch you, little dove."

His thumb slipped between her lower lips, finding the hidden bud of pleasure. She'd only let one other man touch her here, but it became hard to think of him now as Adam stroked her in slow circles, the calloused pad offering delicious friction.

"Oh," she whimpered, small shudders of pleasure rippling out through her body with every pass of his digit over her clit.

He deepened their kiss, his tongue tangling with hers as he dipped his thumb lower to discover the wetness seeping from her core. Smearing it over her pearl, he increased the pressure of his caresses, changing his rhythm as if he noticed she angled her hips toward him more when he touched her a certain way. As if he knew, by simple touch, what she craved.

"That's it, love," he grunted, his voice thick and heavy with the lust causing his cock to bulge against the front of his breeches. "Relax and let me touch you. Doesn't that feel so good?"

Biting her lower lip, she choked back a moan. He was touching her as if he existed in her dreams and knew what she imagined a lover doing to her as she lay alone in her bed. As if he'd touched her before and already knew every contour and pleasure spot to be found.

As if he wanted to ensure no man could ever touch her this way again without causing her to think of him.

The bloody bastard.

She could not fall prey to his seduction, to let him make her forget why she was here. Her family was destitute, and he held the funds she needed to set things right. All she had to do was let him use her without losing hold of her good sense in the process.

"Aren't you going to fuck me?" she asked, panting her words out between ragged breaths.

With a grin, he tickled her entrance with his index finger, still steadily plying her clitoris with his thumb. "Eager for my cock already? Sometimes, a man simply wants to sample the goods before the plunder."

Meeting his gaze with a defiant tilt of her head, she sneered. "Or maybe a man simply isn't *up* to the challenge?"

He froze, his fingers stilling between her thighs, his eyes flashing with golden lightning strikes. The feral gleam there warned her she'd gone too far, but she remained powerless to avoid her fate as he snatched one of her hands up from the table, causing her to fall onto her back. Dishes rattled when she hit the surface, and as she attempted to prop herself up on one elbow, he took her other hand and pressed it to the fall of his breeches. She gasped at the feel of his cock against her palm, the organ seeming to have grown even more since he'd pressed it against her earlier. It fairly throbbed with power and promise, a threat too large to be ignored.

"Does it *feel* as if I'm not up for the challenge of fucking you until you beg me to stop?" he challenged. "Or maybe you won't beg me to stop ... maybe you'll plead for more."

Even knowing that needling him would be dangerous to her well-being, Daphne could not resist. "*Me*, beg *you*? Never."

Pressing his thumb to her clit again, he smirked. "Never? Are you certain?"

Her mind went vacant, all rational thought fleeing as he began stroking her again, this time with increased vigor. Her chest heaved with the effort it took to hold in the moans simmering in her throat, begging to be released along with the tension coiling low in her groin.

Bloody hell, she had gotten herself in over her head. It wasn't supposed to be like this. His touch was supposed to repulse her, not make her feel ... feel ... well, like the surface of her skin had been set on fire. Like she would die if he ever stopped.

"Do not make the mistake of thinking me some ham-handed Neanderthal who will spend the next thirty days rutting on top of you for less than a minute each night before falling into a sound sleep," he said, his gaze boring into her as he joined his hand with the other, his thumb steadily circling her clit while a finger stroked the entrance of her channel. "I intend to savor you, little dove ... take my time and use you in every way I can think of. By the time I'm finished with you, there won't be a place you haven't felt me in, a body part your future lovers will touch that I have not touched first."

Bending down over her, he rocked his hips, adding more of his weight against the hands tormenting her dangerously closer to the edge. The moan she'd been holding back spilled out, the sound high and keening—completely foreign and driven by the primitive need driving her to buck her hips up against his hands.

"You will take my cock into every orifice," he taunted. "First here."

His tongue came out to lap at her lips, and he plunged it inside as if to mimic an act that made her face flame hot.

"Then here," he added, his index finger gaining an inch into her cunt, and then another.

Her eyes slid closed, and she buried her face against his shoulder, too far gone to care about his crass words and their implications, too overcome with pleasure to think past the thumb pleasuring her most sensitive place while his finger slowly stroked her inner walls.

"And here," he groaned, sliding a second finger past the first and toward the tight hole of her back passage. "Fuck, your tight little arse will feel so good around my cock."

She choked on a gasp when his second finger slipped into the tight ring of flesh, just enough to send another jolt through her. This pleasure was foreign to her, tinged with a slight burning sensation. Taking a man there was a prospect she'd have never thought possible. It made her flush with embarrassment, discomfiture and curiosity mingling in a way that seemed to enhance the pleasure of his thumb against her clit. No matter how much her mind told her the mention of such acts should revile her, her body came alive at the promise of what his words and touch offered.

What the devil was wrong with her? She needed to put a stop to this, to push him away and demand he unhand her unless he claimed to get on with deflowering her. This had not been part of their agreement—him forcing pleasure on her, taking away her determination to lie beneath him and passively surrendering her maidenhead.

God help her, she was spiraling, her entire body going rigid as the tension unfurled in a fell swoop she had no choice but surrender to. Throwing her head back, she let out a keening cry, her back arching as currents of pure pleasure jolted through her, all converging between her legs in pounding spasms that sent her eyes rolling back into her head.

When it had calmed, she went still beneath him, her body now limp upon the table. Her limbs went slack, and she doubted she could even find the strength to lift her head.

Her eyes stung, hot tears pooling in the depths. What had she been thinking challenging this man? Not only had he stripped her of her armor, he had proven to her that she possessed not a single weapon with which to fight him.

Adam gazed down at her, seemingly unruffled by what had just passed between them. And why should he feel anything? This had been about proving he could make her desire him—that she stood no chance of simply lying passively beneath him and pretending to be someplace else. He would not allow it.

Backing away from her a step, he continued staring down at her in a way that left her on edge. It was the same way he'd looked at her just before offering to buy her body for thirty thousand pounds. His upper lip curling as if she disgusted him now that it had ended, he hurled his words at her in a tone that made the warmth following her climax die a swift death.

"Your father ... your uncle ... your precious brother ... they are not the men you think they are."

Turning on his heel, he left the room as if he couldn't be away from her fast enough. Behind him, the door slammed, rattling in the frame and causing her to flinch. A cold numbness washed over her, his words penetrating her middle like a sharp icicle and lodging deep.

Slowly sitting up, and then standing from the table, she began to shiver, her entire body as cold as if her blood had suddenly turned to ice water. His words echoed in her mind, tumbling over and around each other as if some part of her could not make sense of them. What had he meant by them, and what had he hoped to achieve by hurling cruelty at her after making her feel such pleasure? It was as if he'd purposely timed it to ruin the moment, to tip her back off balance.

It had worked, making her head spin and her gut churn as she tried to pull herself together.

She wrapped her arms around herself and walked to where he'd left her dress, kneeling to pick it up in a stupor. Her hands shook too badly for her to put it back on, so she simply held it up over her naked breasts as she crossed through the connecting door to her chamber.

3

D aphne awakened a few hours later with a pounding headache. After breakfast with Adam, she'd been unable to do anything other than retreat to her guest chamber and crawl into the bed, leaving her clothing in a pile on the floor. Pulling the blankets up over her head, she'd curled into a ball, hiding from the world ... from the man who had so easily controlled her body before waging war on her mind.

Your father, your uncle, your precious brother ... they are not the men you think they are.

The words had haunted her dreams, and now, they reverberated from the walls of her chamber. She needed to escape them, as well as this room, for a time. She located the garments she had discarded that morning and quickly put them back on. The blue ribbon she'd worn as a choker remained on the floor. She made sure to step on it as she walked toward the door, giving her heel a little twist. If she never saw the scrap of satin again, it would be too soon.

Planting her hand on the doorknob, she yelped and backpedaled as it moved against her fingers. The knob turned, and the heavy panel swung open to reveal Adam. Inclining his head, he smirked at her—as if he knew he'd frightened her out of her wits, appearing on the other side of the door just as she was about to open it.

Sweeping into the room, he paused just before her. He smelled of horse, leather, and the outdoors. His hair had been pulled back and tied with a scrap of ribbon, but stray tendrils framed his face as if tugged free by the wind.

He'd just come back from riding, if Daphne hadn't missed her guess.

"How fares my little dove?" he teased, folding his hands behind his back and giving her a once-over with his eyes.

"Tired of staring at these four walls," she confessed.

He nodded. "I assumed as much. I've come to give you a tour of Dunnottar, should you be amenable."

"Yes," she agreed quickly, choosing to be grateful for the chance to walk freely instead of annoyed by the company she'd be forced to keep.

She could not avoid him for the entirety of her stay if she wished to earn the promised thirty thousand pounds, so she might as well accept the fact that she'd be forced to cater to his whims. Perhaps acquiescing instead of fighting would earn her better treatment.

"Excellent," he said, standing aside and gesturing toward the open door. "Shall we?"

She moved past him as swiftly as she could, her shoulder brushing against the door frame as she tried to avoid walking too close to him. After his unpredictable behavior this morning, she half expected to be pounced upon, dragged to the bed, and ravished.

But no. He had assured her he had no interest in taking her maidenhead quickly. He would prolong the act, leaving her wondering exactly when she could expect him to ruin her.

It was far more frightening than the prospect of being pounced upon, dragged to the bed, and ravished. At least if he did those things, it could be done with swiftly. This game would wear on her before long, the wait becoming unbearable. She would need to steel herself for the days to come. Thus far, he had managed to disarm her in a matter of minutes, and it was only the first day.

"Come," he commanded, turning left to guide her down the corridor.

The directive bristled along her spine, stirring her ire at him. Yet, she said nothing about the way he'd barked the order at her as if she were a dog. Desperate for some exercise—even if it was only a walk through the massive castle—she pressed her lips together and fell in line.

"Are you familiar with the history of Dunnottar?" he asked as they neared the main hall.

"I'm afraid not," she replied, turning in a slow circle to take in the light streaming through large stained-glass windows.

The colored glass sent rainbow prisms dancing across the stone floor while the rich tapestries adorning the walls filled what might have otherwise been a dreary room with rich bursts of color. It looked like the sort of place where a king might hold court, and she could imagine a large throne against the far wall.

Adam stood beside her, hands folded behind his back, seeming content to let her take it all in. "In the beginning, there was only a chapel here upon the rocky headland. St. Ninian founded it sometime in the fifth century. No one is quite sure when it became a fortified keep, but over time, walls went up and additions to the property came and went, some eventually torn down to create better ones."

"That would explain the assortment of outbuildings I passed on my way in last night," she replied.

"Quite right," he said. "One thing that never changed ... Dunnottar has always been one of the most impregnable fortresses in all of Scotland. The sheer cliffs and the flatlands around it ensured no one could approach unseen, and they would have a steep climb to the gates. There are only two ways in or out—the front gate, which would make raiders vulnerable to attack from all sides, and an underground tunnel on the northern side."

Her eyes widened at the thought of being able to explore the underground entrance. She'd always read of places like Dunnottar in her novels—dark, gothic castles filled with mysterious secret passages. Adam's home seemed like a place from a dream.

"How utterly fascinating," she said.

Feeling his stare on the side of her face, she turned to meet his gaze. He studied her in silence, his face inscrutable, his eyes betraying none of his thoughts. Almost as if he wondered whether her interest could be real, or feigned in order to gain his good favor.

"I think I'd like to see the tunnel," she added sincerely.

He gave a curt nod. "Perhaps another time. There's more for me to show you. Come."

This time, she was happy to follow as he led her toward another corridor stretching in the opposite direction.

"Dunnottar has changed hands many times over the years," he continued as they walked. "During King William the Lion's reign, it was the administrative center of Kincardineshire. It fell to King Edward I at one time, only for it to be snatched away from him a year later by Sir William Wallace."

"Sir William Wallace," she repeated. "The knight who led the rebellions during the war for Scottish independence?"

Pausing near a closed door, Adam turned to her and smiled. "The lady knows her history. Aye, the very same Sir Wallace. Dunnottar would not fall back into the possession of the English until 1336. Sometime in the sixteenth century, it was granted to the Keith family —the Earls Marischal—by King James the fifth. It remained the seat of the Marischal for over one hundred years. During that time, the keep was transformed into the lavish palace you stand in now. I've had a bit of work done to refurnish much of the place, but have kept it mostly the way I found it."

He opened the first door to reveal a large library, each wall covered in shelves upon shelves of books. A hearth remained cold, but she could imagine the space becoming quite cozy with a crackling fire casting light and warmth into the room.

"So many books," she murmured as she glanced about the large space. "Our library at Fairchild House could fit inside this one several times over."

"If you ever wish to visit and read, inform Maeve ... she will see to it that the hearth is lit," he said.

Following him back into the corridor, she smiled. "That is generous of you, Adam. Thank you."

He waved her off as if it were of no consequence and led her on, opening doors as they continued down the long hall. There were several drawing rooms, all decorated in an intriguing mixture of old and new. In the midst of the corridor lay the study she'd been ushered into—Adam's domain.

"How did Dunnottar fall to you?" she asked as they reached the end of the corridor and a winding set of stone steps leading upward.

"In 1715, the Earl Marischal was found guilty of treason and stripped of his titles and lands—including this castle. It was acquired by the York Building Company, and remained in their possession until I purchased it five years ago. A lavish expense, some might think, but as a direct descendant of William the Lion, on my mother's side, I thought it a necessary one. A piece of my heritage, I suppose."

"I had wondered which of your parents was the Scottish one," she mused as they came to the landing of the second floor.

He raised an eyebrow at her and smirked. "Was it the burr that gave me away?"

Despite what he'd done to her this morning, she could not help but smile back at him. It seemed a genuine grin, unlike the flash of teeth and snarl he'd flashed at her previously, reminding her of a predator preparing to attack its prey.

"It isn't strong," she assured him. "Just pronounced enough to be noticeably Scottish."

"I can make it stronger when I'm of a mind to, lass," he said, the accent becoming more pronounced with every word. "Most cannae tell when I dinnae want 'em to."

Daphne suppressed a giggle, reminding herself who this man was. This was no courtship—he was not a suitor flirting with her while giving her a tour of his home. He was a lecher who had stripped her naked in front of his butler before throwing her onto a table to do wicked things to her. He was the man who had ruined her family.

Adam's demeanor shifted as if he'd had the same thought at the exact same time. His expression hardened, his jaw clenching as the humor fled his eyes. Jerking his gaze away, he inclined his head down the corridor.

"Shall we?"

Holding her head high, she kept pace with him as he led her down a corridor which opened into a long gallery at the end. They paused there so she could inspect the paintings hanging on the wall, with stained glass windows appearing here and there along the stone. Instead of the family portraits she had been expecting, the gallery had been filled with art—expensive paintings commissioned by some of the most famous artists in London. In some places, she found stone sculptures and busts. Aside from those things, the gallery remained mostly empty—except for the weapons rack she found at the very end of the hall.

She gasped in delight when her gaze fell upon the fencing rapiers hanging there, along with a selection of face masks. A trunk lay on the floor beneath them, and she would be willing to wager it contained the necessary padding needed for the sport of fencing.

"You fence?" she asked.

"Aye," he replied, opening the trunk and revealing that it did, in fact, contain fencing attire. "Do not tell me you have taken up the sport of fencing, little dove? Do ladies of your social standing not indulge in the typical pursuits of sewing, singing, and the pianoforte?"

Daphne huffed. "I become all thumbs with a sewing needle, am an abominable singer, and find the pianoforte to be a tedious instrument. I'll have you know, I've been fencing since the age of twelve."

The mocking smirk that set her teeth on edge returned, and he advanced on her, his eyelids drooping seductively.

"Naughty little dove. Engaging in a man's sport when no one is looking. What else do you indulge in when no one is watching, I wonder?"

A lump lodged itself in her throat, and she backed away from him, unable to help the instinct for self-preservation warning her away from him. The memory of what had occurred over breakfast was not far from her mind, reminding her of how easily an encounter with him could change on the whim of his mood.

He followed, pressing her against the wall with his body, stunning her into submission with the raw power emanating from his hard muscles.

She stiffened against him, sucking in a sharp breath, causing him to smile—a feral display of teeth that sent a shiver down her spine.

"N-nothing, really," she demurred, turning her head to avoid his gaze.

It was too probing, too *knowing*.

His breath huffed against her neck, his nose sliding along her jaw as he moved his mouth toward her ear.

"Oh, come now, little dove. There must be something. Tell me something naughty, a secret you would never dare utter aloud."

Her face flushed as she thought of days spent hidden in the woods, grass staining her gowns as she lifted them to allow a pair of hands beneath. Pulse quickening, she closed her eyes and recalled the feel of his lips on her neck and breasts, his groans in her ear as he taught her how to touch him the way he touched her.

No. Those summers spent in bliss, roaming the lands between her parents' estate and his were too precious to speak of.

"Truly, there is nothing," she whispered as he went on nuzzling her neck, his arms a menacing cage trapping her against the wall.

"Liar," he growled, his teeth scraping against her earlobe. "Come now, Daphne ... tell me one of your secrets, and I will tell you one of mine."

Her heart stuttered as she realized what he must mean, and she forced herself to meet his gaze and not look away. "A secret about my family ... about why you ruined us."

He laughed, his chest rumbling against her breasts and causing her nipples to pebble. She shuddered, but held his gaze, determined not to back down from a direct challenge.

"A fair exchange," he relented. "You first, little dove. Tell me something wicked."

She tried to think of something—anything that would placate

him enough to earn the promised secret. She'd come here for answers, and thus far had only been told that the men responsible for protecting her were not who she'd made them out to be in her mind. How could that be when her father had always doted on her—even when her willful nature had frustrated him? How could that be when Bertram had always been the man she trusted more than any other in the world? Her uncle had had his faults, but he certainly hadn't deserved to be coerced into murdering himself.

She must think of something, but would not betray the memories of those summers spent in the country with the man she had once hoped to marry. There were some parts of her Adam would never touch.

Reaching for the first memory she could fathom—one of the few which could be considered naughty—she blurted it out without thinking.

"I once stole an erotic novel from my brother."

Adam drew back slightly, his lips quivering with amusement. "Is that all?"

Shock dropped her jaw. "Well, of *course* that is all. You needn't sound as if I've confessed to pilfering a biscuit from a bakery, as if what I did was of no consequence. The novel was quite explicit in detail and rather shocking to read. Not to mention the scandal that would have ensued had anyone known I'd read it. My reputation—"

"It has always amused me how easily a woman's reputation can be ruined," he interjected. "How adorable you are, little dove ... so pure and sweet, your white wings untouched and pristine. I am going to enjoy sullying them."

A shiver shot through her at what his words implied, and the promises he'd made over breakfast of the different ways he would go about ruining her.

"Did you blush as you read the erotic novel?" he teased. "Did the words cause your cunt to grow wet?"

Her neck grew hot as she remembered reading page after page of filth—of being both titillated and intrigued by it.

"Of course not," she lied.

He chuckled again, the sound a grating reminder that he was laughing *at* her. "How easily you lie, little dove. I know they taught you it is safer to pretend—to lie to yourself about the things you think about when you are alone at night in your bed ... to be ashamed of the things you desire. No one is here. You can admit it to me."

Shame fell on her like a crushing force, but she forced her chin up and speared him with a defiant glare. She would never confess to being wanton, to have come close on quite a few occasions to becoming the whore he now tried to make of her.

"There is nothing to tell," she insisted. "I stole the book, read it, and put it back before Bertie was the wiser."

He scowled, moving away from her with a heavy sigh. "You disappoint me, Daphne. Our time together will become so much more enjoyable once you cease playing the lamb to my lion. You called me a villain last night; yet, I have never been dishonest about the sort of man I am. I told you what I want from you, and the price I am willing to pay for it. But you insist upon playing the coquette, lying both to me and yourself about who you are and what you desire."

How did he see through her so easily when he had barely known her an entire day? She'd spent her life hiding behind a carefully cultivated mask of innocence, holding her tongue when she'd rather speak, spurning kisses when all she'd ever wanted was to be kissed, pretending to be embarrassed by the reaction of her body to certain stimuli when she'd wished to revel in it. What good was her pretense if a man like Adam could see straight through it?

"I do not know what you expect from me," she replied, injecting as much coolness into her voice as she could muster. "But I will never play your whore."

"My whore," he murmured, reaching up to cup her face, his thumb tracing over her lower lip—still tender from his earlier assault. "Perhaps not, but you will be mine, Daphne. I will have you whether you play the innocent or the wanton."

He stroked her lip with the pad of this thumb, pressing down enough to pull her mouth open. Her breath quickened, and the response he'd coaxed from her this morning roared to life once more, leaving her feeling off-balance and dizzy.

God, why can't I fight him? What is it about him that makes me feel so weak?

"You promised me a secret," she reminded him—because she needed him to talk, to return to their original conversation before she lost her head again.

He gave her a slow smile, lowering his hand and allowing it to brush against her breast on its way down. "So I did. You wish to know about how your uncle met his demise."

"At your hands," she snapped, taking the opening his lowered arms offered and slipping out from between him and the wall.

He fell in step beside her, and they walked back the way they'd come. "Are you sure? I feel certain I'd heard he killed himself."

"Because of you!" she bellowed, turning to face him with her hands balled up at her sides.

Unruffled by her outburst, he paused and leaned against a closed door they had not yet explored beyond.

"No," he retorted, grinding the words out from between clenched teeth. "Allow me to let you in on a little secret about your uncle. The man was a known gambler, a habit only exacerbated once he began over-imbibing ... something he did much more frequently toward the end of his life. Haven't you ever wondered *why* he'd taken to drinking so heavily, drowning himself in spirits from sunup to sundown?"

Daphne wrinkled her brow, her ire cooling as confusion pushed to the forefront of her mind. It was true, Uncle William had always had a bit of a gambling habit, though he'd never lost so heavily until ... well, she was not entirely certain. Five years ago, perhaps. That was when he'd begun a swift descent into near poverty, taking her father with him.

"Of course I wondered," she whispered, wracking her brain for some clue as to the reason for her uncle's drinking. For the life of her, she could conjure nothing.

"The reason was hidden from you, naturally," he replied, folding his arms over his chest and causing his coat to strain at the seams along his shoulders. "Poor, sweet Daphne, too innocent to know the truth."

"And what truth is that?" she demanded, narrowing her eyes at him. "What did you do to my uncle to drive him into the bottom of the bottle?"

Adam laughed, the rough sound lacking humor. "When a man drinks like that, there is only one cause ... the demons he runs from. I did nothing to your uncle to cause him to drink himself half to death. Guilt drove him to drink, which drove him to gamble, making it easy for me to take everything he ever owned."

Her chest tightened, gripping her heart in a vise as she studied the cold-hearted man before her. Jaw clenched tight, eyes dark and lifeless, mouth a cruel snarl. Despite his rugged beauty, the disdain he felt for her family overshadowed it all.

"You purposely pushed him to gamble away his livelihood," she accused.

He shrugged as if they spoke of the weather instead of his methodical destruction of Lord William Fairchild. "Was he not a man with a mind of his own, capable of standing up from the table and leaving?"

"Yes, but—"

"Your uncle was irresponsible with his property, gambling it away as carelessly as a child tosses a toy across his nursery," he interjected. "If I am to blame for anything, it would be simply reminding him that after the pain he had inflicted upon others, he no longer had any reason to live."

Shock rippled through her, swiftly giving way to outrage. Her spine snapped straight, her fists tightening until her fingernails bit into her palms.

"You bastard," she rasped, her voice tortured from the grief tearing her up inside. "You ... you ..."

"Murderer?" he offered, remaining as stone-faced as he had since beginning this conversation. "No court would convict me. Perhaps your uncle knew I was right ... he took his own life because his sins had made his existence worthless. The pain he felt the moment that bullet tore through his skull was nothing compared to the pain he'd inflicted upon someone else."

Someone else? Could the person Uncle William had hurt be Adam? The man seemed a force of nature, like a mighty oak tree, unable to be bent by even the strongest winds. How on Earth could her uncle have hurt him? And if William had committed some wrong against Adam, what role had her father and brother played?

"Whatever he did, I am certain he regretted it," she managed, her head beginning to pound again from the effort it took to understand what was happening. "He did not have to pay for it with his life."

Coming close again—near enough that she could see the molten gold and green flecks swirling within his brown irises—he dropped his arms to his sides. She stiffened, but he only came closer, so close his lips brushed her cheek, his breath tickling her skin when he spoke.

"A life for a life," he murmured. "His final debt ... repaid in blood."

She gasped, her eyes going wide. "A life for a life? He *killed* someone?"

Backing away from her, he turned and began walking back down the gallery. "Come."

She flinched as if he'd doused her with a bucket of frigid water, but quickly recovered, trotting to catch up with him as they went back the way they'd come. "Will you not answer me?"

"That is the extent of what I wish to divulge to you at the moment," he replied, his tone dry as if he'd grown bored with both the conversation and her.

"But you cannot leave it there," she argued. "You cannot accuse my uncle of murder and then refuse to speak more on the matter."

His eyes darted toward her, and he smirked. "The weight of my secret was a match for yours. Perhaps, if you wish to know more, you will not hold back when I ask you for something. You will get from me as much as you give, little dove. Remember that next time you wish to make demands of me."

She opened her mouth to argue, but then swiftly snapped it

shut. Arguing would clearly get her nowhere with him. He'd given her a piece of the puzzle, one she could think over further once she returned to her chamber. Perhaps some hint of her uncle's misdeeds stared her in the face—she only needed to think harder. She did not want to believe any of the men in her family were capable of the sort of thing Adam had implied, but something told her there must be some truth here. From the moment she'd met Adam, he'd been forthright, even when he'd been cruel. He had looked her in the eye and admitted to purposely setting out to ruin her father, uncle, and brother. Why would he then lie about the reasons?

Whatever the case, she *would* know the entire truth by the end of her thirty days here. She had come all this way and put her virtue on the line—leaving without answers would not be an option.

She followed him in silence, numbly inspecting the contents of each room—her glance sliding unseeingly over opulent sitting rooms, a sun room, more guest chambers than she could count, and a small dining room meant for intimate meals. Another, much larger dining area could be found off the main hall, with a table long enough to seat fifty.

"That will conclude our tour for today," he announced once they'd come back to the corridor where her room was located. "There is still more to explore, but Dunnottar is too massive for you to see all in one day. I will see you back to your room."

Nodding, she trailed him back down the hallway toward her chamber. As they paused before the door, she gazed further down the corridor and frowned. Now that it was more brightly lit, she noticed the hallway curved to the left, likely leading deeper into the palace.

"What's down there?" she asked.

Adam followed her gaze, his expression growing even more shuttered as he shook his head. "That part of the palace is forbidden to you, Daphne. Do you understand? You may venture to any other place I have shown you except that wing of the castle. The moment you step foot in that corridor, I will eject you from the premises with nothing more than the clothing on your back and the horse you arrived on. Our agreement will become null and void, and you'll receive nothing from me."

The sudden harshness of his tone took her aback, and as she gazed toward the forbidden wing, a shiver rolled down her spine. What could possibly be down there that he did not wish for her to see? His private chambers? Something more nefarious?

Get a hold of yourself. Your imagination will run away with you and ruin everything.

Knowing what lay in that corridor was of no consequence while learning the truth Adam would reveal to her was imperative. She could not leave Dunnottar without answers.

"Daphne," he barked, drawing her attention back to him. "I asked you a question. Do you understand what I've just said?"

She nodded quickly and found her voice. "Yes, of course. I understand."

With a curt nod, he opened her door for her. "Maeve should bring you the afternoon meal shortly. Tonight, you will dine with me in the room adjoining yours—where we shared breakfast."

Nodding again, she moved past him as swiftly as she could—the instinct to avoid his reach as strong as ever. He grinned at her, as if very much aware of how he set her on edge.

"Until dinner, little dove," he purred before leaving the room and pulling the door closed behind him.

Daphne exhaled, the breath she'd been holding coming out in a rush. His threat of dragging out the inevitable breaching of her maidenhead proved more frightening than anything else she might endure while here. Not knowing when he might strike—when he might strip her naked and use her body for his own pleasure—would keep her constantly on edge. Which, she supposed, must be his aim.

"Well, you are alone now," she muttered to herself. "No need to fear that when he isn't even in the room."

Instead, she would turn her thoughts to the things Adam had revealed a moment ago. Wandering aimlessly around the room, she found an old but polished and well-preserved writing desk with a rough wooden chair pushed beneath it. Pulling out the chair, she sank down and opened the drawer. Inside, she found a stack of stationary, along with a quill pen and full inkwell.

Intriguing.

Had these items been placed here for her use? Perhaps Maeve had thought she'd want to write to her family while living at Dunnottar.

For now, she had nothing to say to her father that Adam had not already revealed in the missive he'd sent to London. What else could she tell him, other than 'I'm doing it for you, Papa, and Bertie, and Uncle William.' Her father would know without her needing to divulge it in a letter, and writing it would only bring her to tears. He would likely write back pleading with her to come home, crumbling her resolve. It was best if she did not make contact until she was ready to return, thirty thousand pounds richer.

Pulling out a sheet of the stationary, she unstopped the inkwell and wet the tip of the quill. In the haphazard scrawl that had always vexed her governess, she quickly recorded her thoughts on Adam's revelations.

Uncle William, drinking led to gambling.

Coerced into gambling away his fortune and property by Adam. Why?

A life for a life. Uncle William, a murderer?

Pausing for a moment, she absently toyed with the quill while staring at what she'd written so far. Adam had implied her uncle had caused someone pain—that it had not compared to the pain of the bullet wound he'd inflicted upon himself. Who could he have hurt so badly that Adam felt William no longer deserved to live?

In her experience, the male sex only reacted this strongly to the pain of another when it was inflicted upon a female in their care, or a child from their loins.

Furrowing her brow, she added another note.

A woman or child?

Had Adam ever been married or sired a babe? She could not think of a single bit of gossip she had overheard about Lord Hartmoor's family life. Being of both English and Scottish heritage, and owning property in London as well as in Scotland, he divided his time between the two places. Though, she could not recall hearing of him visiting London in quite some time. She had certainly never encountered him in town.

Five years ago. Adam's return to London coincides with Uncle William's sudden drinking?

She stared at the note after she'd jotted it down, and she fixated upon it. Daphne did not believe in coincidence. He had returned to London just before her family's troubles had begun. But, had his dastardly plan run its course? Or would her father and brother suffer even more of his wrath?

Rubbing her tired eyes, she decided it all required closer investigation. She would be prepared to give Adam whatever he asked in return for another piece of the puzzle.

She corked the inkwell and ensured her writing had dried upon the stationary before storing everything back inside the drawer. Shortly after, Maeve arrived with a lunch tray. After the events of the long morning and afternoon, Daphne was positively famished. The maid left the tray and retreated, apparently to see to some pressing task—which left her alone with her thoughts.

Thoughts that, despite her best attempts at avoidance, continued straying to Adam—his hands undressing her, touching her body, his lips claiming hers in a way she would be hard-pressed to forget.

Lord Adam Callahan had destroyed her family and purchased her body as he would a brothel whore ... yet, these things seemed minor in comparison to the way he'd set her body on fire, causing her to crave his touch when she should have found it repugnant.

That, Daphne realized, made him far more dangerous than she could have ever imagined.

4

aphne's second night at Dunnottar passed uneventfully, much to her surprise. As promised, Adam came to dine with her in the drawing room adjacent to her chambers— the same room where he'd shamed her in front of Niall and done wicked things to her on top of the table. Her face burned with excruciating embarrassment as she sat there, forced to eat at the same table upon which he had demonstrated how easily he could bend her to his will. He seemed to know it, casting her knowing glances from across the table, smugly smirking as he brought bits of lamb up to his mouth with his fork.

She half expected him to lunge across the table and take her down to the carpet, perhaps indulging in a repeat performance from this morning. Maybe he would push things further. Her throat had constricted at the thought, making it difficult to breathe, let alone eat.

However, Adam proved capable of behaving like a gentleman. They ate together in near silence, the only words exchanged comments on the spread laid out between them. Once they finished, he bid her good night and left her alone in the drawing room. He did not even touch her, though he did pause in the doorway and rake his gaze over her in that way of his—the way that reminded her that for the next twenty-nine days, she was this man's property. She'd barely survived the first day, feeling several times as if she might break under the strain and suspense. Yet, she had persevered.

"One down, twenty-nine more to go," she muttered to herself as she left the drawing room and returned to her own chamber.

Tomorrow, she would not spend so much of her time in this room alone. Perhaps she would explore more of the areas Adam had given her permission to enter. Though, curiosity had her wondering what lay in the wing just off the one she occupied. The one he had explicitly warned her away from.

"Don't be daft," she chided herself. "The man will throw you out without the money, and then where will you be?"

The sound of a throat being cleared startled her, and she fought to calm her racing heart as Maeve came into view, approaching from the corner of the room.

"Beg your pardon, my lady," she said with a quick curtsy. "I did not mean to frighten you. I was waiting up to prepare you for bed."

Lifting her chin, Daphne pretended to be unperturbed by having been caught talking to herself. "That would be fine, Maeve."

As the young maid approached, Daphne held still and allowed her to begin unfastening the gown. She released a sigh of relief as the constricting garment fell away, heedless to her nudity underneath. Despite being annoyed with Adam for insisting she have new clothing during her stay, she found herself looking forward to wearing garments that fit.

Maeve hummed happily as she gently laid the gown across the bench sitting at the foot of the bed, then took up the nightgown she'd draped beside it. Daphne studied the maid with curious eyes, wondering why she would willingly work for a man like Adam. Yes, work could be hard to come by for a servant, but there was no shortage of homes in London where Maeve could work as a lady's maid. What inspired such loyalty in her for the 'Master' of Dunnottar? Did she know about the things Adam had done to her since her arrival? Perhaps it was not surprising because he was in the habit of debauching young maidens of the *ton*. Or worse ... he had done them to Maeve.

For reasons she did not understand, the notion of Adam kissing Maeve the way he had her—touching her ... stripping away her clothing with a single gaze—caused anger to flare in her gut.

"There," Maeve said once she'd finished brushing and braiding Daphne's hair for bed. "Would you like anything before you go to sleep, my lady? A nightcap or tea, perhaps? A book to read? The Master gave me a collection of tomes he thought you might enjoy."

Raising her eyebrows, she paused in the middle of climbing into the bed, the covers turned down and one knee upon the mattress. "He did? When?"

Maeve smiled, beaming as if proud of her 'Master' for doing something so thoughtful for his guest. "Just this evening before dinner. I placed them on the bedside table."

Glancing to her left, she found a stack of books waiting for her beside a lit lamp. With a frown, she glanced back up at Maeve. The maid went on smiling, giving her an encouraging nod, her gaze darting to the pile.

Settling against the pillows, she sighed. "Thank you, Maeve. I will read one of these books, but the nightcap will not be necessary. Good night."

The maid curtsied and picked up her discarded dress and slippers before leaving. "Good night, my lady."

Once she had been left alone, Daphne reached toward the books, taking the one on top of the stack. Just because she hated Adam and the things he'd done to her family did not mean she couldn't enjoy what his extensive library had to offer. From what she'd seen during her tour today, there was more where these books had come from.

She glanced down at the front cover of the tome in her hands and gasped, her breath catching in her throat and beginning to burn. Her heart thundered in her chest as she read the inscribed words, her face growing hot.

The School of Venus, or the Ladies' Delight, Reduced into Rules of Practice.

An erotic novel. Adam had sent an erotic novel to her room.

Tossing the book aside, she reached for the next one in the stack, her jaw clenching as she read the second title.

Venus in the Cloister.

Yet another salacious and indecent work of fiction.

Daphne rifled through the others, her jaw dropping as she found more of the filth, more than she could possibly read in a night.

A Dialogue Between a Married Lady and a Maid.

Memoirs of a Woman of Pleasure.

The Tale of Two Lovers.

Fanny Hill.

Les Bijoux Indiscrets.

She shoved the books away, causing them to spread across her duvet. The covers stared up at her accusingly, the knowledge of their contents flooding her with shame, even though she hadn't read them.

Damn Adam ... he was making fun her and her confession from this afternoon. In fact, he'd probably known she would react this way —with maidenly outrage. He and Niall likely shared a good laugh over it in his study over tumblers of brandy. The thought infuriated her, and the urge to throw the books into the fire seized her.

Yet, as she glanced down at the tomes spread out in front of her, she decided not to stoop so low. If she destroyed his property, he might think of some way to make her pay for it—or worse, throw her out without the bank draft or the answers she'd come for.

Stacking the books neatly, she laid them on the bedside table. Then, plopping back against her pillows, she closed her eyes and waited for sleep to claim her. Exhaustion had been nipping at her heels all day, despite the nap she'd taken that afternoon. The long journey to Scotland and the emotional turmoil Adam had put her through since her arrival had wrung her dry. A few seconds with her eyes closed should have been enough to send her drifting off.

However, one minute passed, and then another, and another. The longer she lay there, counting the minutes as they passed her by, the more she thought of the books beside her. Like some unholy beacon drawing her in, the erotic novels seemed to call to her, to dare her to open their covers and discover the naughty delights inside.

Heaving a sigh, she opened her eyes and stared up at the canopy above her. He had been wrong about her. She was not a hypocrite—a lion in lambs' clothing. She had allowed a man to take a few liberties with her body and had enjoyed them. It was no more than some of her friends had done. That did not make her a whore, or a wicked person. If feeling such strong desires was unnatural, why did so many fall prey to scandal? Why countless women disgrace themselves for a stolen moment of pleasure?

Yet, the books continued to taunt her, the firelight flickering over them and casting their shadow against the paneled wall.

If her desires were normal, then reading about the desires of others couldn't be so bad. And, truly, reading them would mean she had won, not Adam. He wanted her to feel ashamed, to make fun of her confession. She would show him. She would read every one of these books, and when he asked how she enjoyed them, she would hold her head high and tell him her favorite parts.

That decided, she reached for the copy of *The School of Venus* and pried it open. Curling up against her pillows and angling the book so the candlelight shone upon the pages, she began to read.

THE NEXT MORNING, Daphne woke with a pounding headache. She hadn't slept much, becoming so engrossed in *The School of Venus* that she'd hardly been able to put it down. The titillating story of Kate and her intimate education at the hands of her suitor, Roger, had captured her attention thoroughly. Aside from putting heat in her cheeks, it had also made her giggle, proving to be quite witty in places. It had reminded her of those summers spent in the country, exploring new desires and passions with her dashing neighbor. In fact, those exploits proved fodder worthy of an erotic novel themselves.

She'd smiled to herself while reading, wondering if she could ever be bold enough to chronicle her own exploits. They might not be as salacious as the contents of *Venus*, but they certainly made her pulse race whenever she thought of them. Besides, by the end of her thirty days with Adam, perhaps she'd have even more material for such a project. The thought had dampened her excitement a bit. If she was going to explore her own sensuality with a man, she would never have chosen Lord Hartmoor with which to do it.

She'd had someone once, but had not seen him in years. Now that her family stood on the fringes of high society, he would likely shun her should they cross paths again. The notion made her chest ache, but she steeled herself against the sensation of heartbreak. She might never marry now that she had given herself over to Adam to be ruined, but she would be the savior of her family. It was all that mattered.

Morning seemed to arrive far too quickly after she'd finally set the novel aside to sleep, but once Maeve entered and threw open her curtains to allow in sunlight, Daphne could not coerce herself back to sleep. The maid cheerfully announced that her new wardrobe had arrived, before ushering in an army of footmen, all of whom toted shop packages wrapped in brown paper. Her eyes widened as the boxes slowly filled the room—covering the bed and every other available surface. Maeve turned in circles, her smile wide as she seemed to try to decide which to open first.

Approaching the bed, Daphne began tearing the paper off the first box her hand fell upon. "Why so many?"

Maeve joined her at the bed, lifting the lid off a hatbox and revealing a straw bonnet adorned with flowers along the brim. "The Master wanted you to have clothing for every possible contingency."

Frowning, she lifted a morning gown from her own box. "I cannot imagine why. I had thought I'd spend most of my time ..."

She paused and cleared her throat, pushing the first box aside to reach for a second. Maeve hummed quietly as she went about opening another. The unspoken thought lingered between them unsaid. Daphne had expected to spend most of her time nude in Adam's bed. It would seem her captor had other ideas. Not knowing what he could be thinking made her blood run cold, her mouth becoming dry while her head spun at the possibilities.

"Allow me to dress you and finish this on my own while you have breakfast and explore a bit, my lady," Maeve chirped, pulling a pair of slippers out of her hands.

Restlessness and the urge to leave this room caused Daphne to acquiesce. Perhaps some time spent exploring the castle would help pass the time until Adam decided he wanted her.

"Where is Lord Hartmoor?" she asked while the maid helped her out of her nightgown and into one of the new morning gowns—without undergarments.

"Had a bit of business to attend this morning," the maid replied. "He says you're to have breakfast on your own and occupy yourself until he's finished."

Maeve brushed her hair and secured a jeweled pink comb into one side, sweeping the hair away from her ear. Then came her stockings and slippers, before another ribbon tied around her throat—pink trimmed in white lace. Inside one of the boxes, she spied several spools of ribbon in an array colors—some trimmed in lace, others with false gemstones. Also Adam's doing, she supposed. He'd seemed to like the blue ribbon she'd worn yesterday. With a disdainful snort, she realized that, of course, he'd enjoyed a piece of clothing meant to make her look like a pet. A possession. His to use and toy with.

Giving her a curious glance, Maeve announced she was finished and that breakfast would be served in the adjoining drawing room as before. She left the maid to her work and walked into the drawing room to find the table laden with several dishes and the same silver tea service. Only, this time, she ate alone, without even the imposing presence of Niall to disturb her. Once she'd eaten her fill, she left the drawing room through a door leading into the corridor. Pausing, she glanced toward the sharp turn leading to a different wing of the castle. The forbidden corridor.

Realizing Adam would likely become angry if he caught her even contemplating going down there, she turned the way she'd gone with him the day before. Walking at a leisurely pace, she opened doors and peered into the rooms to familiarize herself further with this wing of the palace.

Most of them turned out to be guest chambers with adjoining sitting rooms, but one door not far from her own room drew her in. Stepping through the doorway, her eyes wide and jaw slack with awe, she observed the impressive collection of instruments making up a music room. A long, low table against one wall held several violins, flutes, a clarinet, and a lute. A collection of polished brass music stands gleamed in the light of several lamps, while stacks of sheet music littered the end tables situated between oversized pieces of furniture. A harpsichord and spinet took up opposite corners of the room.

However, the two instruments filling the center of the room drew her eye and held her attention. The first was a large, golden harp— the most beautiful she'd ever seen. Its pillar had been adorned with the painted figures of angels taking flight. As she came closer, unable to keep her hands off the instrument, her gaze roamed over the angelic fixtures, their hair billowing as if they flew into the wind, their golden wings stretched behind them. She smiled as memories of learning the instrument came back to her. It had been ages since she'd touched a harp, but as she caressed the strings of this one, something within her resounded with overwhelming force. Should she decide to attempt it, she had a feeling her fingers would return to the practice with stunning accuracy. A part of her, clearly, had not forgotten.

Beside the harp rested the largest, most beautiful pianoforte she'd ever seen. Its polished surface, the worn cushion of the bench resting before it, and the lit lamps told her someone used this room quite often. Obviously, the servants took care to ensure it would be ready for said person's use.

Adam, perhaps? Or someone else in his household?

Was there even a household here at Dunnottar? From what she'd seen, Lord Hartmoor resided here alone.

"Do you play an instrument?"

His deep, resonant voice caused her to flinch, her blood rushing as her skin seemed to vibrate in response to his presence. Resting one hand on the surface of the pianoforte, she turned slowly to face him, taking a deep breath and gathering her wits. Her breath came out in a rush as their gazes collided—hers wide and frightened, his feral and primitive. He leaned against the door frame, his casual posture belied by the capacity for destruction radiating from his eyes.

His hair had been pulled back and secured with a ribbon at the nape of his neck, though his attire proved downright indecent. He wore no coat, and his shirt lay open to reveal most of his chest. Coils of dark hair drew her eye, blanketing bulging muscles which made her mouth go dry. His breeches were so snug, there was no disguising the steady swell of his cock as he stood there staring at her. Despite his distance from her and such dim lighting, she could see he was only half-aroused. Even then, the masculine organ appeared as intimidating as the rest of him.

Raising one eyebrow, he smirked at her as if discerning the direction of her thoughts. "I asked you a question, Daphne."

Shaking her head, she blinked and forced her gaze away from him, focusing on the wallpaper. "I was never any good at the pianoforte ... much to my mother's chagrin. But the harp ..."

Her gaze strayed to the beautiful golden instrument, though Adam's never left her. She could feel his gaze caressing her form, undressing her with his eyes. Her throat seized as she wondered if she would surrender her maidenhead here, on the carpet, in this music room, with the painted angels gazing down upon her.

"Would you like to play it?" he asked, straightening away from the door frame and entering the room.

The hard muscles now moved fluidly beneath his clothing and his skin as he approached her slowly, like a hunter stalking its next meal. She backed away from him until the pianoforte halted her progress. Her rear struck the keys, sending a discordant collection of notes floating through the air.

"I ... I would," she stammered. "If you will allow it."

He paused when only a bare inch of space separated them, bracing his hands on either side of her against the instrument, his arms trapping her. She tried to hold her breath, but after a while, found it necessary to inhale—drawing his fragrance into her nostrils. Her head spun as that spicy scent of his seemed to imprint itself on her from the inside.

"Perhaps I will," he murmured in a teasing tone. "Perhaps I will not. It all depends, Daphne."

Lifting her chin and fighting to maintain her dignity, she met his piercing gaze with a level stare of her own. "Upon?"

"Upon what you are willing to give me in return," he replied, reaching up to stroke the line of her jaw. "Are you ready to reveal more of your secrets to me, little dove?"

Goosebumps pricked along her skin as his touch skimmed the side of her neck, pausing over the ribbon as if in approval, then moving farther down.

"What would you like to know?"

Suddenly taking hold of her waist, he lifted her onto the surface of the pianoforte. The backs of her thighs struck the keys, filling the room with more disjointed notes. He sank onto the bench before her, their positions bringing his head level with her knees. Grasping her ankles, he gazed up at her, a wicked gleam creeping into his eyes.

"Did you choose a book from among those I sent?" he asked, tightening his hold on her legs, his large hands akin to shackles.

"I did," she replied. "*The School of Venus.*"

"Ah," he said. "The salacious adventures of the virginal Katy. Quite a … stimulating read."

One of his hands slid up over her calf, sending a shiver down her spine. Stimulating, indeed.

"I found it interesting," she admitted, her defenses melting away as both his palms stroked her legs, his rough callouses abrading the silk covering them.

He was doing it again, battering her defenses, tearing down her guard and forcing her to feel … to acknowledge how the pleasure affected her, how *he* affected her.

"Did you?" he prodded. "Perhaps it was also educational?"

Pursing her lips, she refused to break his gaze as he slid her gown up to her knees, his fingers curling around her garters. He moved his knuckles languidly against her skin, curling his digits around the lace and ribbon-adorned garters.

"The content, thus far, is hardly shocking," she replied, raising her eyebrows at him. "It was nothing I was not already aware of."

Releasing her garters with a tug, he smirked when she gasped at the feel of the fabric snapping against her skin. His hands glided higher, skimming her thighs, his fingers digging in once he'd reached her hips. She stiffened, her breasts lifting as she sucked in a deep breath and it caught in her lungs.

"My little dove has been naughty," he teased, shifting closer and wedging his broad shoulders between her knees. "Tell me, Daphne, how many men have plundered your body ... and I will allow you to practice the harp whenever you wish."

"Th-there has only been one before you," she whispered, closing her eyes against the shame flushing her cheeks as he nuzzled her mons through her gown—reminding her that only one layer of thin fabric separated him from her.

"A lucky bastard," he growled, his breath heating the flesh between her legs. "Did he find his way beneath your gown, like this?"

She squirmed, her breath coming out in a rush when he gave her hips a squeeze. "Yes."

Another growl emitted from his throat ... primal, masculine. "How old were you the first time you let him touch you?"

"Ten and six, the first time. His family's country estate bordered ours, and we were of an age."

She had promised herself that she would not reveal these things to him, but he was leaving her with no choice. Just as he had that morning he'd thrown her, naked, onto the table, he was giving her no room to deny him.

Closing her eyes, she tried to pretend she could not feel his burning gaze on her. She reminded herself that giving him this secret would allow her something she wanted ... and she'd already lost the fight over underthings with him. It would injure her pride to lose ground here, as well. Besides, these mundane details did not give him the full picture of her feelings for the young suitor of her past ... nor did they ruin them. She would not let him ruin them.

"How romantic," he grumbled, clear disdain tingeing his words. "The lord's young daughter and the neighbor's son ... sneaking away to steal kisses when Papa isn't watching. Such a wicked girl you were."

Her response died on her lips as he suddenly jerked her gown up to her waist, baring her body from the hips down. Despite the fact that he'd already seen her naked, instinct caused her thighs to clench inward. They met the resistance of his shoulders, and he chuckled, seeming to sense her distress over being unable to cover herself.

She kept her eyes closed, hoping that detaching herself from him would make this easier for her. Perhaps she could pretend he was her first lover—a man who had touched her with such reverence and care.

His hand cracked against her inner thigh in a reprimand, and a gasp lodged in her throat as her eyes flew open. Gazing down at him in shock, she bit back a whimper at the stinging pain blossoming where he'd struck her.

His gaze burned into her, his voice clipped and abrupt when he spoke. "Always keep your eyes open. I don't want you escaping me."

It lay on the tip of her tongue to argue that she hadn't been trying to escape. But they would both know it to be a lie. That was precisely what she'd been trying to do. As he turned his head and began kissing her reddened flesh, Daphne realized she should have known he would never allow it.

So, she kept her rapt attention upon him as he went on kissing the inside of her thigh, as if to soothe the skin he'd bruised. He hadn't shaved this morning, and his sharp stubble prickled her skin, exacerbating the sting from his blow. Yet, his lips skimmed her in a pleasant counterpoint. The dual sensations did queer things to her belly, twisting her in knots until she was left uncertain of how to feel.

"Tell me more about your first lover," he mumbled between kisses, bracing his large hands upon her thighs to hold her open.

She shuddered in his grasp, but could not move otherwise, forced to rest on her elbows as he turned his attention to her other leg, kissing her and running his nose along her skin as if breathing her in. The longer she watched him, the more some hidden part of her reacted ... the more she enjoyed what he did to her.

"He was no one important," she lied.

She might reveal her secrets, but she would not utter his name.

"Of course he was," Adam countered, lifting his head and meeting her gaze once more. "He must have been quite special to you ... if you allowed him access to your body. Did he touch you, little dove?"

His breath tickled her mons, the sensation lodging her breath in her throat. She could only manage a swift, jerky nod, which prompted a feline smile from Adam.

"Like this?" he asked, slipping a thumb between her nether lips, seeking out the little bud of her pleasure.

She gasped when he pressed down upon it, then began moving his thumb in slow circles. Her insides fluttered, her hips bucking against his hand.

How did he do this ... understand what her body would respond to with such accuracy?

"N-no," she panted out between swift breaths. "I mean ... yes, but ... not the way you are doing it."

He chuckled, the golden flecks in his eyes becoming downright molten as he held her gaze while still steadily stroking her clitoris. "Do you not like the way I'm touching you?"

The shudder that tore through her answered his question, even as she struggled to find words. Her mind had begun to fade as her body seemed to practically hum with pleasure from the press of only his thumb.

"His touch was lighter than yours," she whispered. "Gentler."

He laughed again, the one hand holding her thigh tightening, sending a jolt of pleasure straight to her core.

"What a gentleman he must have been. I'd wager he did not open you up and spread you out wide like this, did he?"

Her face flamed hot as she recalled the slender hands of the man in question slipping beneath her skirts, touching her through her drawers. She did not need to answer for Adam to know to truth.

"His loss, I say," he declared. "How about this, little dove ... did he touch you like this?"

She mewled when he pushed a thick finger inside of her, the wetness he'd coaxed from her core slicking his path. One of her feet slipped and struck several keys of the pianoforte, sending notes of music floating through the air to mingle with the soft sounds he pushed out of her with each slow stroke of his finger inside her. A familiar sensation began winding in her middle, growing tighter and tighter until she felt as if she might snap. Arching her back, she struggled to keep her eyes open as Adam had demanded. But she was spiraling, her body hovering on the verge of release.

"Did he?" he asked again, his voice growing sharper as he suddenly pulled out of her.

"No," she exclaimed, the word coming out on a cry of regret at the loss of that thick digit filling her.

"How about like this?" he asked, pressing both thumbs to the lips of her mons and parting them to reveal the tender flesh inside.

Before she could reply, he laid his tongue against her, dragging it up and over her folds, then swirling it over her clit in one long lap. She cried out, her eyes falling closed again as the unfamiliar sensation sent fresh waves of desire through her. Now beyond caring about who he was or what he'd done, her body simply craved release. For thirty days, he would possess her body, use it as he saw fit. Why should she not derive pleasure if he wanted to give it? The alternative was something she did not wish to think of.

"N-no," she whispered, trembling in his hold. "No one has ever done that to me before."

He made a little sound in the back of his throat just before surging forward and putting his mouth on her. His tongue laved her clit while he suckled at her tender inner flesh, his hands holding tight to her thighs. Her head fell back, and she melted, her limbs becoming heavy as he nibbled upon her as if starving. He licked and kissed, suckled and tugged, causing her to squirm beneath him, her feet and legs striking the keys when he struck a particularly sensitive place and caused her entire body to quake. Then, he centered all his attentions upon her clit, drawing it into his mouth and sucking it with deep, merciless pulls that made her toes curl.

The tension in her core unfurled in a torrent that stole her breath away. Her lips parted on a silent cry as the tremors of a climax ripped violently through her, accompanied by a flood of moisture. Adam held her down when her hips lifted from the pianoforte, refusing to pull his lips away from her until the spasms had ceased and she'd gone still beneath him.

Opening her eyes, she found the ceiling above her spinning, her entire world tilting and swaying precariously. She'd achieved climax many times—both at the hand of her first lover, and at her own once she'd figured out that she need only touch herself the way he had—but it had never been so explosive, so all-encompassing. And he'd only been touching her with his mouth.

Struggling back up onto her elbows, she forced herself to look at him. It would not do to lose what she'd gained if he caught her trying to avoid looking at him. He was watching her with a smirk curving his arrogant mouth, the twinkle in his eye unmistakable. He knew what he'd just done to her and must be feeling quite proud of himself. He stood abruptly, forcing a gasp from her as her heart began to pound in anticipation of what he would do next. Her legs flailed, her instinct for self-preservation flaring to life as he loomed over her—so overwhelmingly large and masculine.

With a throaty laugh, he hooked his fingers into the ribbon tied around her neck and pulled, hauling her up against him. His wide body forced her legs to remain parted, leaving her open and vulnerable to him as he kept hold of the ribbon, his knuckles digging into her throat.

Lifting his other hand to her face, he held her captive with his fiery eyes, locked in her stare as he ran his index finger over her lips. The scent of her own arousal flooded her senses, mingling with Adam's earthy, masculine aroma. It proved a heady fragrance, making her head spin and her body relax against his. He flicked his tongue out, tickling her upper lip, then her lower, then the seam of her mouth. She opened for him with a sigh, whimpering as their mingled taste overwhelmed her palate, causing desire to flare back to life deep in her belly.

Pulling away abruptly, he sat her up, taking both her hands in his and pressing them against his middle. She gasped at the feel of him through his shirt. Without the layers of a waistcoat and coat between them, she could feel every hard inch of his abdomen, his skin radiating heat through the linen.

"Now you," he demanded. "Show me how you touched him."

Her hands trembled as she wrinkled her brow, her mouth going dry as she realized what he was asking her to do. She'd only ever been so bold once, after much cajoling.

His hand shot up in an eye's blink, his fingers biting into her jaw. She gasped at the naked intensity she found in his gaze, a quiet threat lurking in the depths.

"Obey, Daphne," he said in a low whisper more threatening than any roar would have been. "If you fight me, I'll only enjoy it more."

His words spurred her into action, and she dropped her hands to his breeches, her fingers fumbling to get them open. Clenching her teeth, she forced her shaking hands into submission and managed to open his fall, freeing the heavy root between his thighs. Her mouth fell open in a shocked gasp as she glanced down at his cock, the long, thick organ stretching out toward her through the opening of his breeches, the head dripping with wetness.

She'd only touched one other man's cock, and his hadn't been half as big as this. Her gut churned as she tried to imagine him putting it inside of her and wondering if he might not split her in two. Shaking herself out of her reverie, she reminded herself of his threat. If she didn't do what he'd demanded, who knew what he'd do to punish her.

Wrapping one hand around him, she tested his weight and length, curiosity propelling her past fear. When she had touched her previous lover, she'd been too ashamed to look at him, too young and afraid to be so bold. This would be her first unobstructed view of a man's cock, as well as her first thorough exploration.

His skin was hot and smooth, so soft against her palm. Yet, when she gave him a little squeeze, he felt as if he were made of iron inside, hard and unrelenting. Grunting, he surged his hips, stroking it against her palm. She followed his lead, closing her hand around him, her fingers barely meeting her thumb as she stroked in time with his thrusts.

He grasped her other hand and urged it toward his cock, wrapping it around him just above the other. But he did not let go this time. Instead, he kept a tight hold on her fist and guided her, shifting his hips to meet each downward motion. His breath grew harsher, and against the base of his throat, his pulse hammered wildly.

"That's it, little dove," he groaned, quickening their strokes by coaxing her hands faster, the moisture urged from his head causing skin to glide easily over skin. "Stroke me with those soft, pretty hands."

He captured her lower lip between his teeth, making her whimper and flinch at the stinging nip of his teeth. Then he soothed it with his tongue, plunging it into her mouth while he kept thrusting his cock into her hands.

"Fuck," he muttered, jerking against her and gritting his teeth, the corded muscles of his neck straining.

A shudder wracked him, and then he spent, his cock shooting hot spurts of his seed onto her. She gasped when it splattered her lower belly, another sudden stream of it staining one of her thighs, even more of it dribbling over the back of one hand. Staring at him open-mouthed, she remained speechless as he straightened and tucked himself back into his breeches.

Still breathing heavily, his chest stretching his shirt with each inhale, he gave her a wicked grin. "The harp is yours, little dove ... whenever you wish."

Then, he was turning to leave, striding for the door with all the swagger and cocky assurance of a man who'd just gotten exactly what he wanted.

Daphne remained where she sat on the pianoforte for a moment, still shocked. She trembled, her body humming as if her blood rushed hotly through her veins. As promised, he'd used her, and it would seem he was now finished.

Carefully lowering herself to the floor, she cringed as her gown fell to cover her. Adam's seed still marked her, sticky and wet against her belly and one thigh. Hoping Maeve would not be in her chambers so she could clean the evidence of the encounter off her body in private, she left the room.

5

After cleaning herself up, Daphne left her chambers and continued exploring the castle alone. Despite now having Adam's permission to use the harp in the music room, she had grown too restless to sit still and practice. Her encounter with the Master of this imposing palace was never far from her mind, each touch of his hand and stroke of his tongue indelibly imprinted on her memory. As she walked through the house, taking her time to inspect more of the rooms more closely, just the thought of the wicked things he'd done caused her face to flush. Her nipples grew tight beneath her gown, her thighs becoming slick from the moisture pooling there.

Lord Hartmoor had achieved the very thing she had hoped he would not by making her desire him. While it should relieve her that she would at least find pleasure during their encounters, it also frightened her. The man had paid to use her body as if she were no better than a prostitute, and now, he would make her like it. If the way she was feeling right now were any indication, he would make her crave it.

Turning her thoughts away from him proved impossible when she remained always aware of her surroundings, the ominous castle a reflection of its owner. A bit of fresh air would help to clear her head before she would inevitably face him again. She returned to her chambers for a shawl, uncertain of the weather, but knowing protection from catching a chill would be needed when she traipsed about with only one layer of fabric between herself and the elements.

As she left her room, she nearly collided with a maid carrying a basket full of freshly laundered clothing. She gasped as the woman fell onto her rear on the ground, several items falling out of her basket.

"Oh, I beg your pardon," she said, reaching down to offer the maid a hand up. "I'm afraid my mind was elsewhere."

The maid smiled, but it seemed forced. She pointedly avoided Daphne's gaze as she crouched to begin picking up the things that had fallen out of her basket.

"It's quite all right, m'lady," the maid mumbled.

"Here, let me help you," Daphne said, kneeling to lend a hand.

The maid gasped, snatching the items she held and shoving them into the basket. Daphne frowned while the maid swiftly gathered the other articles as if offended that she would dare touch them. Shoving them quickly under a stack of linens, she straightened and bobbed in a swift curtsy.

"Sorry to have troubled you, m'lady," she mumbled before moving quickly around Daphne and disappearing down the corridor.

Brow furrowed, she turned and watched the maid retreat, her curiosity growing as she turned left and ventured down the forbidden corridor. Lingering where the maid had left her, Daphne's mind spun as she considered what she'd just seen. The only indoor servants she'd encountered since arriving at Dunnottar had been Maeve and Niall. Her assumption that there must be a larger staff here rang true now that she'd spotted a chambermaid in the halls. More disconcerting proved the clothing she'd noticed in the woman's hands. Clothing trimmed in bits of lace.

Clothing which clearly belonged to a female.

And since the maid had taken them, freshly laundered, into the forbidden corridor, Daphne could only conclude that Dunnottar had a female resident. Bile rose up in the back of her throat, acidic and bitter as she wondered who the woman might be. A wife, a mistress? Another unsuspecting chit like her, who had been coerced into selling her body?

The thought caused her throat to clench, anger fisting her hands at her sides. She must know the truth—especially if there turned out to be a Lady Hartmoor she'd known nothing about. She could not —would not—lay with another woman's husband, not even for thirty thousand pounds. Not even for the answers she had come for. It was one thing to sell herself ... it was quite another to commit a sin so grievous as to participate in adultery.

That decided, she made her way to Adam's study. Her shoulders slumped when she found it empty, the fire in the hearths burned down to nothing but embers. In a huff, she stomped back to her room, determined to find answers. There, she found Maeve hanging the last of her gowns in the armoire.

"Oh, my lady!" Maeve exclaimed, turning to face her with a bright smile. "Is there something you're needing?"

"Yes," she declared, closing the door firmly and crossing her arms over her chest as she faced the rosy-faced young woman. "You can tell me who else resides here with Lord Hartmoor."

If she weren't mistaken, the maid's cheeks flushed scarlet, her gaze lowering to the floor.

"Well, there's Niall and me, of course," she murmured, her voice so low, Daphne had to edge closer to hear.

"Of course," she prodded. "And a host of other servants, I imagine. A castle of this size must require a large staff to see it run efficiently."

Maeve nodded, forcing a smile and timidly meeting Daphne's gaze. "You've the right of it. There's the cook and the scullery maids, the footmen and grooms ... chambermaids and the like."

Inclining her head, Daphne raised one eyebrow. "And who, besides Lord Hartmoor, do these servants tend to? A wife? A mistress? Members of the Callahan family?"

Lifting her chin, Maeve folded her hands neatly before her. "Now, my lady, it will not do for you to ask such questions of me. The Master will not like it."

"Hang what your Master does or does not like!" Daphne spat, her nerves already frazzled by the explosive encounter in the music room, and now the realization that she might be cuckolding the lady of the manor in her own home.

Maeve gasped, flinching as if Daphne had blasphemed. "My lady, please ... your time here could be so much more enjoyable if you do not go putting your nose where it doesn't belong. The Master wants you here, in this corridor, where you'll be comfortable and—"

"And ensconced away from his lady wife?" she interjected.

"No, my lady," Maeve replied, a pleading tone in her voice. "It is nothing like that."

"Then why will you not simply tell me?"

Moving around Daphne and busying herself with tidying the surface of the vanity, the maid went on avoiding her gaze. "Please, speak of this no more. If the Master knew we'd discussed this, he'd be furious."

Scoffing, Daphne waved a dismissive hand at Maeve. Her long legs carried her quickly to the door, which she threw open and slammed behind her in her frustration. She was not usually so petulant, but the unwavering loyalty of this woman to her so-called 'Master' irked her to no end. With a sardonic smirk, she wondered what Maeve would think of Adam if she knew of the things he'd done to her on top of his pianoforte. Her face flushed at the thought, and she supposed the maid might not hate him for it. After all, he'd ensured Daphne received her pleasure before taking his own.

But, at what cost could she enjoy his hands on her body, and eventually the coupling he was parting with a small fortune for?

Daphne would never be able to live with herself if he turned out to have a wife, closeted away in some far-flung wing of the castle while he took up with her. Determined to know the truth before she allowed him to lay another hand upon her, she set out to find him.

However, a quick sweep of the areas she knew of the house turned up nothing, and an inquiry of the imposing butler revealed

Adam had left Dunnottar on urgent business in Kincardineshire. He would return for dinner and had requested she join him.

Daphne would be prepared to meet him, and she would not rest until she'd gotten the answer to at least this one burning question. Perhaps then, the guilt of what she'd allowed herself to sink to would not be so unbearable.

DAPHNE ARRIVED in the dining room that evening to find Adam already there. For the first time since they'd met, he was dressed appropriately—his shirt buttoned to the throat and a simply-tied cravat adorned with an onyx stickpin, a brocade waistcoat hugging his chest and waist, a black coat clinging to his shoulders. Not a strand of his hair appeared out of place, combed back from his forehead and tied neatly at his nape.

Still, even dressed so finely, the subtle air of danger remained. In truth, these clothes only heightened the effect, the stark shades making his hair and eyes darker. His body appeared even bigger wrapped in a waistcoat and breeches, the thick column of his neck and rigid slash of his jaw hardly softened by the white linen neck cloth.

He stood behind the chair at the head of the table, hands clasped behind his back. When his gaze fell on her, she froze in the doorway, held captive by his eyes. While his expression remained unmoved—stern, emotionless—the pools of his eyes changed, becoming more liquid, like molten bronze. As those eyes of his lowered, his gaze caressing her from across the room, she supposed he found her attire acceptable.

Maeve had dressed her in burgundy satin trimmed in black lace, the matching gloves covering her arms to the elbow. Despite her protestations, the maid had also tied a length of matching ribbon around her throat, insisting the Master would like it. Daphne supposed it could not hurt to try to appeal to his baser urges. Perhaps if he was pleased with the way she looked, he would be more amenable to answering her questions.

"You look ravishing, little dove," he declared, coming around the table toward her. "Will you stand there all night for me to admire you, or will you join me at the table?"

The softness of his tone, as well as the humor dancing in his eyes, disarmed her as he approached, offering her a hand. Was this some sort of trick? This was, perhaps, the politest he had been to her since their first meeting. As she placed a hand in his and let him lead her to her place to the right of his setting, she could almost imagine he was escorting her at a London dinner party.

Someone had gone through a great deal of trouble for just the two of them, laying out a variety of sumptuous dishes and adorning the table with beautiful Wedgewood china. Candles lent an ethereal glow to the darkened room, the drapes shut against the light of the moon.

If she did not know better, she would think the man was attempting to be romantic. She decided to play along, and hoped it would smooth the way for her inquiries.

"You look quite handsome this evening," she remarked, reaching for her napkin and neatly draping it over her lap.

He grinned, leaning back in his chair far more casually than would be acceptable in a London dining room. The posture reminded her how little Adam seemed to regard propriety.

"Do I?" he teased. "Well, that is good to hear. I shall convey your appreciation to Maeve, who insisted I must dress properly when dining in such fine company."

She gave him a smile, hoping it appeared genuine. Her hands trembled in her lap, and her body seemed to remain on high alert, as if remembering how easily and quickly he could have her naked and spread out wherever he pleased. He'd already proven he wasn't above draping her over a table and having his way with her.

"Would you care for wine?" he asked, gesturing toward the two bottles resting on the table between them. "I dismissed the footmen so we could dine alone, so we are to serve ourselves this evening. I was not sure which you would prefer, so I ordered both sherry and Madeira brought from the cellar."

"I would love the Madeira, thank you," she replied. "That was thoughtful of you, Adam."

He filled the empty goblet beside her place setting, then his own. After placing the bottle back between them, he eyed her with open curiosity.

"So amenable this evening," he remarked. "To what do I owe the sudden shift in your demeanor?"

Daphne took a quick sip of her wine to avoid answering right away. His query made her pulse race, worry that he could see right through her making her antsy. The fortifying swallow of Madeira took a bit of the edge off, and she relaxed a bit in her seat.

"Perhaps you allowing me to use the harp has pacified me," she hedged, shrugging one bare shoulder.

Adam reached for one of the platters and began serving himself, so Daphne followed suit. She was ravenous and took a large helping of venison before reaching for the turnips.

"Hmm," he murmured while he helped himself to a healthy portion of lamb. "Yet, I did not hear one note of music before I left for Kincardineshire."

She lowered her eyes and bit back the words hovering on the tip of her tongue. Instead of informing him that she'd been too busy scrubbing his seed off her skin, then trying to unravel the mystery of the hidden woman in his house, she cut her meat and avoided his gaze.

"I plan to take up my practice tomorrow," she said. "It has been ages, but I do not believe I've grown too rusty since the last time I touched a harp."

"I fully expect to hear sweet music drifting down the corridor to my study," he said, glancing up at her between bites of food. "After all, you more than earned as much time with the instrument as you wish."

The reminder of what she'd had to do to 'earn' the harp almost caused her to choke. She cleared her throat and forced a swallow, taking a sip of wine to wash it down. His teasing set her teeth on edge, but she managed to keep her composure as they ate.

He asked he why she'd learned the harp, and she answered that she'd been terrible at the pianoforte so her mothered had hired someone to teach her a different instrument. From the moment she'd first touched the harp, she'd excelled.

She asked him about his business in Kincardineshire, and whether he owned lands here in Scotland. He informed her that Dunnottar was simply a castle, not a grand estate with farms and tenants. He did, however, own two larger holdings, both with lands and tenants to be managed—one in Scotland, and the other in England. The time in his study must surely be spent safeguarding his assets.

He spoke of the fair weather today, informing her she was free to take a horse out for a ride tomorrow if it held up, providing she took Maeve for an escort. She thanked him for his generosity and praised the efforts of his chef as she tasted a bit of everything before serving herself dessert.

Daphne was almost loath to destroy the easy camaraderie they'd found during dinner. For at least an hour, he'd been polite, a perfect gentleman who seemed to listen to everything she had to say, answering her questions and asking a few of his own.

Still, the nagging suspicion concerning what he hid in that forbidden corridor would not allow her to enjoy his company with ease. Not when his wife could be eating her own dinner alone in her chambers right now.

The thought washed over her like a frigid douse of water, and she dropped her fork to her plate, the loud clangor drawing his sharp gaze. He frowned as she straightened, lifting her chin and narrowing her eyes at him.

"Is there something wrong with your dessert?" he asked, a look of genuine curiosity plastered across his face.

Instead of answering his question, she volleyed one of her own at him. "Is there a woman living here?"

Pausing with his wine goblet halfway to his mouth, he gave her an amused smirk. "Aye, little dove ... you."

Scoffing, she shook her head, annoyed with his avoidance of her question. "I meant, other than me. A wife? A mistress? Someone you don't want me to encounter during my time here?"

For a moment, something flickered in his gaze, but it disappeared as quickly as it had appeared. Had that been shock—anxiety, even? As if she'd struck a nerve.

He inclined his head. "What does it matter?"

"It matters!" she exclaimed, her voice raising as the annoyance and anger she'd been trying to hold back all evening boiled to the surface. "It matters if you are keeping both your wife and your ... your ..."

"Whore?" he finished for her with a sarcastic smirk.

After coercing her into this agreement, humiliating her in front of his butler, then subjecting her to his debauched attentions, he had the nerve to refer to *her* as a whore?

Rage gripped her so swiftly, she could hardly register the emotion before it propelled her to act. Wrapping one hand around the stem of her goblet—which he had just refilled for her—she tossed its contents in his direction. The amber liquid splashed his face, soaking his cravat and front of his shirt. He flinched, closing his eyes and reaching quickly for his napkin, using it to clear his vision before settling his gaze on her.

Dread coiled in her belly at the predatory gleam in his eye, his jaw hardening as he glared at her, nostrils flaring like an animal scenting its prey. She realized her error far too late, and now could not find the strength to stand and run. Her legs had turned to jelly, and she remained frozen in his stare, even as his upper lip curled back from his teeth in a snarl. Even as he took up his own glass and flung its contents at her, returning tit for tat.

She gasped when his wine missed her face but soaked her neck and chest. It sluiced into her cleavage and down her belly, causing her bodice to cling to her breasts. As she stared at him in open-mouthed shock, he reached out and grasped one of her wrists.

Before she knew what was happening, he had hauled her out of her chair and into his lap. She struggled in his hold, but he quickly captured her other wrist, winding it behind her back. Then, bending the other arm so both were trapped behind her, he secured her wrists with one large hand. He used the other to grasp her throat, the light hold just enough of a threat to frighten her into submission.

He was looking at her the same way he had before stripping her naked and humiliating her in front of Niall. The same way he had when threatening to debauch her in every way he could think of. Had she angered him enough that he would simply throw her onto the table and ravage her?

A shiver raced through her—though, with the way her traitorous body behaved in his presence, she could not be certain whether it was from fear or excitement.

"Shocked, little dove?" he growled, his teasing tone edged like the blade of a knife. "Perhaps I should have forewarned you, I am no gentleman, and your maidenly outbursts and childish tantrums will not endear you to me."

"That you are no gentleman has been quite apparent to me from the beginning," she snarled.

Tightening his hold on her neck just enough to kick her pulse up a notch, he leaned closer ... so close, his mouth brushed the line of her jaw. She shivered, her body now chilled by the Madeira soaking the front of her gown.

"One turn deserves another, does it not?" he murmured, his lips gliding along her jaw line and toward her chin.

He opened his mouth and lapped at her skin, now sticky from the wine. He made a sound low in his throat, like a purr, then closed his lips around her chin and suckled.

"If you wanted me to lap wine off your beautiful tits, you should have simply said so, Daphne," he uttered, the rumble of his deep voice stroking down her spine as he kissed her jaw, then lapped at it with his hot, rough tongue.

"I do not ... oh!"

Her protest broke off on a surprised cry as he lowered his head toward her collarbone, then licked his way slowly up the side of her neck. Latching on, he suckled, drawing a breathless sound from deep in her throat.

"Of course you do," he whispered, his breath tickling the areas he'd left damp with his tongue. "I can feel you responding to me ... hell, if you were any more aroused, I'd be able to smell you."

His crude words stunned her; yet, her cunt throbbed in response, her nipples tightening and her breath quickening. He continued lapping at her, like a cat enjoying a saucer of cream, forging a slow path down toward her décolletage. Releasing her throat, he gripped the front of her bodice, snatching it down to free her breasts. He paused, his lips poised just above the fleshy mounds.

"Christ, you're a bonny thing," he murmured, his breath causing goose bumps to spread over her naked chest. "No, little dove ... to answer your question, there is no woman here. Only you. Mine to do with as I please."

"For the next twenty-eight days, at least," she replied defiantly, despite the urge to arch her back and place her nipple within reach of his mouth striking her hard and deep.

He chuckled, nuzzling one of her breasts and teasing it with a quick swipe of his tongue. "Of course."

She gasped when he continued licking her clean, delving his tongue between her breasts, then tracing the crest of each one, pointedly avoiding her nipples. She squirmed in his lap, beyond caring that each movement caused her bottom to surge against his cock. The organ was full and thick, throbbing against her through his breeches.

"I will not lie with another woman's husband," she managed between pants, her resolve slipping away as he went on teasing her, taking little nips at her breasts, nuzzling her neck, teasing her collarbone with his teeth. "Not even for thirty thousand pounds."

"I have no wife," he grunted. "Now cease your prattling."

She gasped when his lips closed around her nipple, finally giving her what she wanted. The pleasure of his tongue circling the tight bud struck her deep, causing answering twinges of longing deep in her core. He suckled her with relish, his cheeks caving in as he drew as much of her into his mouth as could fit, as if he wanted to devour her whole.

She became pliant in his hands, a bit of clay for him to mold how he wished. Even the discomfort of her arms being held behind her back faded as he released one breast and moved to the other. Nipping at her with his teeth caused her to cry out at the slight sting, then sigh, melting from the pleasure of his tongue soothing it away.

When he stopped, she wanted to weep, the pulsing between her thighs now unbearable. She wanted to twine her fingers through his hair and hold him to her breasts, arching her back and inviting him to consume as much of her as he desired. Yet, the unrelenting hand wrapped around her wrists reminded her she was in no position to make demands of him.

She'd lost her grip on rationale, craving the mouth of a man who, when he wasn't making her feel this way, was hurling insults at her and speaking ill of her family. It defied explanation and reason, this notion that she could desire someone she loathed. She had always thought of softer emotions and desire to be intertwined, but Adam proved her wrong with every kiss, every touch.

As if to further prove his point, he released her wrists and pushed her to her feet. Then, moving his chair back from the table a bit, he grabbed hold of her again, swiftly upending her so she lay over his knee. A gasp of dismay lodged in her throat as he began pulling up her gown with one hand, bracing the other against her back.

"What the devil are you doing?" she screeched, kicking her legs once the cool air of the room kissed her backside, and shocking her out of her lustful daze.

A large hand collided with the back of one thigh, stilling her movements. The blow had been a warning, she realized. She had already angered him with her questioning ... perhaps it would be best to avoid pushing him any farther while he had her in such a vulnerable position.

"Teaching you a lesson, little dove," he replied, slowly smoothing one hand up the thigh he had abused, resting it upon the swell of her buttocks. "Should you fail to obey when I require it, or act like an uncultured harridan, I will take you over my knee."

The words to upbraid him came readily to her tongue, but died a swift death at the first blow of his hand to her bare arse. A gasp lodged in her throat as the thud shifted her body, her skin blossoming with a sting that spread from the point of impact. Before she could recover, his hand rose and fell again, this time punishing the other cheek. Again and again, he struck her, increasing his force every other blow, until she felt certain she would be unable to sit for days. But then, the burn of pain faded into something else, a warmth that infused her entire body, causing her to relax against him, her head falling forward as she ceased fighting the punishment.

Yet another new sensation she did not understand. His blows hurt, truly punishing her for acting out of turn. However, her body had translated the pain into something else ... something frightening and exquisite all at once. She could hardly fathom it before it had ended.

Seeming satisfied with her submission, he stopped spanking her and began caressing her sore buttocks, his touch so feather-light, it felt like a soothing balm. She sighed, the tension in her body melting as he kneaded and massaged her buttocks, easing away the pain as effortlessly as he'd caused it.

Then, he delved two of his large fingers between her legs, slowly sliding them down toward her quim. She gasped at the first touch of his fingers to her folds, and he made an answering sound as he began to caress her.

"So wet for me, little dove," he said, his voice hoarse and gruff as he found her clit and gave it a little pinch.

She gasped at the pressure, then moaned when he dipped one finger inside her. The digit merely caressed her inner walls before pulling out again, and she issued a grunt of annoyance.

He chuckled, stroking his fingers over her in circles, his touch gliding over her silken wetness. "And such a greedy thing you are ... needing pleasure again so soon after this afternoon. If you aren't careful, I'll make you burn for me ... day and night, yearning for my touch."

She wanted to deny it, to declare he could never do that to her. Giving him the satisfaction would just be one more thing he could laugh at her over ... just one more thing he would take from her.

Aside from that, she needed to deny it for herself, to reassure herself that she had not fallen too deeply into this pit of depravity.

Nevertheless, she was burning for him now, whimpering and arching her back, attempting to urge his fingers where she wanted them, where she needed them.

"Yes, that's it, Daphne," he whispered, grasping her clit and pinching it again, harder this time. "Stop holding back and let yourself feel. There is no one else here but you and me ... No one ever need know you enjoyed it."

No ... no one would ever know. Just as no one had ever known about the secret passion she'd shared with her neighbor, or the times she'd given in to her debauched urges and teased herself toward climax with her own fingers. But, she would know ... she would always remember.

In spite of that, she could not make herself put a stop to this ... could not conjure words like 'stop' or 'no.' Not that she believed he would heed them. He was paying quite a bit of money to do what he pleased with her, and refusing him might cause him to renege.

Closing her eyes, she bit her lip as he slipped his finger back into her slick entrance, teasing her clit while delving the digit in and out. Her insides snapped, the tension of her need dissipating and spreading outward on waves of euphoria. The strength of her rapture shook her to her core, making her grateful for Adam's strong hold keeping her from toppling off his lap. He went on stroking her, his touch gentle and light as he eased her back down slowly.

When she went still and silent, he withdrew his finger, the sound of him licking it clean causing her core to clench once more, an echo of her fading orgasm.

Swiftly snatching her skirts down, he righted her so quickly, her head spun. Falling back into the chair she'd previously occupied, Daphne hardly realized he had stood before he was striding for the door. Dumbfounded, she lifted her bodice back over her breasts with shaking fingers, the chill of the wet fabric shocking her into lucidity.

Shame washed over her at the realization of what she'd just done —reveling in the touch of the man who had destroyed her family—

not just once, but twice within the same day. She'd brazenly lain across his lap and allowed him to debauch her, to make her forget who he was and why she was here.

Pausing in the doorway, he glanced at her over his shoulder, his expression as unreadable as always.

"Have a care, little dove," he said, a heavy warning in his tone. "The next time, my punishment will not be so merciful."

Slowly rising on shaking legs, she curled her hands into fists and met his gaze, refusing to be intimidated into looking away. "You are, by far, the most despicable man I have ever been forced to lay eyes upon."

He laughed, the sound dry and humorless. His face almost appeared haunted, the color of his eyes so dark from this distance, they appeared fathomless.

"Poor Daphne," he said in a tone tinged with regret. "You haven't the slightest idea. The most despicable men you've ever known are the ones who claim to love you ... the ones you trust to protect you. I almost pity you for the lesson you are about to learn."

Outrage bristled her spine as she thought of her father, of dear Bertram, of her uncle who had taken his own life because of this man. How could she have forgotten that so quickly and allowed him to seduce her?

"Say what you will about the Fairchild men," she ground out, her entire body fairly trembling with rage. "But they do not need to force a woman into their bed using tricks and bank drafts."

Adam's menacing smile appeared, the one that reminded her of the grimace of a lion. "No, they resort to brute force and threats to take what they want from the fairer sex."

His words slapped her in the face, the accusation echoing through her mind so loudly, she could never hope to block it out. "How dare you? My father and brother—"

"Oh, not your father," Adam amended quickly with a casual shrug. "Just Bertram. You know, the brother you braved disgrace and scandal to rescue."

"No," she whispered, shaking her head rapidly from side to side. "You're lying."

"Why would I?" he challenged, his hold tightening on the door-knob. His voice began to quake, the only hint of any emotion. "It would gain me nothing to lie to you."

"It would!" she accused, unable to help that her voice had risen enough to echo from the high ceiling. "It would destroy my love for my brother, just as you have destroyed everything else!"

What he was accusing Bertram of was unconscionable, the complete opposite of her brother's nature. No one knew him the way she did; they'd been the best of friends since she'd been old enough to follow him about, wanting to do all the things he did. And he'd let her ... indulged her in a way no one else ever had. More than that, he'd never told her to be anyone other than who she was. Unlike her father or mother, he'd never tried to change her.

"Yes, that's right, blame me ... the heartless villain," he taunted with a derisive snort. "It will not change what Bertram is ... or the things he has done."

Without another word, he quit the room, slamming the door so hard, the walls around her seemed to shake. Hands trembling, Daphne sank back down into her chair, ignoring her stinging bottom. Her head spun with the ramifications of what Adam had just revealed.

The things he'd said about her uncle had rung true, lining up with his penchant for over-imbibing and gambling. But this ... it was not true. It simply made no sense. Her brother was a man the debutantes of London flocked to. Bertram could have had any woman he wanted for marriage, or in his bed.

It simply did not make sense for him to force anyone into anything when there existed so many who would do whatever he asked with nothing more than a sweetly whispered word and a smile. Just the thought of him losing everything had sent her from London to Scotland, seeking answers on his behalf. It was for him, above her uncle and father, that she had done this.

She simply refused to believe she'd risked ruin and her own body to avenge a rapist.

There must be some mistake ... some rumor that cast Bertram in a bad light. Adam was wrong ... he must be. And the moment she saw him again, she would tell him so.

6

Daphne woke the next morning feeling as if her mouth had been stuffed with cotton. Her head pounded like the devil, and when she sat up in bed, the room began to spin. She could not remember how much Madeira she'd drunk the night before and did not know whether she suffered the aftereffects of overindulging or of encountering Adam. His accusations hung over her head like a cloud, the implications of what they could mean having kept her awake for most of the night. When she'd finally fallen asleep, it had been restless, her mind refusing to allow her peace in slumber now that Adam's words had sowed themselves in her mind.

Finding a glass of water on her bedside table, she took it up and drained it, flopping back onto the pillows and pulling the blankets over her eyes. She drifted back to sleep for a while, relieved to find her dry mouth and pounding head less acute when she awoke the second time. Leaving the bed, she stretched and blinked as her eyes adjusted to the brightness of the sun streaming through her parted drapes.

Reaching for the dressing gown laid across the bench resting at the foot of her bed, she covered her thin nightgown and strode over to the writing desk. The inkwell, quill, and notes she'd jotted down concerning her uncle remained inside the drawer, but on the desk's surface, she found a sealed envelope with her name scrawled across the front. She recognized the writing as Bertram's, the seal on the back revealing itself to be his.

Her heart leapt into her throat and remained there as she swiftly broke the seal and retrieved the letter inside. Maeve must have delivered it while she slept, and its appearance here surely meant her father and brother were now aware of her location.

Sure enough, the letter had been written by her brother just the day before. Her eyes grew watery as she detected his familiar scent on the paper, his words swimming before her eyes. She missed him ... just as she missed her parents and their home in London. Blinking to clear her vision, she focused upon the letter.

My dear sister,

Word has reached us concerning your whereabouts. While Father and I do not approve of you rushing off to Scotland and risking your reputation to confront Hartmoor, we certainly understand why you would do such a thing. Oh, Daphne, why would you put yourself within reach of that lecher? I've been fit to kill since Father read me that blackguard's letter informing us he has you in his clutches. Nevertheless, he has reminded me that going after you would cause an even greater scandal. So, please know we will do everything we can here in London to keep gossip about your disappearance to a minimum. In the meantime, do what you must to return to us. We will be waiting with open arms when you make your way back home.

All my love,

Bertie.

Folding the slip of stationary, she lowered her head, her throat constricting so tight, she could hardly breathe past the sob lodged there. It hurt to know her brother would not come rushing to Scotland to save her; yet, even if he did, she would not wish to be rescued. She'd come here of her own free will and agreed to Adam's shocking proposal all on her own. She was doing what needed to be done for the sake of her family, and she could not leave without the promised funds.

Bertram's letter reminded her of Adam's revelation the evening before, and she clenched her jaw at the thought. The man might hate her family, and the things he'd said about her uncle might prove true, but this ... the very thought of her brother being the sort of man who would abuse a woman went against everything she knew about Bertram. It simply could not be true.

Rising from the writing desk, she placed the letter in the drawer and turned away, determined to get to the bottom of this. She started with a gasp when she found Maeve in the room, her concentration upon the letter having distracted her from hearing the woman enter.

"Apologies for startling you, my lady," Maeve said with a soft smile. "Are you ready to dress for breakfast?"

"Yes," she replied. "Is His Lordship in his study, or will he be joining me for the morning meal?"

Maeve smirked as she removed an emerald green gown from the armoire. "The Master rose early and has already taken his breakfast. He went to the stables just now to prepare for a morning ride."

Despite her empty belly, Daphne would not be able to keep down a single bite until the inevitable confrontation had passed. "Then I would like to dress for riding ... quickly, please, so I might catch up to him."

Maeve's smirk turned into a full-fledged smile, and she gave Daphne a knowing look.

She fought the urge to roll her eyes and inform the maid that she did not seek out her 'Master' for any amorous reasons she might be imagining. Quite the contrary—she pictured ripping his tongue out for the slanderous things he'd said about Bertram.

She hurried Maeve through helping her into a plain brown riding habit, her hair hastily braided into a single plait before she rushed from the room. The habit was well made, fitting her like a glove, and it reflected the latest military style with brass buttons and braided rope draping her from shoulder to shoulder. She felt very much like a soldier marching off to do battle with the man who had destroyed her family ... who seemed determined to destroy *her*, despite the fact that she'd never knowingly done him harm. If she unraveled the entire mystery, surely, she would discover the answer.

Bursting through the front doors of the palace, she trotted down the front steps, hands balled into fists as she spotted the stable and Adam standing just outside it, the reins of a massive black stallion held in one fist. He turned as if feeling her heated gaze upon him and leaned against the animal's flanks, raising an eyebrow when she drew near. He had done away with the finery of last evening, his white shirt unbuttoned to bare a wide swath of his chest, worn buff breeches clinging to his thighs.

She drew up short, self-preservation warning her not to come within arm's length of him. He seemed to notice, his lips widening into a teasing grin as he raked her body from head to toe with his gaze.

"Well?" he prodded. "Will you tell me why you've come running from the house like your arse is on fire, or will you tell me what it is you want?"

Crossing her arms over her chest, she fought for composure. If she allowed him to rile her, she would surely strike him, and after last night's 'punishment,' she could not be certain what he would do to retaliate.

"There must be some mistake," she blurted, not caring that the pleading tone of her voice made her sound desperate. "I know Bertram like no one else, and I could assure you he would never ... he is not a rapist!"

Adam's expression did not allow her any insight to what he might think of her outburst. His voice remained flat, indifferent, when he responded.

"A mistake," he repeated, saying the words slowly as if tasting them, weighing them with his tongue.

"Yes," she said with a resolute nod. "Some rumor you have heard, stories about my brother that could not possibly be true."

Inclining his head at her, he scowled. "Are you in your brother's company at all times, little dove?"

"Of course not," she snapped.

"Then you cannot possibly know for certain, can you?" he countered.

She opened her mouth to reply, but then snapped it shut, realizing he was right about that, at least.

"Tell me what you know," she whispered, lowering her eyes.

She had come here for the truth, after all. Perhaps someone had told Adam something that was untrue, or the situation had been misconstrued. A woman could be ruined for something as simple as a kiss ... maybe what Bertram had done wasn't as bad as he had been led to believe.

"Ride with me," he replied. "And I will tell you."

As if on cue, the dark stallion nickered and tossed his mane, impatient to be on their way. Glancing toward the stables, she realized her gelding had been trapped inside it since her arrival. It would be good to spend some time out of doors and get a bit of exercise. Besides, she was dressed for riding.

"Very well," she relented.

Adam bellowed for a stable groom, who quickly went about preparing her horse. Daphne was pleased at the sight of her gelding, who seemed to have been well taken care of in her absence. She thanked the groom, then allowed Adam to help her up into the side saddle someone had placed on her horse's back. Since she'd come wearing breeches, she had ridden astride, which left her wondering whose saddle she now occupied. Perhaps the woman who also happened to own those lace garments she'd seen.

One mystery at a time, she admonished herself.

Giving her horse a little nudge with her heels, she trailed Adam from the stable, following him between the cluster of outbuildings filling the bailey. Then, they approached the gatehouse, pausing long enough for the old gatekeeper to raise the portcullis for them. The moment it had lifted enough to allow them beneath it, Adam spurred his mount forward, and together, they left the imposing stone walls of Dunnottar. The morning sun shined into her eyes, causing her to squint as she tried to adjust to the change after days cloistered inside the castle.

Riding down the sloping pathway leading down the escarpment to the plains below, Daphne ignored the man at her side and drank in her environment. The Scottish countryside surrounding Dunnottar had seemed threatening in the dark of night—an expanse soaked by rain and cloaked by blackness. Today, with the sun shining over the plains and new blades of spring grass bending in the breeze like ripples on the surface of a pond, it proved simply breathtaking. With only an unpaved road leading away from the castle to disturb the natural landscape, the entire surrounding area looked like something out of a painting.

As they reached the bottom of the steep, inclined path, Daphne noticed clusters of whin, bell heather, and harebell in full bloom, their yellow, magenta, and lilac blossoms offering bursts of bright color here and there among the vibrant, green grass.

Adam's horse broke into a canter, so she urged her gelding at the same pace, her mood lifting a bit as the sway of the animal beneath her and the familiar thrill of being able to ride uninhibited brought a smile to her face. She had not been free to ride like this since before leaving the family estate to go to London for her first Season—had never been able to do so in the cramped lanes of Hyde Park.

Ahead of her, Adam rode with a skill and ease that hardly surprised her. His Corinthian frame had hinted at athleticism, and she knew he fenced. It only made sense that he would ride with such control, his big body relaxed in the saddle, his hands firm on the reins.

As her horse came abreast of his, she glanced over and found the hard lines of his face softened, the tightness around his mouth banished away. Locks of his hair fell loose from their binding to frame his face, glittering with golden strands in the light of the sun.

Turning to meet her gaze, he smirked before giving his stallion a nudge with his heels and pursing his lips, a sharp whistle ringing out over the meadow. His horse was off like a bullet leaving a gun, Adam's laughter ringing out through the air. Grinning, Daphne followed suit, her mount breaking into a gallop.

For what felt like hours, she allowed herself to forget about the events of the previous evening, of the circumstances that had led to her being in Adam's clutches. She simply enjoyed the freedom of riding across the Scottish countryside with the sort of wild abandon she could never surrender to in a London park. Here, no one could see her except Adam, and he would hardly judge her for riding so hard and fast that her braid began to unravel, her hair flying about her face and shoulders like a banner. And if he did think her uncivilized, what did it matter? She hardly cared what a man like him might think of her. She hated him ... hated what he had done to her family.

That thought almost ruined the ride, but she pushed it aside. She would pretend he was not here, that she took this ride with someone she actually liked.

But her fantasy, as well as their thrilling ride, had to come to an end. Her gelding slowed first while Adam's stallion carried him a bit farther before he wheeled the beast around, circling back toward her. They stood in a patch of grass almost completely covered by wild daisies and other blooms she could not identify, the bursts of white and yellow surrounding them as he dismounted and came toward her.

She stiffened when he reached for her, taking her waist in his hands and lifting her easily from the saddle to set her on her feet. Relief swept through her when he released her and backed away, running a hand over his mussed hair. He breathed a bit heavily, just as she did, his chest heaving beneath his half-open shirt. Her gaze fell to the exposed patch, the stretch of skin made golden by the sun and sprinkled with sparse coils of hair matching that on his head.

When she glanced back up into his face, she found him watching her in that way of his, the gold flecks in his eyes gleaming as he seemed to undress her with his gaze.

She knew without having to ask that what he would reveal to her would shatter her, something she was not quite ready for. Grasping her skirts to lift them with one hand, she dodged him, edging around him and pacing over the soft blanket of flowers. Bending to pick a daisy, she lifted it to her nose as she straightened.

"I can see why you spend most of your time here," she said, the scent of the daisy flooding her senses, its petals tickling her upper lip. "The countryside is so beautiful."

"Daphne."

His tone held a warning to it, but she babbled on, not ready to stand here and listen to the words that would change everything—perhaps for good.

"The air is so clean here ... not at all like the smog of London," she said, keeping her back to him and staring out at the picturesque meadow surrounding them. "The quiet is comforting after the constant whirl of the city."

"Daphne," he said again, his voice sounding closer this time.

She whirled to face him, startled by his sudden nearness. Being so close to him still unnerved her, the memories of the things he had done to her body causing her pulse to race. He stood over her with his hands clasped behind his back, his gaze holding hers without wavering. His scent swirled up her nostrils, strong and masculine, combining with the clean, fresh scent of the outdoors with a pleasing effect.

"You are better than this," he said, his tone softer than she'd ever heard it. "Stop your inane prattle. You are rambling to avoid what is to come, but this cannot be evaded."

Shaking her head, she widened her eyes in an unspoken plea. "When I was a little girl, I almost died from a fever. Bertram, only a few years older than me, refused to leave my side, even when Father tried to coerce him from the room. The doctors and maids came and went, as did my parents ... but it was Bertram who coaxed me to sip broth and drink tea ... Bertram who mopped the sweat from my brow and changed the linens on my bed when I soaked them with perspiration."

Inclining his head, Adam studied her with a glance she might almost interpret as pitying—if not for the harsh gleam in his eyes. "He was a child then ... nothing like the man he has become."

"He taught me how to waltz when the teacher Mother had hired grew frustrated," she continued, knowing she was avoiding the inevitable just as he had accused, but now unable to stop. "He comforted me after my first Season, when the man I'd taken a liking to proposed marriage to someone else. H-he taught me to fence and never told our parents when I rode astride on my horse or did things they might have called unseemly."

"Daphne—"

"My brother cannot be a rapist!" she blurted, her eyes welling with tears. "I know him ... he is a *good* person! It is not true. It cannot be."

Folding his arms over his chest, he sighed, avoiding her gaze and staring at the horizon over her shoulder. "I am going to tell you a story, without mentioning any names, and you are going to listen. And when I am finished, you may decide to believe me, or you may go on believing in the grand delusion you try so ardently to convince me of."

Her throat constricted, her tongue seeming to swell in her mouth, rendering her speechless. Straightening her spine, she braced herself for what he would say, remembering that she had asked for this. Adam had warned her to run, that she was not strong enough to endure the promised thirty days or the truth they would reveal.

She would show him. She would listen to every word.

"There was once a young man about town ... the heir to a lordship and a charmer known for his quick wit and easy smile," Adam began. "Mamas pursued him for their daughters while young debutantes giggled behind their fans whenever he glanced their way. Admired by most of his peers, he seemed to have the entire world upon a platter, his for the taking. Someday, he would inherit his father's wealth, title, and lands ... and everyone knew he would soon need a wife to bear his own heir with."

Daphne clenched her trembling hands together, his description bringing Bertie to mind so easily, it was uncanny.

"Season after Season, he could be seen courting some of the year's most beautiful debutantes," Adam went on. "Flaunting them about town on carriage rides, escorting them to the theater along with their chaperones, signing their dance cards at Almack's. Before the eyes of the *ton*, he appeared the perfect picture of a gentleman going about the marriage hunt. Yet, when no one was looking, he would lure the lady of his choosing to a private place—a garden, an empty drawing room, a carriage. He was never violent with them ... oh, no, not this young charmer. It would all begin with chaste kisses and passionately whispered words. Then, a hand beneath a skirt, passing the edge of a stocking, perhaps the touch of a breast or taste of her throat. But once her defenses had been lowered, the young man would strike, pressing for other liberties. If the lady demurred, he might allow it the first or second time while pushing each encounter further and further, luring them into believing he would always respect their wishes and stop when asked."

Shaking her head, she closed her eyes, her blood running cold. "That's enough."

"But you see," he snapped, his voice growing sharp. "This man was actually a snake ... a conniving, manipulative bastard with no conscience."

"Please," she whispered. "No more."

His grip on her face startled her, and as she opened her eyes, he tightened his hold, stepping so close, she could feel the heat radiating from him like a tangible force. Her breath quickened, fear lancing through her as he held her chin and sneered at her.

"Do not close your eyes, little dove," he growled. "For once in your pampered, sheltered life, you will know the truth, no matter how ugly. Would you like to know what the young man would do when he attempted to initiate intercourse, only to be spurned by his chosen debutante?"

No.

The word lodged in her throat, thick and heavy. She could only stand there and stare at him as he held her face, his fingers biting into her jaw.

"He forced them," he rasped, his voice low and grating. "He ignored their pleas and cries ... pinned them down ... and forced himself inside them, ruining them, then tossing them aside when he'd finished."

"No," she sobbed, her chest panging as the agony of Adam's revelation swept through him. "No ... please."

"Please, what, little dove?" he taunted, derision radiating from him so strongly, she could feel it to her core. "Please keep the truth from you, just as the men of your family have? Please lie to you, so you can feel better about selling yourself to me to save a man who forces women against their will?"

"Just as you have forced me?" she countered, her voice growing shrill and echoing through the air around them. "How is it any different for you to hold thirty thousand pounds over my head to coerce me into your bed?"

Releasing her face as if she'd burned him, he sneered. "Do you think I *care* if you remain? That I'll come running after you like a dog chasing a bitch in heat? I enjoyed the taste of you, little dove, but you are not *that* good."

She flinched as if he'd physically struck her, the insult washing over her and filling her with shame. Of course, she meant nothing to him, and he'd never given her cause to believe otherwise. Yet, she had been foolish enough to think that perhaps he might respect her. They'd struck an agreement in the same way two men might have, agreeing on terms. However, he made his disdain for her clear every chance he got. As much as she hated to admit it to herself, it stung.

"Good enough for you to pay a small fortune to have," she countered, tearing her gaze away from his.

Why should she care if he did not think her worth the paper his bank draft was printed on?

Stepping toward her again, he leaned down until they were nearly nose to nose, his jaw ticking with what appeared to be barely contained fury. "The money isn't for the joy of taking your precious little cunt ... though it certainly does sweeten the deal. But

I would gladly pay that amount three times over for the pleasure of ruining the only female Bertram Fairchild seems to give a shite about."

Daphne's throat tightened until she could hardly draw breath, the edges of her vision growing hazy as her despair crumbled away, leaving nothing but rage. This man ... this conscienceless *bastard* had destroyed everything she held dear, and still, it was not enough. He must also destroy her pride, her love for her brother, her faith in the goodness of the people she loved.

A foreign, animalistic cry ripped from her throat, and she lunged at him, her body slamming into his unrelenting one. She swung, and her palm connected with his cheek, once, twice. He took hold of her wrist and spun her about—but not before her nails had raked down the side of his neck. Pulling her back against his front, he imprisoned her with his arms, the thick bands of muscle biting into her chest and stomach.

She screamed again, kicking and flailing as tears filled her eyes, her fury dissipating as he seemed to squeeze every ounce of it out of her. He bore it all in silence, keeping her against him until she sagged in his hold, her legs giving out.

Kneeling on the ground, he allowed her to sink into the grass, her hands shaking as she lifted them to swipe at her eyes. The almost comforting presence of his body against hers was taken away, and he moved to crouch beside her.

If she did not know any better, she might have thought she read pity in his gaze as he reached out to wipe away a stray tear with his thumb. She sat torn between slapping that expression right off his face and clinging to him and weeping until she could not weep any longer.

Sniffing, she reared away from his hand, angry with herself for finding relief in the touch of the man who had caused her pain.

"What have I ever done to you to deserve this?" she whispered, her voice hoarse and strained from screaming.

He shook his head slowly. "Nothing at all, little dove ... the sins of the brother have fallen upon the head of the sister. But it is your own fault, is it not? You came here to confront me, to learn the truth, and to stand in Bertram's place and receive his penance."

"No," she protested, shaking her head. "That isn't what I thought this would be."

"Is it not?" he challenged, his voice softer than she'd ever heard it as he studied her pensively. "I warned you it would hurt ... that I would hurt you. Perhaps you thought I meant physically ... which, I still might. But when you placed your hand in mine and agreed to thirty days and nights, you purposely stood in the place of the men of your family. How courageous you are, to want to save them, even though they are beyond saving."

Narrowing her eyes at him, she wrapped her arms around herself to attempt to still the shudders wracking her body.

"I *despise* you," she spat, each word dripping venom.

He nodded, giving her a sad half-smile. "Aye, I gathered as much."

"Have you always been such a relentless bastard?" she accused, tearing her gaze away from him and staring off across the countryside.

He laughed, the sound rough and sarcastic. "No, actually. You would have your precious brother, father, and uncle to thank for my present state ... though, I suppose the blame cannot rest entirely upon them. We may as well throw my own father into the fire."

Wrinkling her brow, she tried to make sense of his words. "What did my father do, Adam? What did *your* father do?"

"You will know ... in time," he hedged.

She grunted in frustration, sick of him constantly speaking to her in riddles. "Damn it all, I do not understand!"

Taking her chin gently in his hand, he tipped her head so she looked at him again, his expression hardening once more. His voice came out gentle, but each word was edged with cold, hard steel.

"I do not want you to understand, little dove ... I only require you to pay."

Without another word, he stood, turning his back to her and tramping across the field toward his mount. The stallion stood grazing nearby, her own gelding having strayed just a bit farther. He did not so much as glance in her direction as he hauled himself up into the saddle and issued a terse command to his horse. Then, master and rider were gone, hurtling across the fields and back toward Dunnottar.

Daphne collapsed back onto the ground with a sigh, her body cushioned by the blanket of flowers blooming all around her. Overhead, the sky was as blue as she'd ever seen it, the clouds fluffy and white. The beauty surrounding her seemed sickening now, tainted by the man who had just left her here, bleeding internally from wounds he'd inflicted. Her entire body ached as if he'd pummeled her, when in truth, he'd barely laid a hand upon her.

In the back of her mind, she wondered if he would punish her for slapping him. Had he not promised her one turn would earn another? If he would take her over his knee for a glass of wine thrown in his face, what would he do to her for assaulting him?

Despite knowing she ought to be anxious, she remained numb, unable to conjure any emotion beyond the pain radiating from her heart. While she wanted to accuse him of lying, her rational side argued she had no proof otherwise. Besides, she knew how much her brother loved to court debutantes. He and his friends approached it as sport—competing to see who could sign their names upon the most dance cards, who could secure the most beautiful of them for waltzes or rides in Hyde Park or evenings at the theater. It had all seemed so harmless, a group of young blades testing the waters, enjoying courtship before inevitably becoming leg-shackled.

But what if it had all been more nefarious than that? What if her brother turned out to be the manipulative snake Adam had named him?

Could she ever forgive him for the things she'd endured for his sake?

7

Once she had recovered from her encounter with Adam in the meadow, Daphne returned to Dunnottar alone. Leaping astride her horse, she'd ridden back to the castle as fast as the beast would carry her—so fast, the lash of the wind dried the tears upon her face. She'd galloped as if the hounds of Hell nipped at her heels—and in truth, she'd felt as if they did. The ugly accusation Adam had hurled at her feet had chased her relentlessly, echoing through her mind, reverberating like the voice of a phantom through a darkened corridor. No matter how she tried to outrun it, the realization that her brother might be a debauchee followed her, calling to mind memories long forgotten.

Bertram signing dance card after dance card at Almack's ... disappearing for hours on end during various soirées ... pouring attention upon a different woman every fortnight.

What had, at first, seemed like nothing more than a young man enjoying his days as a bachelor and engaging in light courtship had now been cast in a nefarious light. She could not help but imagine Bertram signing those dance cards in order to ease young chits into a false sense of comfort, or slipping into darkened gardens with unknowing women in order to have his way with them where no one could see and then moving on to the next victim once he had finished with her.

As she'd entered the courtyard and approached the stables, her mind had whirled, her stomach lurching so violently, it was a wonder she had not cast up her accounts. Handing her reins off to a groom, she'd pressed a hand against her middle, choking down bile and telling herself it could not be true. This was Bertram, her brother, the kindest man she knew. The sort of man every man wanted to be friends with and every young woman wished to wed. Why would he need to force a woman into his bed when he could have his pick of any chit in London?

No, Adam must be mistaken ... someone had given him false information. It did not make sense.

However, as she entered her chamber and ambled toward the little writing desk, her certainty began to waver. The things she'd learned about her uncle had held the ring of accuracy to them, and she'd been forced to admit they might be true. She must put aside her love for Bertram and think objectively. Adam had warned her his version of the truth would be difficult to fathom, which meant she must examine this new piece of information from every possible angle.

When Maeve entered the room to offer tea and a light afternoon meal, Daphne dismissed her. She could not even think of trying to eat. Instead, she retrieved the stationary, inkwell, and quill pen she had stored inside the desk, spreading them out upon the surface. Setting her notes concerning Uncle William aside, she reached for a fresh sheet. Her other notes had indicated that Adam's return to London five years ago after a long absence seemed to align with her uncle's swift descent into poverty and despair before his death. At that time, she'd just begun her second Season, right before their financial difficulties had begun.

Bertram had danced attention upon several young debutantes, whose names Daphne jotted down as they came to mind.

Lady Cassandra Lane. Miss Caroline Redgrave. Lady Avis Urswick.

As her list grew, she tried to recall whether Bertram had

expressed interest in marriage to any of them. The more names she added, the more frustrated she became, realizing he'd never paid attention to any of them for longer than a few weeks. In truth, her brother had never seriously courted *any* woman.

"I'll marry when it becomes necessary, Daff," he would say whenever she teased him that he would die a bachelor. "Father is still in good health, so it seems unlikely I will inherit the title in the near future. You don't want just any chit to become the next viscountess, do you?"

Having arrived at the age of four and twenty without choosing a husband, Daphne had never found Bertram's desire to remain unattached odd. After all, she had yet to find a man she would wish to spend the rest of her life with and did not intend to wed until she had. Was it so odd for her brother to hold out for love ... or at least, passion?

Yet, staring at her list of names, her heart sank. The sheer number of them did not indicate the predilections of a man holding out for love. They seemed the mark of a predator ... a rake ... a scoundrel who preyed upon the innocent.

Setting the quill aside, she buried her face in her hands with a heavy sigh. If Adam's claims proved true, then perhaps the man's vendetta against her family had something to do with one of the women on her list. A woman Bertram had ruined ... one who was important to Lord Hartmoor in some way.

During her short time at Dunnottar, she had yet to encounter anyone other than Adam and the servants who catered to him. However, the palace was massive, with plenty of floors and wings unexplored by her—plenty of places the debauched woman could be hiding. There were also the unexplained women's clothing; both the items she had worn during her first day here and those within the laundry she'd spotted in the basket of a maid.

The more she thought on it, the more it all began to make sense. If her brother had ruined someone Adam cared about, then he might feel obligated to defend her honor. Yet, the actions of the man who'd paid a grand sum for access to her body didn't seem in line with that notion. When a woman was found to be ruined, her father or guardian typically sought restitution from the man—usually ending in a hasty marriage in order to salvage the lady's reputation. Why, then, had Adam not visited her father, demanding something be done about the situation? Why set about the systematic destruction of her entire family? He had told her he did no more than take an eye for an eye, but he had chosen to target three men for the alleged sins of one.

For that matter, who could this faceless woman be? Despite being several years her senior, Adam was not old enough to have a daughter who might encounter Bertram. Had it been someone he'd wanted for his own? A woman he had courted, loved, and hoped to marry? A sister, a cousin, a ward?

Issuing a grunt of frustration, she lifted her head. She must ferret out Adam's secret, learn more about his family and his past ... it was the only way she could untangle this convoluted web of secrets and lies.

Resolved, she swiftly returned her notes to the desk drawer, then stood. Not long ago, she had been desperate to get away from him, to escape the truth he wielded against her like a weapon. Now, she must purposely put herself in harm's way, endangering both her body and soul in order to bring more of his torment upon herself.

She steeled herself for what was to come, prepared herself to be awakened by his wicked touch ... to retreat with a mantle of shame draped over her shoulders and her logical mind doing battle with her undiscerning body.

Leaving the room, she set off to find him, wrestling with the right words in her mind. She could not simply approach him and demand answers; he would laugh in her face before doing something to remind her she was subject to his whims. She hadn't wanted to play his games, but had been left with no other choice. She needed to know the entire truth—to put to bed the voices in her mind telling her she was sacrificing herself for nothing, that she would allow this monster to tear her apart and send her back to her family in tattered shreds.

Pausing outside of the door Niall had led her to her first night here, she raised her fist and knocked before she could change her mind. When no answer was forthcoming, she knocked again, pressing her ear to the heavy panel to listen for the deep, rumbling tones of his voice.

After a while, restlessness prompted her to reach for the knob. She pushed the door open just wide enough to peer through the crack, searching for his large, imposing frame in the dimly lit room. When she did not find him, she pushed the door open wider, quickly realizing he did not occupy the study. His presence seemed to fill any space he occupied—some elemental *thing* that never failed to make the hairs on the back of her neck stand on end.

That feeling was distinctly absent; yet, she continued into the cavernous room, curiosity drawing her toward the massive desk resting on its other end. Both hearths had been lit, the crackling fires surrounding her in a comforting warmth. Despite the size of the study, it felt oddly intimate, a scent that was distinctly Adam's permeating the space—cedar, spice, and musk—intertwined with leather and the lemon oil his desk and bookcases had been polished with. Drawing closer to the desk, she spied a crystal ashtray upon the surface, the stub of a cigar lying amid a pile of ashes. Its aroma lingered in the air, mingling with the other scents.

The strength of his fragrance and that of the cigar told her he had been here recently. Glancing over her shoulder to ensure he, or a servant, did not approach, she quickly rounded the desk. Curiosity drove her now, the need to learn something—anything—about Adam making her reckless. She did not allow herself to think of what he might do if he found her here. It could not possibly be any worse than the things he'd already done—or the things he'd promised he would.

Sitting in his chair, she sank into the worn, comfortable leather, the masculine scent even stronger here. The surface of his desk was immaculate, free of the sort of clutter and disarray she had expected. A large, leather-bound book rested in the center, turning out to be a financial ledger of some sort once she opened it. His handwriting proved even neater than hers, the pleasing lines and slopes of his letters and numbers coming as an odd surprise. Picturing him sitting at this desk, his long hair spilling down his back, face fixed into that expression of disdain, she found it difficult to imagine him executing such flawless penmanship—as opposed to stabbing at the pages while huffing smoke and snorting fire.

She chuckled at the image she had conjured and closed the book, observing the other contents of the desk. An inkwell and quill sat perpendicular to the book while an open, wooden box displayed several sticks of red wax and a large, ornate seal fob. Taking up the fob, she turned it over in her hands, noting that the warmth still clinging to its gilded surface meant he'd just used it. Its bottom had been etched to create the imprint of a castle upon the wax, the word 'Dunnottar' scrawled elegantly beneath it.

Replacing the fob, she sat back in the chair, reaching for the long, slender drawer built in just beneath the top of the desk. Inside rested several stacks of neatly placed stationary, several beautiful, filigreed quill pens, an extra inkwell, and a collection of other odds and ends. Among it all, a handful of square envelopes rested, stamped with the wax and seal she'd just inspected.

She furrowed her brow, retrieving one of the envelopes from the drawer and turning it over in her hands. Its shape and size left no question that she held an invitation in her hand. The other identical envelopes numbered few, leading her to believe they must be for a dinner party. Invitations would likely number in the hundreds for a ball hosted at a home the size of Dunnottar. No names had been scrawled on the front of them, so she could not know who he would be inviting to the keep. With a sigh, she placed the envelope carefully back in its place before closing the drawer.

In a typical household, invitations of this sort would be chosen by the lady, sent off with her seal. Bachelors might rely on a man of business or even their mothers to see the job done. Yet, in the absence of either, it seemed Adam took the task on himself. Who had he invited to Dunnottar, and for what purpose? Would they arrive while she resided here?

Shaking her head, she decided it had no bearing upon her quest for the truth. Unless her father or Bertram were among his guests—a highly improbable possibility—it was none of her concern.

She made quick work of exploring the rest of the desk, opening two larger drawers to the left of his chair to reveal a humidor filled with cigars and a cedar chest holding a pair of revolvers.

Having now grown bored with the desk and study, she stood and made a hasty exit, pausing at the door to peer into the corridor and ensure no servants happened past. Slipping out into the hallway, she continued on her way, uncertain where to go now. Adam had not divulged which rooms in the castle might be his favorites, nor had she seen him anywhere except this study, the drawing room where they had taken breakfast, and the music room.

The gallery, she recalled suddenly, spinning on her heel and heading in the opposite direction.

Her steps quickened as she neared the great hall and the corridor stretching toward the other wing of the ground floor. The fencing equipment she'd seen in the gallery meant he must spend time there practicing. That he had left his study when the day had hardly begun told her be must be restless. She found a bout of fencing to be just the thing when her mind became disquieted and wondered if he could be of a similar mind.

Sure enough, the sound of metal striking metal reached out to her as she neared the gallery, the shuffle of footsteps mingling with panting breaths. As she turned into the long, wide space, she spied two men in fencing attire, masks obscuring their faces. Despite being of large stature, they both moved with fluid dexterity, displaying impressive skill with the épées they wielded.

The first man was, undoubtedly, Adam, his large body moving with all the grace of a big cat, his long hair spilling from beneath his headwear and hanging down his back. The other must surely be Niall—the only other man in the castle as large and imposing as Adam.

Leaning against a nearby wall, she watched them go at each other, duly impressed with the way they seemed to know each other, moving back and forth as if in a dance instead of a fight.

Within minutes, Adam had bested his butler, striking the winning point and bringing an end to their bout. Niall removed his mask first, slipping it up to rest on top of his head. Unlike the other times she'd laid eyes upon him, he smiled, easing the harsh lines of his face into an almost handsome visage. Adam followed suit, pulling his mask away completely and shaking his head, causing his hair to undulate, the wavy strands kissed by the sunlight streaming through the large gallery windows.

The two spoke, but she heard nothing more than the low rumble of voices, her distance from them too far for her to discern words. Suddenly, Niall lifted his head and glanced in her direction. She felt it the moment his gaze fell upon her, all the warmth fading from his expression. A chill raced down her spine, followed by a tremor when the butler murmured something to Adam, prompting him to turn and glance at her over his shoulder.

Her throat constricted when he crooked his finger at her, demanding her to come to him without speaking. She'd wanted this, hadn't she? To find him, speak to him, figure out a way to uncover the things he hid from her.

But as she forced her legs into motion and began the long walk down the gallery toward them, fear lanced through her, turning her stomach. The two men had turned to face her, watching her approach, and the memory of the last time she'd been caught between them opened a pit of anxiety in her gut.

Choking down bitter bile, she fixed her face into an expression of indifference as she came near, the mingled scents of both males and the tang of their sweat making her stomach lurch, heat blossoming in her middle. Adam studied her with unguarded interest, his gaze raking her from head to toe. Conversely, Niall watched her with clear derision in his eyes, as if he would rip her to shreds with his bare hands should he be given half a chance.

"Well," Adam drawled when she stood before them, hands clasped demurely before them. "When Maeve told me you'd refused lunch, I did not think to see you again until dinner. What brings you here, little dove?"

His downright jovial manner took her aback, a complete departure from the man who had confronted her in the meadow, demanding she open her eyes and face the hideous truth.

"I ... I have a proposition for you," she stammered, her face heating when Niall chuckled in reaction to her statement.

Adam raised an eyebrow and traded amused glances with his butler. "A proposition, eh? Niall, you'd better make yourself scarce ... the lady wishes to *proposition* me."

Pursing his lips, the butler leveled an annoyed glare at her, but swiftly removed his headgear and fencing attire he'd donned over his breeches, shirt, and waistcoat. Hanging them on a nearby rack, he retrieved his tailcoat, swiftly slipping it on before executing a stiff bow.

"As you wish, Master," he murmured, casting her another malevolent glare before leaving them.

His footsteps echoed over the polished marble tiles, eventually fading altogether as he disappeared from sight.

Resting his épée over one shoulder, Adam probed her with a curious gaze. Sunlight flooded the room, causing the golden strands of his hair to shimmer and his eyes to take on the hue of warm honey.

"Well?" he prodded when she'd stood there for several seconds without speaking.

Clearing her throat, she lifted her chin. "I had hoped to challenge you to a duel."

He chuckled, twirling the grip of his épée, the sunlight glinting off the blade's edge. "Is that so?"

She nodded. "Yes ... but I want to attach a wager to our bout. If I win, you must answer a question for me. Any question I ask."

Creasing his brow, he nodded slowly, as if digesting her proposition. "Did you not learn enough this morning?"

The reminder of the revelation he'd made left a bitter taste in her mouth. "I do not relish being made to wait for the answers I seek. If you are bold enough to allow me a chance to earn more, I'd like to try."

His smirk spread into a grin, exposing his teeth. "What do I receive when I trounce you?"

She bristled at his teasing, annoyed he thought so little of her skill. That he underestimated her would prove his downfall in the end. She could beat him ... she *would* beat him.

"You may have ..."

She bit her lip, knowing she must offer him something enticing; otherwise, he would simply laugh her off. Yet, offering him too much too soon would make it more difficult to attempt this tactic in the future. It would lose its allure for him if, for instance, she offered to give up her maidenhead here and now without a fight. No, it must be something that would please him enough to make him risk being forced to reveal something before he was ready.

"M-my mouth," she offered before she could lose her nerve.

His grin faded, and his pupils expanded, turning his eyes into fathomless bronze. Nostrils flaring, he took a step toward her, reaching out with his empty hand to grasp her chin. His thumb rested against her lower lip, his gaze dropping as he contemplated her offer.

"A bonny mouth it is, little dove," he murmured. "What, exactly, are you offering to do with it?"

Her chin trembled, her breath hitching as his nearness washed over her like a roaring ocean wave, muddling all her senses. He filled her vision with his large frame, his scent flooding her nostrils—so heady and masculine, she could practically taste it. Primitive. Wild. Spicy with just a hint of sweat from his exertions. Her knees grew weak, her legs turning to jelly.

"You threatened to use it, did you not?" she managed, her words coming out low and husky.

"Aye. That, I did," he replied, slowly tracing the line of her lower lip, then pressing down on it to part it from the upper. "And you understand what that means, do you not? You are not quite as inno-cent as I first assumed, are you?"

He sank his thumb into her mouth, and she lifted her tongue to meet it, lapping at the tip of it in answer to his question. She had never performed fellatio before, but believed she grasped the basics. It should not be difficult.

"Say it, little dove," he growled, going back to stroking her lip, biting his own as if tamping down the urge to devour her whole. "Say out loud what you're going to do with that pretty little mouth."

The words hovered on the tip of her tongue, embarrassment making it difficult to say them. She had insisted he'd never make a whore of her; yet, here she stood, bartering a sexual favor in exchange for something she needed.

"Say it, Daphne," he growled, an edge of annoyance creeping into her voice. "I want to hear it."

"I-I will ..."

He leaned closer—so close, she could feel his breath fanning against her face, tickling her cheek.

"Suck your cock, Adam," he finished for her.

"I will suck your cock, Adam," she said, lowering her eyes—but not before heat and satisfaction flared in his, searing the surface of her skin like a branding iron.

His smile returned, slow, teasing, and feline, drawing her gaze back up to his face. "You have yourself a wager, little dove."

Releasing a sigh of relief, she stepped away from him, squaring her shoulders and stepping around him to approach the rack arranged against one wall. She swiftly unbuttoned her jacket, exchanging it for the protective clothing Adam already wore. After adorning herself in the padded jacket and gloves, she selected a mask, holding it beneath one arm while inspecting the row of épées mounted upon the wall beside the equipment racks. Flanked by foils on one side and sabers on the other, the épées all appeared identical, so she selected one, testing its balance.

She held it up by its grip and inspected it, then turned it on its side, letting it go and catching it with the tip of her first finger, balancing it by the blade. A trick Bertram had taught her. Satisfied with the épée, she flicked her wrist and caught the weapon by its grip before turning to face Adam.

Eyebrows raised, he inclined his head at her. "The lady knows her way around a weapon."

She shrugged one shoulder, brushing past him and pulling on her mask. "I told you ... I've been fencing since I was a girl. I am no novice."

"We shall put your skill to the test," he replied, walking down the gallery a few paces before turning to face her. "*En garde!*"

Daphne reacted swiftly to the command, assuming her starting position and thrusting her épée out before her, legs bent, one hand folded behind her back.

"Rules?" he asked once he'd sank into his own beginning posture. "First to five points wins the bout ... three bouts total?"

She nodded in agreement. "The winner of two out of three bouts claims their prize."

"Very well," he affirmed. "Ready?"

"Yes," she replied just before he called out the starting word.

"*Allez!*"

He followed the command with a swift lunge, his long limbs serving to thrust the épée squarely at her center. She danced back and circled her own weapon to parry the thrust, easily knocking it aside. He lunged again, feinting left, then swiftly striking right when she moved to defend herself. The tip of his épée struck her shoulder, earning him one point.

Clenching her teeth, she moved away from him, sinking back into her beginning stance while he did the same.

"*En garde,*" she growled, thoroughly irritated that he'd scored the first point.

Bertram had always accused her of being competitive in everything, often goading her into wagers over even the most mundane thing. Her need to win was now more than a desire to ferret more secrets from Adam. It had become a matter of pride. This man had humiliated her far too many times since they'd met, and she was owed recompense.

"Allez!"

This time, she attacked first, lunging, then backpedaling when he feinted and tried to counter-attack. She feinted again, lower this time, forcing him to protect his legs. Then, she swiftly flicked the épée, striking his lowered shoulder.

Glowering at her through the mesh front of his mask, he backed off, taking his position once more. They went at each other three more times, dancing around one another as they learned each other, testing with various attacks and discovering each other's weakness.

After becoming tied with four points each, Adam managed to beat her in the first bout, countering her attack and landing his épée upon her thigh. Despite the loss, Daphne grinned, circling him to get back in position for the second bout. She'd always enjoyed fencing and had not faced so worthy an opponent in quite some time.

"You possess admirable skill with the épée," he said as he faced her and crouched into position. *"En garde."*

She rolled her eyes and snorted. "Funny ... I was going to say the same thing about you ... *Allez!*"

He laughed, swiftly backpedaling away from her attack before countering with one of his own. The second bout lasted longer than the first, both of them giving as good as they got, the tentative learning from the first fight making way for displays of style and flair. She proved lighter on her feet than him, her slender figure making her a smaller target and therefore harder for him to strike.

She stole the second bout, gaining her five points to trounce his three.

"Well met, little dove," he panted, lifting his mask for a moment and using his sleeve to dry the sweat causing his brow to glisten. "But you shall not fare so well in the final bout. I can feel your sweet lips around my cock already."

Determination clenched her jaw, and she ignored his teasing, remaining silent as she resumed her starting position. Laughing as if he knew he'd struck a nerve, he circled her, returning to his place and preparing for the third round. She fought against the urge to so much as blink lest she miss any hint of his moves as he went on the offensive, using brute force to beat her back. She danced away from him, spinning and parrying to avoid the touch of his épée. Yet, he did not allow her to land a single blow, becoming far more ruthless in this bout than he had been in the previous two. He landed two blows in quick succession, sacrificing himself and allowing her to land one in the process.

His laughter taunted her, her breath quickening into enraged pants as he landed a third blow and then a fourth. He'd thrown her off balance so quickly, causing desperation and anger to make her careless. The fifth blow fell so easily, she might as well have stood still and allowed him the point.

The épée landed in the center of her chest, its blunt edge resting between her breasts. Adam kept it there while he removed his mask and tossed it aside. Sweat dampened his forehead, but his eyes danced when he grinned at her, triumph squaring his shoulders and lifting his chin.

Tossing her épée to the floor with a huff, she tore off her own mask and dropped it, hands clenching into fists at her sides. She wanted to bat his sword aside and rush him, pummeling him with her fists, possibly even delivering a slap that would leave a handprint upon his face.

However, she had been fairly beaten and could find no fault with him this time. Remembering how he'd punished her for acting like a harridan the night before, she took a deep breath and calmed. No need to provoke him further, especially when he would now have her in a vulnerable position.

"You aren't half bad, little dove," he quipped, lowering his épée and bending down to retrieve hers before going back to hang them on the wall. "Only Niall ever proves as much of a challenge, so it is nice to have someone new about to cross swords with."

As he began stripping away his jacket, she was taken aback by his downright jovial tone. Just that morning, he had been so harsh with her; yet, it would seem fencing had put him in a good mood. She had expected him to tease her, to rub her nose in her defeat before throwing her to her knees to claim what he'd fairly won.

"I am out of practice," she admitted, reaching up to begin unbuttoning her own jacket. "It has been some time since I've had someone to spar with daily. Bertram and I ..."

She lowered her eyes when his gaze fell upon her, heavy with reproach at the mention of her brother's name. The urge to kick herself overwhelmed her, and she could not believe she'd gone and said the one name guaranteed to drag him back into a dudgeon.

Clearing her throat, she glanced back up at him, fixing her face into a placid expression.

"If you wish to begin—"

"Not here," he interjected, shaking his head. "Come."

Turning and setting off across the gallery, he left her with no choice but to follow.

8

Daphne remained silent as she followed Adam away from the gallery and down the winding corridor back toward the great hall. His long strides were swift and sure, as if he had a particular destination in mind. At first, she assumed he meant to take her to his study—the only room in the palace she had seen him occupy aside from the gallery and music room. Yet, they breezed past his domain, the door remaining tightly closed. He led her through the main hall and toward a door she had never noticed before—one she assumed led outdoors.

Sure enough, when he swung the heavy panel open, sunlight flooded the gap and stung her eyes. Squinting against the glare, she followed him into a large, square courtyard. Coming to a stop at his side, she gasped in awe, soaking in every detail of the little space. The sides of the quadrangle-shaped palace folded in around the courtyard, closing it off from the world. Stone paths guided the way toward a green hedgerow maze while iron benches here and there invited visitors to sit and absorb the scenery. Bursts of color drew her eye to the blossoms someone had carefully cultivated—roses, edelweiss, lilies, iris, tulips, and a plethora of others, complementing the green hedgerows with bursts of red, yellow, purple, and pink. In the center of it all sat a large well, the low edge allowing her to glimpse the clean, clear water inside.

"Oh," she whispered, the reason she'd followed him out here forgotten. "It's so …"

A breathless sigh escaped her as she approached the closest plant, reaching out to caress the delicate petals of a blood red rose.

"You must really love these flowers," she murmured, the tranquility of the garden all but demanding a lowered voice. "They're well taken care of."

"My gardeners are compensated well for keeping them," he replied.

Despite his attempt to sound nonchalant, she could hear the strain in his voice. Turning to peer at him over her shoulder, she frowned. He avoided her gaze, his hair falling over one shoulder as he gazed out over the courtyard.

"Still," she offered tentatively. "This must be the most pristine, well-maintained part of the castle I've come across. It has to mean something to you."

Uncertain why the sight of him surrounded by so much light and life tugged upon her heartstrings, Daphne approached the well, putting him behind her. She did not want to see that haunted look in his eyes, or wonder what it might mean. This man had destroyed her family, and, if he had his way, would tear her apart, too. He did not deserve her pity.

"Someone who lived here once planted the flowers," he hedged, following her to the well. "I can take no credit for them."

Bracing her hands upon the stone lip of the well, she gazed down at the water. It reflected her image back to her, as well as Adam looming behind her. She held her breath as he braced his hands on either side of hers, trapping her between his arms and pressing his body up against hers.

"This cistern supplies the entire castle with fresh water," he said conversationally, as if he were not pressing the thick root of his erect cock against her back. "A system of pipes built into the palace walls allow us to pump it into the kitchen and the water closets."

She wanted to ask who had planted the flowers and why they no longer lived here—if they also happened to be the same person her father, uncle, and brother had somehow wronged. Yet, the hard press of his chest against her back, the heat emanating from him and sinking through her skin, and the warning of his breath teasing the nape of her neck stole the words from her lips. Holding her back erect, she fought the urge to sink against him, to arch her spine and rise up on tiptoe so she could nestle her hips into the cradle of his groin.

"Why must you fight me, little dove?" he murmured, lowering his head and pressing his mouth against her ear.

His lips skimmed the back of her neck, his facial hair tickling the delicate skin, his breath caressing her like the brush of insistent fingers. With a whimper, she closed her eyes, her body jerking from the shivers she tried to keep at bay, the desire she tried to hide from him.

"The things you want ... the things you need ... I know what they are," he whispered, grasping her hips and pulling her back into him. "They are why you have remained unmarried for so long, despite being the sort of woman the men of London clamor for ... despite having your pick of eligible bachelors. They are why you stayed, even when I promised to hurt you, to break you."

"You know nothing about me," she retorted despite the pleasure causing her toes to curl in her boots, her eyes rolling back into her head as he brushed his lips against the back of her neck, his tongue creeping out to taste the ridges of her spine.

He chuckled, the rough sound causing liquid heat to pool in her middle and her cunt to clench with longing.

"I know you do not want courtly manners or sweet kisses," he countered. "You do not want to be cherished or coddled. You want to be used, defiled ... broken. You want to be spread apart and plundered until there's nothing left."

She could not suppress her shudder this time, her mouth going dry when he took hold of her hair, wrapping her disheveled braid around his fist before giving it a rough jerk. Her neck arched, her scalp stinging from his brutal hold as he contorted her, seeming not to care that the angle he held her in might cause discomfort. Her heart pounded so hard and fast, she would not be surprised if he could hear it, her veins fairly humming from the heady rush of her blood, the excitement that had ramped up her pulse.

"Keeping you here for thirty days and sending you back to London would be more than enough to ruin your reputation," he rasped, his whiskers rasping her cheek, his lips soothing where the coarse hairs abraded. "But I knew the moment I laid eyes upon you that it would not be enough—not for me, and not for you. It will go easier for you if you submit and obey, Daphne... if you surrender to what we both want."

Snorting derisively, she squirmed in his hold, determined to win the battle against her body, which seemed to react to him of its own volition, even as her mind screamed that she stood in the arms of a monster.

"How can I desire someone I hate?" she retorted.

He laughed again, the rumbling of his chest resounding through her back, warming her entire body and causing prickles of awareness to sting her skin.

"So naive of you to think lust has anything to do with softer emotions like admiration or respect. When you return to London with your reputation in tatters, what will it matter that you enjoyed it, that you craved it ... even begged for it?"

"I will never beg you," she ground out from between clenched teeth, even as he rubbed his pelvis against her, filling her mind with all manner of erotic thoughts—imaginings of all the things he could do to her with that cock.

"Perhaps not," he relented, letting go of her hair and spinning her to face him.

His eyes glittered like brilliant gold in the light of the sun, green prisms appearing in the depths, an unmistakably predatory gleam radiating at her with destructive promise.

"But it does not matter in the end," he reminded her. "I fully intend to take what I want. Whether you fight me, or give in and let yourself enjoy it, is not my concern."

Raising her chin defiantly, she met his gaze silently, determined not to be defeated, to let him force her to feel things she did not wish to feel. He was wrong about her—she did *not* want what he threatened her with, the pain or the defilement. She did not want a monster in her bed, laying claim to her body, filling her with his poison.

Even if her body practically sang in response to his touch.

Taking hold of her shoulder, he pushed, commanding her to her knees without a word.

"Will you give me what I am due, or will you force me to take it from you?" he asked, staring down at her from his position of dominance.

He seemed larger this way, his shadow blotting out the sun, his thick, sinewy legs spread to either side of her, his big body trapping her against the stone side of the cistern. The hard ridge of his cock showed against the front of his breeches, straining toward her against the fabric. Remembering the feel of the large organ in her hands, both hard and soft, made her throat constrict.

"You won our wager fair and square," she declared, tearing her gaze away from his prick and forcing herself to look up into his eyes. "I am a woman of my word."

He nodded, his rigid frame relaxing a bit, the muscles that had coiled to spring and attack unwinding. Reaching down to grasp her arm, he trailed his hand along the limb until finding her hand. With a tight grip on her wrist, he urged it toward the fall of his breeches, laying her hand flat against him. She sucked in a sharp gasp, the heat of him radiating through the fabric setting her palm on fire. The organ leapt in response to her touch, seeming to fairly pulse with raw power and masculinity. He grunted, pumping his hips and grinding his cock against her palm, rubbing himself against her.

Then, releasing her hand, he let his arms fall to his sides, gazing expectantly down at her. "Take it out."

She hastened to obey, not wanting to make this any harder upon herself than necessary. If she pleased him, perhaps he would be kinder to her in the future, more likely to exercise care when taking her maidenhead. Steadying her shaking hands, she swiftly opened the fall of his breeches, revealing his cock inch by inch. It sprang free after she'd finished unbuttoning him, the absence of smallclothes allowing it to practically fall into her hands. It was just as menacing as she remembered, swollen and straining toward her, gone nearly purple at the tip from the blood filling and stretching it to near impossible proportions. Yet again, she found herself wondering how it would ever fit without tearing her in two once he finally decided to claim her.

Sparing a glance up at Adam, she found him watching her impassively, his expression betraying nothing. He took a step closer to her, forcing her to lean her head against the stone well, crowding her vision with the sight of his prick jutting out from the confines of his clothes and the thatch of dark hair blanketing his groin. His bollocks hung heavy and full between thighs made like tree trunks—all sinews and bulging muscle. His scent made her head spin, his unique musk mingling with the aromas of cedar and cigar smoke that seemed to always cling to his skin.

"Take me in your hand," he snapped, impatience edging his voice.

She quickly obeyed, wrapping her fingers around his shaft, her hand just barely enclosing his entire width. He gritted his teeth and thrust into the opening of her hand, his seed welling up in the slit of his head. Despite the hard, angry length of him pulsating in her grip, he did not seem affected by her touch, his face remaining as expressionless as ever.

"Both hands," he rasped, his voice coming out rough and shaky.

She smirked, giving him her other hand, the evidence of his lust now beginning to show through his mask of indifference. He grunted when she enclosed him with her second hand, slowly surging his hips to create friction between them. His cock seemed to grow and swell with each thrust, the plump veins throbbing with each beat of his heart. He added his hand to hers, tightening her grip and showing her the rhythm he wanted. His breaths came out in harsh pants, his eyes sliding closed as he helped her pump him, their hands moving in tandem over the hard ridge of his prick.

Staring down at her from beneath lowered eyelids, he released her hands. "Your mouth, little dove ... fuck me with that pretty little mouth."

Dropping her hands, she gathered the courage to do what he instructed. What if she was horrible at it? What if he became annoyed with her for not knowing what she was about and found some other way to satisfy his urgings instead?

Fear only held her back for so long, the realization that making him wait might prove the greater offense prompting her into movement. Leaning forward, she brushed her lips against his flared head, tentatively kissing him. He held perfectly still, even the sound of his breathing dissipating as he seemed to wait, anticipating what she might do next.

Opening her mouth, she flicked her tongue at him, surprised at the taste of him. The bit of seed that fell onto her tongue proved wild and primitive—what she must assume constituted the taste of pure, raw *male*. Slightly salty, slightly sweet, completely and wholly masculine. She lapped at him again, this time dipping her tongue into the slit. He made a little sound in the back of his throat that made her skin tingle and emboldened her. Exploring him more with her tongue, she circled the tip, then stroked the underside, licking down to the base, then slowly working her way back up.

He was breathing again, the harsh sound sawing in and out of his parted lips, chest heaving as he clenched his hands into fists at his sides. She took him between her lips, instinct driving her to suck him, moving her mouth over him the same way she had with her hands. Adam trembled, one hand shooting out to grip the edge of the cistern.

"More," he growled, thrusting his hips at her face and urging his cock deeper into her mouth. "Take more."

Breathing through her nose, she closed her eyes and obeyed, tightening her lips around him while stroking the underside of his cock with her tongue.

"Aye, little dove ... just like that," he urged, finding a steady rhythm in her mouth as she took to it easily, urged on by the low grunts and swift breaths he seemed unable to keep quiet.

His words lit a fire in her belly, its tendrils licking at her cunt, sparking a longing only he could fulfill. Her empty channel clenched with need, her breasts tightening at the tips.

Muttering an oath, he took hold of her hair with his other hand and surged even deeper, sending his tip to the back of her throat. He groaned, even as she choked, rearing away from him and fighting to breathe.

His fingers tightened around her braid until her eyes watered, and he thrust at her mouth relentlessly.

"Take it all," he ground out before shoving her head back down onto his length.

Her chest burned from the effort it took to draw breath as he forced his way to the back of her throat again, holding her there without mercy.

"Breathe," he commanded, stroking her hair before taking it into his ruthless hold once again. "Through your nose ... relax your jaw ... take me in."

She did as he suggested, tamping down the urge to fight against the rigid flesh demanding access to her throat, easing her jaw open and drawing air in through her nose. She swallowed the saliva pooling in her mouth, and he gasped, falling even deeper into her before withdrawing, then plunging in again. He stretched her mouth wide, his grip on her hair never letting up as he fucked her mouth, slowly at first, and then with mounting speed as she grew accustomed to it.

Squeezing her eyes closed, she surrendered to his control, let him use her, the way made easier by her nonresistance. Each breath she took through her nostrils flooded her senses with his scent, each thrust of his cock inside her mouth resounding through her body and causing a pang of longing deep in her core with every stroke. She needed relief, to press a hand to her clit and stroke until she spent, to ease the agony twisting in her womb, growing more acute with each rough sound she pulled from him.

"Shite, that's good," he groaned, his knees buckling as his strokes became wilder and less controlled. "Aye, little dove ... God, you're so perfect ... so good ..."

Her eyes flew open, and she stared up him, an unexpected triumph swelling her chest at the sight he presented. Eyes tightly closed, head thrown back to expose the thick cords of his neck, lips parted as he moaned his pleasure. Even as he used her, took from her, placed her in the demeaning position at his feet, she felt as if she had won this little game, nearly bringing him to his knees with nothing more than her mouth.

"Fucking hell, I'm going to come," he panted, his knees buckling as he gripped her head with both hands, angling her the way he wanted. "Take it all, Daphne ... every single drop."

She made a little noise of acquiescence, staring up at him and watching as he fell apart, shuddering and shaking as he seemed to fight for more time. Yet, the moment he looked down into her eyes, he gasped, doubling over as he began spilling in her mouth. Hot spurts of his seed flooded her palate, each thrust of his hips bringing on more and more of the salty, tangy fluid. She swallowed every drop, just as he'd commanded, keeping him in her mouth until the last wave of it had left his body, until he went flaccid against her tongue and eased his way out of her.

Breathing heavily, he stared down at her with heavy-lidded eyes, the golden gleam hinting at satisfaction. Releasing her hair, he cupped her face, stroking his thumb over her lips.

"Such a bonny mouth," he murmured. "And a wicked one, too. Well done, little dove."

His words had a strange effect upon her, warming her chest and causing pride to lift her chin. He'd thrown her off-balance from the moment she'd arrived here; yet, for the first time, she felt as if she had gained some ground in their battle of wills.

Releasing her face, he pushed his cock back into his breeches and quickly buttoned his fall. While tucking in his shirt, he studied her with amusement dancing in his eyes.

"Look at you ... as wanton a creature as any I've ever seen," he teased. "And I've had my share of wantons."

Glancing down at herself, she flushed, embarrassment heating her cheeks. The position on her knees had caused the skirt of her riding habit to ride up to her thighs, revealing her stocking-clad legs. Her blouse had become wrinkled beyond repair, the pristine white sullied by her proximity to the ground. She was certain the back had fared no better from being pressed against the well, the blouse likely ruined. The points of her nipples were visible through the thin shirt, with no chemise giving her the benefit of modesty. An unmistakable scent floated on the air—her arousal.

She glared back up at him in silence, shame washing over her as she realized he'd been right about her. If he tackled her to the ground then and there and plundered her body, she would hardly put up a fight. Just as she had every other time he'd touched her, she would go up in flames, consumed by desire and seized with an insatiable need.

What the devil was wrong with her?

"Why won't you just get on with it?" she asked, shaking her head in disbelief. "I've agreed to give you my body ... I am here day and night dressed like a prostitute and at your disposal. Why will you not simply put an end to this?"

She bit her lip as she realized her questions had sounded too much like begging for her peace of mind.

Adam flashed his cat-like grin at her. "Where's the fun in that, little dove?"

With that, he turned and walked away, his long legs carrying him swiftly back across the courtyard. Then, he disappeared into the castle, leaving her sitting on the ground with an aching cunt and a muddled head.

. . .

THE NEXT FEW days passed with a sort of stillness Daphne found unnerving. She and Adam seemed to have fallen into a sort of limbo, leaving her on edge and wondering when he might strike again.

Each morning after her breakfast, she would venture to the gallery, sure to find him fencing with Niall. She would watch him spar with the butler, studying his smooth grace and the fluidity with which he moved—with the same surety and confidence he displayed in every other aspect of his life. When he was finished with Niall, he would take her on next, seeming to enjoy crossing swords with her. Upon being dismissed, the butler never failed to make his displeasure known, his disdain for her clear as he stripped off his fencing equipment all the while ripping her to shreds with his gaze. It sent tremors down her spine and settled a cold mass of dread in her gut. The man studied her as if she were no more than a loathsome insect he would crush beneath his heel if given half the chance.

However, Adam's presence put her at ease, and a part of her seemed to innately understand that he would not allow anyone within the household to harm her. She was not dense enough to believe it could be due to any affection or care on his part. The man would simply wish to protect his thirty-thousand-pound investment. An investment he had yet to take full advantage of. He seemed content to adhere to his plan, to draw it out and leave her guessing when he would take from her the one thing she could never recover once he'd had it.

And so, in the days following the wager and his subsequent claiming of the spoils, she forced herself to relax and take things as they occurred. For a time, they came with alarming predictability—fencing bouts in the mornings, time spent reading in her room while Adam tended to business matters in his study, rides across the Scottish countryside, hours in the music room practicing the harp.

She'd been as rusty at the harp as she had at fencing, but a few hours on the little stool plucking the instrument and it was as if she'd never stopped. These moments were her favorites—the times she could closet herself away in the music room and touch her fingers to strings. The music would float around her, and she could close her eyes, imaging herself in some other place—perhaps on a grand stage with scores of people watching her, listening, soaking in every note she coaxed from the instrument. And a beautiful instrument it was—the heavy gold resting upon her shoulder like an old friend, its winged angels taking flight and carrying her music with them.

Before long, Adam began appearing in the music room, standing in the doorway or lounging about on the oversized furniture. One afternoon, he'd brought along a stack of ledgers and a quill, quietly settling in a corner of the room. When she'd paused in the middle of Charles Oberthur's *Harp Concerto* to cast a wary glance at him, he'd met her gaze and smirked.

"Play, little dove," he had urged, his voice low and quiet in the stillness of the room, sending a flush of warmth to her palms. "Do not stop on my account."

She'd continued the concerto, keeping her eyes on him, certain he must have some ulterior motive for disturbing her solitude. Half expecting him to pounce on her and finish what they'd started the last time they had occupied this room together, she'd played with her gaze fixated upon him.

As she'd finished *Harp Concerto*, flowing easily into Jean-Baptiste Krumpholz's *Symphony No. 1*, it became clear he simply meant to sit and listen, his head lowered over his ledgers as he went about his work. Closing her eyes, she'd returned to her own private world—the space inside her mind where only she and the music existed, notes flowing from her fingers like feathers on the wind. One concerto had turned into two, then three, and before she knew it, she'd opened her eyes hours later to find him watching her, his ledgers closed, his gaze intent.

Breath quickening and pulse racing, she had clung to the harp, registering the beading of sweat on her brow and the fatigue in her hands. She had not played for so long or so passionately in ages.

"You play beautifully," he had said, keeping his voice low as if loath to break the spell. "It has been some time since a person with your skill has laid their hands on those strings."

Her brow furrowed as she studied him, taken aback by the way that confession transformed his face, his eyes darkening as if storm clouds had gathered, his mouth pinching at the corners. Like the garden, he spoke of the harp as if it belonged to someone important, someone who no longer resided at Dunnottar, but who had meant something to him.

"Did you love her?" she'd asked, uncertain why anticipating the answer should make her hold her breath.

He'd held her gaze for a long moment before answering, a thousand expressions warring with each other upon his face, even as it remained implacable, unmoving. His eyes had betrayed him, giving Daphne her answer before he spoke.

"Aye," he'd rasped.

The single word had held within in notes of anger and rage, which had only baffled her more. If he'd loved her, then why such bitterness at the reminder of her?

"What happened to her?"

Then, it had dawned on her ... the reason she was here, the reason Adam had declared war upon her family.

"Bertram," she'd declared before he could reply. "He happened to her."

Nodding slowly, he had crossed one leg over the other, his hands flexing and clenching as if he wished to use them upon something— to break and destroy. The power in those thick, blunt fingers, the veins pulsing along the backs of his hands, had sent a shudder through her.

"Now you've begun untangling the threads," he replied. "It is quite a bit more complicated than that, little dove, but in short ... aye. Bertram happened to her."

Without another word, he'd stood and quit the room, taking his things with him and leaving the door hanging open. She'd sat upon the stool for what had felt like countless more hours, turning over the mystery Adam had presented in her mind. Someone he loved—a woman—had been ruined by Bertram. Who had the woman been? He'd claimed to have no wife; yet, the harp and the garden here at Dunnottar told a different story.

Shaking her head, she'd sighed, realizing it still made no sense. Lord Hartmoor was known as a confirmed bachelor and had not been publicly attached to any woman that she was aware of. Perhaps a mistress or lover, some woman he had lived with in sin or had a secret liaison with.

Yet, there remained the accusation leveled against her uncle ... the charge of murder. If Adam believed Bertram had raped this woman, then surely, he also believed William had killed her? What part did he believe her father had played in all this? What reason would they have for preying upon a presumably innocent woman?

The questions plagued her for days, robbing her of sleep and focus, the only times she could cast off the thoughts being her time spent dueling with Adam or practicing the harp.

By the fifth night, she had gone nearly mad with wondering. Rising from her bed, she had pulled on a dressing gown over her negligee, hoping some time in the music room could soothe her mind. She did not know where in the palace Adam's bedchamber might be located, but felt certain it was not near enough to the music room that she would wake him. In the morning, she would attempt to draw more answers from him, even if it provoked him to take her over his knee or force his cock down her throat. Anything would be better than this place of stillness, the torment of not knowing enough to understand the things happening around her.

She had just stepped out of her room when a strange sound drew her gaze to the bend in the corridor—the turn leading deeper into the palace, down the hallway Adam had warned her never to trespass upon. Her steps faltered, her throat constricting as the noise came again, reverberating down the corridor and echoing off the high ceiling. Clutching the sides of her robe with shaking hands, she turned to glance down the darkened hallway, only slightly illuminated by the moonlight streaming in from the windows of the main hall.

The sound came again, closer this time, its pitch unmistakable.

The shrieks of a woman.

Whoever she might be, she sounded half mad, howling and crying as if possessed by some unholy demon. Daphne wrestled with herself, half of her wanting to retreat into her room and close the door, blocking out the sound, the other half dying to know who the woman in the forbidden wing might be, and what made her scream as if her very soul had been set on fire.

The decision was snatched from her hands when an apparition materialized at the end of the corridor, glowing white like a specter. It raced toward her, its screams reaching out to her, freezing her in place and causing her blood to run cold.

It was the woman, she realized, a thin, white nightgown draping her body, dark hair streaming behind her like pitch black silk. Her face glowed as pale as her gown, wide, desperate eyes unseeing, unfocused, registering something in the air Daphne could not see.

She ran toward Daphne, tears streaming down her face, her bare feet thudding against the carpet. As she drew closer and it became apparent that she did not mean to slow or stop, Daphne began to backpedal, panic flaring in her gut. Whoever this woman was, she clearly did not possess all her mental faculties and might even prove dangerous.

Before she could duck back into her room, the strange woman was upon her, crying and sobbing as she took hold of the lapels of Daphne's dressing gown.

"Please," she sobbed, the long, heavy strands of her hair falling into her face and obscuring her features. "Don't let them take me away ... don't let them hurt me!"

Pity lanced through her as the woman clutched her, trembling and sniffling, clearly terrified by whatever threat she imagined chased her. She was no more than the slip of a girl, slender and petite, the large eyes peering at Daphne through the curtain of hair seeming overlarge in a gaunt face.

Reaching out to grasp the woman's arms, she forced a smile and tried to steady her voice. "It is all right. I will not let anyone hurt you. I am Daphne Fairchild. What is your name?"

The girl's head snapped up suddenly, large, brown eyes connecting with Daphne's. They widened, and the woman's grip on her arms tightened painfully.

"Fairchild," she growled, her pupils spreading and darkening her eyes, the snarl echoing ominously down the corridor. "*Fairchild!*"

Daphne let out a scream of her own as the woman's body collided with her, throwing her onto the thick rug, falling on top of her in a heap. Hands lashed out at her, nails scraping her face and neck, grasping handfuls of her hair and yanking viciously.

"No!" the woman cried out, attacking Daphne as if her life depended upon it. "No, I will not let you take her from me!"

Raising her hands to defend herself, she twisted and bucked beneath the woman, but madness seemed to lend her strength. A cry for help burned in her throat, lodged there by panic and held there by fear. The woman went on screaming and clawing at her, spittle flying from her mouth, her nightgown falling off one shoulder, hair surrounding them both in a tangled haze of blackness.

Then, as suddenly as she'd fallen onto Daphne, she was gone, a pair of strong hands hauling her up.

Struggling to catch her breath, Daphne crawled swiftly backward, her heart thundering in her chest as she watched Adam wrestle with the enraged woman.

"It's all right, Livvie," he murmured, his voice firm but gentle as he took hold of her arms and gave her a little shake. "I am here. It's me ... it's Hart."

The woman stilled in his arms, stiffening, then deflating, her tiny body wilting like a flower in the absence of sunlight. "Hart?"

Daphne's lower lip trembled. There was awe and love in her voice as she uttered the shortened version of his title as if she cherished it ... cherished *him*.

"Aye, butterfly," he whispered, his voice cracking on the affectionate nickname. "Hart ... I am here. I'm always here."

Nodding, the woman—Livvie, or butterfly, as Adam had called her—fell into another bout of sobs, lowering her head and curtaining her face with her hair again.

"Where were you?" she cried, her tiny voice hoarse and raspy from screaming. "Where were you, Hart?"

He sank to one knee when she collapsed, keeping his arms tight around her as she curled into herself and nestled against him, sobs wracking her body.

"I'm sorry, butterfly," he replied, his voice a low, gruff whisper, as tortured as her scream-roughened tone. "I'm here now ... always."

Another large shadow appeared from the darkness, and Daphne gazed up to find Niall descending upon them, his face white as a sheet, the harsh lines made more prominent by the worry creasing his brow.

Kneeling beside Adam, he ignored her, offering his Master a clear bottle corked with a wooden stopper. The sickeningly sweet aroma of laudanum emitted from the open bottle as it was held to the woman's lips. Her cries subsided as she latched onto the bottle like a babe suckling from its mother, low whimpers sounding in the back of her throat as she gulped the drug that was said to cure all ailments.

Daphne's jaw dropped as the girl consumed an amount that seemed far too much for a person of her size. Yet, once she had finished and Adam removed the bottle from her lips, she closed her eyes and sighed with relief, the tension in her limbs melting away. A soft smile curved her mouth, and her eyes grew glassy and unfocused, peace stilling her.

Studying her features no longer obscured by her hair, Daphne experienced a strong sense of déjà vu. She knew this woman ... or, at least, had been introduced to her in the past. Before she could determine when and where, Adam was on his feet, the woman cradled in his arms like a babe. Handing her, and the laudanum, off to Niall, he scowled.

"Take her to her chamber," he said, the usual sternness in his voice replaced by a weariness that caused Daphne's heart to plummet into her gut. "Stay with her ... she responds more readily to you."

The butler gazed down at the woman in his arms and nodded, a lone tear tracking down his craggy cheek. He glanced up to find her staring and frowned, murder gleaming in his eyes. Daphne swallowed past the lump in her throat, frozen in his fiery stare.

"Niall!" Adam snapped, breaking whatever thrall the butler had fallen under. "Now!"

The man clenched his jaw, but nodded, returning his attention to the woman, murmuring something to her as he turned away and continued down the corridor, eventually falling out of sight.

For a long moment, Adam simply stood there, gazing at her much the same way Niall had—as if wanting to destroy her, tear her apart and leave her lying in pieces on the carpet. But he said nothing, and eventually turned to walk away, taking the opposite direction as the butler.

Scrambling to her feet, Daphne turned to watch him go, her stomach twisting, her heart squeezing painfully.

"Adam," she called out, stumbling after him, her dressing gown tangling with her legs as she struggled to keep pace with him. "Adam, wait!"

His shoulders tensed beneath the wrinkled white linen of his shirt, but he kept walking, refusing to turn back. He continued toward his study, hands balled into fists, his back hard and unrelenting.

Maeve appeared, seemingly from thin air, rushing toward them with wide eyes, her skirts clutched in her hands.

"Master!" she called out. "I came as soon as I heard. Niall ... is he—"

"Tend Lady Daphne," he snapped, swiveling toward the door of his study and throwing it open.

Daphne skidded to a stop before she could bump into him, gasping as he turned to look at her, allowing her an unobstructed view of his face for a swift second. Then, he was gone, swallowed into the cavernous room, slamming the door so hard, it trembled in the frame.

She stood there for a moment in shocked silence, her lips parted and her breath rushing in short pants. Her mind reeled from what she'd just witnessed, still not certain she understood what it meant.

The mysterious woman who had clearly lost her grip upon reality, the tender way both Adam and Niall had handled her, the clear affection between them.

Most of all, she could not comprehend the sheer agony she'd just witnessed upon Adam's face, the hard and rigid lines melting into an expression of despair so acute, she'd felt it to her core.

"Come, my lady," Maeve urged, coming forward to gently grasp her arm. "Oh, you've been gouged something awful. Let's get you cleaned up."

Glancing numbly down at herself, she noticed the evidence of her encounter with Livvie, the deep gouges in her chest and the tiny beads of blood welling in the nicks. She realized she ought to feel something—the sting left over from the rake of nails, the hot, sticky blood. Yet, she remained alarmingly desensitized as Maeve led her back to her chamber, settling her before the vanity.

Staring off blankly across the room, she remained passive, letting Maeve clean her wounds and dab a strong-smelling tincture onto them, then a soothing ointment of aloe. She did not bother to demand answers from the maid, knowing it would gain her nothing. When the time was right, she would have to confront Adam about what she had seen and heard.

One thing she realized without having to be told ... Livvie was clearly the woman her brother, uncle, and father had ruined. Based upon her present condition, Daphne had no doubt in her mind they had deserved every blow Adam had dealt them in retaliation. And, for being ignorant to what the men of her family had done—the grievous sins that had led to the madness of an innocent young woman—perhaps, she did, too.

9

D aphne tossed and turned in bed for hours after Maeve had left her, unable to close her eyes without seeing the tortured faces of Livvie, Adam, and Niall. The few times she drifted toward sleep, the memory of the woman's screams filled her mind, snapping her awake in an instant.

Fairchild ... No ... You will not take her from me!

There could be no denying she'd seen Bertram's features when looking upon Daphne, the blue of her eyes and the red of her hair clearly marking her as a Fairchild. Whatever had been done to her must go beyond simple ruination. It had to have been something so heinous and depraved, the simple sight of Daphne had disturbed the victim to the point of no return.

The guilt that assailed her mingled with the curiosity in her gut—the need to know more, to uncover what remained of the truth. If there was anything she could do to make it right, besides surrendering her pride and her maidenhead to Adam, she must do it. It rested upon her to make things right, even if she had no notion how.

Sighing, she sat up in bed, rubbing her bleary eyes. Despite being more exhausted than she'd ever been, she could not find rest, could not sleep with her conscience weighing so heavily upon her. The four walls of her chamber boxed her in, forcing her into a confined space with her turbulent thoughts and emotions.

Desperate for escape, she stood, pulling on her dressing gown once more. The sun would rise soon, and she had given up all hope of getting any rest. A book from the library might serve to distract her until ... well, until Adam came for her, she supposed. After the way he and Niall had looked at her, as if she were the foulest thing they'd ever laid eyes upon, she should not expect that to happen soon.

She stepped out into the corridor and turned in the direction of the library, her steps faltering as the detected notes of music on the air. Frowning, she looked to the music room door, which stood ajar, the soft glow of yellow candlelight spilling out into the hallway.

Whoever occupied the room played the pianoforte beautifully, with a mastery born from years of practice and dedication. The haunting melody drew her forward, its lilting notes resounding through her entire body from scalp to toes. As if pulling her along with an invisible tether, it urged her to the doorway, lifted her hand to the heavy panel, and prompted her to push it open.

Seated on the cushioned bench with his hands moving lightly over the ivory keys, she found Adam. It was the last person she had expected to discover making the beautiful music—his large hands and meaty fingers seeming made for destruction instead of art. Yet, he hunched over the instrument, his digits moving over it as if he caressed a lover or greeted a long-lost friend.

His hair spilled down his back, the firelight illuminated the golden strands within the brown. The rigid tension in his back had melted away, and even from behind, she could tell the music soothed him—that putting his fingers to keys brought him focus in the same way manipulating harp strings made her feel.

She was not familiar with the piece he played, but it struck her as beautiful in a macabre sort of way. In the way that a blossom growing from a crack in the hard desert floor might be. In the way that his hand striking her arse created both pleasure and pain in one blissful, excruciating act.

Her feet propelled her forward again, until she stood just behind him, close enough to detect the rise and fall of his shoulders with each breath, to smell the aroma of cedar and cigar smoke emanating from him. It tangled with the sting of brandy, and she spied the nearly empty decanter placed atop the instrument, a half-full tumbler beside it.

How long had he been in here, seeking solace with the pianoforte and drowning himself in spirits?

A pause occurred in the music, his fingers pounding a discordant note before going still. He turned his head just far enough to peer at her over his shoulder.

"Why are you here?" he rasped, his voice low and grating, the words slightly slurred from the effects of brandy.

A nodule of anxiety lodged in her throat, but she choked it down, closing her eyes for a moment and taking a deep breath before plunging in.

"I ... I came to say ..."

The firelight illuminated the molten gold pooling in the prisms of his eyes, the rage simmering with a red-orange light within the depths. Coming here—intruding upon his solitude when he was in such a state—had been a terrible mistake.

Throwing one leg over the piano bench, he turned to face her. The half-empty tumbler sat in his large hands, the amber liquid glistening.

"What, little dove?" he snapped, biting off his nickname for her as if it were an epithet. "What have you come to say?"

She cast her gaze downward, unable to abide the revulsion emanating from his eyes ... the evidence of the depth of his hatred for her and her entire family.

"I am so very sorry," she whispered, her voice thick from the tears she fought not to shed.

His upper lip curled back from his teeth, a snarl rumbling ominously from deep within his gut. The sound, filled with turmoil and wrath, sent her skittering back toward the door. Her pulse raced, the instinct for self-preservation prompting her to reach out for the doorknob, to seek escape.

He moved with a swiftness that stole her breath, taking what was left of his brandy in one swallow and tossing the tumbler across the carpet with a thud. Then, he was lunging across the room and reaching past her to slam the door shut before she could slip through. Bracing one hand against the panel, he loomed over her, the burning scent of brandy stinging her nostrils when he parted his lips to speak.

"Sorry," he murmured, scowling as if he found the taste of the word repugnant. "For what, exactly? For the ruin your brother made of her life? For being so naive and sheltered that you could never have fathomed your precious Bertie could be so despicable?"

She shuddered when his body came against her, pinning her to the door. Wedged between two hard, unrelenting things, there could be no escape. The planes and ridges of his torso held her captive, his chest compressing her breasts and one large thigh shoved between hers.

"Yes," she whispered, raising her head to look at him. "For all of it. If I had known—"

He scoffed. "What would you have done?"

"I ... I do not know," she stammered.

He chuckled, the sound lacking humor and making dread curl low in her belly. "That is the problem, is it not? You know nothing ... not even the truth of your current situation. You *dare* come in here to offer me your pitiful apology, as if it would change anything between us ... as if you mean anything more than a means to an end. I do not want your apologies ... I do not *need them.*"

Her chin trembled, but she forced herself to maintain his gaze, to hide her fear in the face of his anger. He would enjoy it too much, knowing he had terrified her to her core.

"I know apologies are not enough," she replied, using her most soothing tone.

She needed him to release her, to let her out of this room. Coming here had been a mistake, but it could not be too late for her to escape.

"I understand you feel the need for vengeance," she added.

"Do you understand, truly?" he taunted, lifting a hand to grasp her face, his fingers biting into her jaw. "How it feels to hold in my hands the object of his affection ... to fantasize about wrapping my fingers around your throat and squeezing until you go limp ... holding you down and fucking you until you scream and plead for mercy ... tearing you to pieces until there's nothing left?"

A sob welled up in her chest, his words striking her as carrying more weight than a mere threat.

"Please," she pleaded, squeezing her eyes shut and trying to compose herself.

Her body jerked away from the door, and she gasped, kicking and flailing as he lifted her off her feet. His fingers bit into her arms as he hauled her to the center of the room, then threw her down on the rug in the center of the floor.

Panic flared in her gut as he knelt over her, reaching out for the belt of her robe. Despite knowing she had given him free use of her body—that she could not deny him without reneging on their agreement—she could not fight the instinct telling her to run, to preserve the parts of herself Adam would surely destroy. She backpedaled, her robe falling open as he snatched the belt loose. The heavy garment fell off one shoulder as she scrambled away from him, her legs tangling in her gown.

With a frustrated growl, he grasped her ankle and gave her a rough jerk, pulling her back to him and straddling her.

"Do you think she begged, too, little dove?" he ground out through his clenched jaw, tearing her dressing gown from her shoulders, then tugging at the straps of the silk scrap she wore, snapping them completely. "Do you think he listened ... that he cared when she cried and pleaded for mercy?"

She bit back a cry when he tore the gown down the front, exposing her breasts. A rough sound emanated from him in reaction to the revealed flesh, his tongue creeping out to wet his lips. Her nipples shrank and hardened beneath his gaze, a twinge between her legs filling her with shame. Despite her fear—or, perhaps, because of it—her body reacted to him, the sensation of arousal unmistakable.

He grasped both her wrists and pinned them above her head with one hand, using the other to pull the bodice of her nightgown farther down. Then, he palmed one breast, squeezing it until she squirmed beneath him, her nipple rasping against his palm.

"So goddamn perfect," he spat, almost as if the perfection he accused her of disgusted him to no end. "So smooth and unblemished ... so breakable. Have you any idea how badly I want to destroy you—how much pleasure it would bring me?"

She gasped again when he pinched her nipple, her eyelids fluttering closed as he plied it with his thumb and forefinger. Her eyes flew open again when he gave it a vicious twist, sending liquid heat and agony spiraling through her belly. It melted and spread to her core when he released her, her sharp cry of pain melting onto a sigh of relief ... of bliss.

"So responsive," he murmured, treating the other breast the same way—teasing her nipple into a stiff peak before torturing it with a twist. "You like this, don't you, little dove? Being defiled ... controlled ... used."

Turning her head and avoiding his gaze, she clamped her lips shut. Answering his question would damn her. More than that, it would force her to confront things about herself she was not yet ready to face.

Lowering his head, he pressed his mouth to her ear, the linen of his shirt teasing the tips of her breasts, his hips fitting into the cradle between hers.

He laughed again, the sound bristling her spine and stoking her ire. "I can see you do, my little wanton ... *whore.*"

A rough cry of rage tore from her throat, and she bucked beneath him, kicking and yanking her arms free of his hold. Lashing out at him, she screamed, raking his face and neck with her nails, squirming to try to work her way from beneath him. Damn him for doing this to her, for poking and prodding at the deeply hidden parts of herself and making her acknowledge them. For making her hate him and want him all at once.

Laughing as if she amused him, he grasped one wrist and then the other, immobilizing her as quickly as he had before, pressing her back against the carpet. Red welts rose up along his cheek where she'd mauled him, the buttons torn off his shirt, the opening exposing a wide swath of his chest.

"Yes, little dove," he said with a slow, predatory grin. "Fight me … you know how I love it when you fight."

Her face went hot when he surged his hips against her, letting her feel the evidence of his words. He had gone hard as stone, the heat of his lust searing her through the layers of his breeches and her night-gown. She went still, hovering on the line between wanting to fight him and being afraid to provoke him further.

Reaching between them, he swiftly jerked open his fall. Her cunt clenched hungrily at the sight of his cock—large, red, and angry—peering at her from the opening in his breeches. Jerking up the skirt of her nightgown, he fell upon her again, keeping a tight hold on her wrists as he fit his cock into the cleft between her legs.

"Deny it all you want," he rasped in her ear, rocking against her and sparking a flame of pleasure in the place where their bodies met. "But we both know no matter how hard you try to fight me, your body craves what I can give it. Isn't that right, my little whore?"

A shudder tore through her, her only response a low whimper as the thick tip of his cock rubbed against her inner folds, pressing down against her swollen clit. Pleasure stole her words, and primitive need overtook all her other urges. The word 'whore' struck her like the lash of a tongue against her clit, sending another ripple of heat and desire throughout her being. She wanted to deny it, to protest his treatment and argue that she would never be his whore, but could not think beyond the steady pressure and friction of his cock against her clit.

She arched her back, tipping her chin up as he began to consume her, devouring her vulnerable throat with his lips and tongue and teeth. He lapped at her pulse point, then sank his teeth into the taut tendons, each suckling pull sending a lightning strike of pleasure straight to her core. One hand tightened around her wrists while the other pawed at her breasts, squeezing, kneading, pinching. Her hips rose up off the floor, undulating against his and adding a sweet coun-terpoint to his rhythmic thrusts.

Her juices coated his flared head and soaked his shaft. A moan fell from her lips, then another, the way between them made slippery by her wetness.

He sank his teeth into her breast, sending another jolt of pleasure stabbing into her core ... and then she spiraled. The climax rushed over her so swiftly, she could hardly catch her breath, the powerful spasms wracking her body with violent shudders. Her cunt clenched around air, seeking more as the flutters of the orgasm began to dissipate, leaving her bereft and longing instead of satisfied.

As if sensing the path of her thoughts, he angled his hips so the tip of his cock kissed her honeyed opening, poising himself to enter her. Her eyes flew open, her lips parting as she tried to wrap her mind around what would come next. It seemed impossible for the large, flared head to fit inside her—for the thick, long root jutting out from his body to follow. She squirmed beneath him, her shoulders burning from the position of her arms, her body balanced on the edge of anticipation and fear.

Adam loomed over her, his eyes glassy and unfocused, his breath coming in harsh pants as if he barely held himself in check. Gritting his teeth, he released a primal growl, pumping his hips with a force that left her stunned.

Her lips parted on a silent cry, a searing pain stabbing between her legs as if a flaming hot poker had been shoved into her sheath. Her back bowed, the tension in her arms and shoulders now unbearable as she fought against his hold, the invasion of his body as he forced his way into her. Her lungs burned from the breath she held, but she could not release it to draw another, could not move. She could do nothing but lie there and feel, the throbbing agony of her channel stretching to accommodate him mingling with the phantom bliss of her recent climax.

"Christ," he groaned, pulling away slightly before plunging again. "So fucking tight."

She bit her lip until she drew blood, tears welling in her eyes as he surged and withdrew, driving himself deeper into her. He had only given her half of his length in the first thrust, and with each surge of his hips, he opened her more, tearing into her, forging a path into her most secret of places. It seemed unending, the slow progress he made as he inched his way through her, the agonizing burn she would be hard-pressed to ever forget.

But then, she exhaled, her body easing back to the carpet as his pelvis met hers, his body coming against her as she sheathed him to the hilt.

He released her wrists, falling onto his elbows atop her as he rested inside of her. She trembled against him, her thighs forced wider by his weight bearing down upon her, her channel throbbing around the thick, intrusive organ taking up space inside her body.

His fingers tangled in her hair, and he shifted his hips, rolling against her. She cried out, the sound reverberating through the chamber and resonating like the notes he'd coaxed from the pianoforte. The stroke of his cock against her inner walls created more of the tortuous burn; yet, his pelvis grinding against her clit created a burst of pleasure. The dueling sensations warred against one another as he moved again, then again, taking up a slow, agonizing rhythm. Her body unwound even more, her back sinking into the rug, her legs falling as wide as they would go. Her body opened to him, her channel stretching for him, more of her wetness easing the way.

"Fucking hell, little dove," he growled in her ear, increasing his pace as he wound a thick strand of her hair around his fist. "You feel … Christ, you feel so bloody good."

She moaned, the sound strangled by a sharp gasp when he gave her hair a vicious tug, tipping her chin up and exposing her throat once more. Then, his body began hammering hers, his hips pounding her against the unrelenting floor.

Her core clenched around him, the ripples of pain intertwining with pleasure until they became one. The deep, throbbing ache radiated outward from her womb, sending tingles of ecstasy over the surface of her skin from scalp to toes. He suckled at her neck like a starving man, biting her chin, claiming her lips with a fervor that took her breath away. She struggled to breathe through her nose, opening her mouth to his thrusting tongue. Her hips undulated on their own accord, meeting his rhythm, the pounding cadence of his pelvis engaging her in a primitive duet.

Tearing his lips from hers, he stared down at her, the blazing fire in his eyes searing her to the soul. The tension in her middle wound tighter and tighter, her thighs trembling on either side of him as he urged her closer and closer to the inevitable end—one she somehow knew would be far more powerful than any she'd ever experienced.

"Please," she panted, groaning and writhing beneath him mindlessly, rational thought fleeing as her body begged silently for what only Adam could give. "Please ..."

She did not know what she begged for; yet, he seemed to. Still fisting her hair in one hand, he slid the other between them, his thumb finding her clit.

"Oh," she whimpered as he began stroking it in rapid circles, the thrust of his hips adding weight behind his strokes. "Oh, God ..."

Release slammed into her with the force of a battering ram, her sheath pulsating around Adam and drawing him in deeper. Her back arched, and her toes curled, her arms coming around him, clinging, pulling at his shirt, her nails digging in to find purchase. He groaned when she dragged them down his back, his hips jerking against hers once, twice, then a third time before he pulled his cock free. He took hold of his shaft, pumping himself with a tight fist until he spent, the hot spurts of his seed staining the silk covering her belly. With a shudder, he lowered his head, releasing his breath on a guttural sound, his hair shadowing his face.

She lay beneath him, suddenly cold despite the fire blazing in the hearth. Shivering uncontrollably, she began feeling about for her dressing gown, her shaking fingers refusing to close around the damask fabric. Her head swam dizzily, her limbs refusing to respond to the prompting of her mind. She needed to stand, to walk, to escape. To run away from the shame that overwhelmed her now that it had ended ... now that he had defiled her and made her enjoy it.

He sat back on his haunches and pushed his hair out of his face, his chest heaving as his breath began to slow, his heavy-lidded gaze fixated upon her. She became acutely aware of the picture she must make as he looked her over—hair hopelessly mussed by his rough handling, face flushed, lips red from the pressure of his, gown ripped and fallen around her waist, the grey satin stained with an offensive mixture of his mettle and her virgin's blood.

More of the same smeared her inner thighs, the red streaks a startling reminder of what he'd just taken from her.

His breeches still hung open, his flaccid cock visible through the gap. She'd torn the buttons on his shirt, and it hung off one shoulder, ripped at the seam. His hair spilled around his face and down his back in a tangled curtain.

He closed his fall with steady fingers, not bothering to right his shirt or tuck it in.

Reaching for her dressing gown, he moved it from beneath her limp hand and draped it in the crook of his arm. Then, he slid a hand beneath her shoulders, manipulating her as if she were a rag doll. She let him, lacking the strength to move on her own. She lay still in his hold and allowed him to drape the dressing gown over her shoulders and take her into his arms like a child. The world tilted and whirled around her as he strode from the room, the warm interior of the music room giving way to the coldness of the corridor.

She shuddered, and a part of her wanted to believe his hold tightened on her in response. Yet, that could not be true ... surely, she imagined it.

He pushed open a door and entered a chamber—her chamber, she realized, recognizing the decor. The light streaming through the parted drapes stung her eyes, a reminder that dawn had come and gone while Adam had torn her apart in the music room.

"Close the drapes," he said in command to someone he could not see.

She wondered how he knew the light bothered her eyes, but then realized it must be because she'd turned her face into his chest, burrowing there to escape it.

"Master, is she—"

"She's fine," he snapped, cutting off the voice she recognized as Maeve's. "But, perhaps a hot bath would be welcomed."

"Yes, Master," the maid said quickly, her footsteps taking her out of the room.

She felt him lowering her onto the bed, the soft mattress a sharp juxtaposition to his hard body. He stood over her, staring down at her with that inscrutable expression he always wore just before saying something he knew would hurt her. The sunlight revealed his exhaustion—the dark circles beneath his eyes, the haggard lines etching his face.

"Do not ever seek to offer me your useless platitudes again," he murmured, though the silence of the room magnified his voice like a cannon's blast. "In the end, they mean nothing to me ... *you* mean nothing to me."

Her eyes stung as she turned away from him and curled into herself, uncertain why his words should flay her open so viciously, like the lash of a whip. Of course she meant nothing to him—and why should she? Yet, his cruel words were like a dagger to her chest, the resounding pain echoing and mingling with the throbbing between her legs. As if he had turned her inside out, exposing all her nerve endings to the elements.

His eyes burned into her back, searing her through layers of satin and damask, as if he could see the stains of his seed and her blood through them. She curled herself tighter, hugging her knees to her chest and squeezing her eyes shut. Tears warmed her face, but she held her breath to contain the sobs. He had hurt her, and he knew it ... but she would not give him the satisfaction of breaking. Not now when he could see and hear her.

Before long, a flurry of motion told her servants had arrived with the tub and hot water. She lay and stared numbly at the wall, uncertain how she knew he'd left the room. His presence simply melted away, and when Maeve came to coax her from the bed, she turned to find him gone.

10

D aphne slept for what remained of the morning, waking hours after Maeve had tucked her into bed. The maid had flitted about the chamber as she'd soaked in the steaming tub, washing her hair and combing out the snarls, soothing her face with a warm, damp cloth, tending to her wounded neck again once she'd left the water.

"You must forgive the Master for his ill temper," Maeve had insisted while slathering the gouge marks with more of the ointment. "It's just ... Livvie's condition torments him, you see. He thinks it's all his fault."

She'd surfaced from the muddled haze submerging her mind at that, turning to glance at the maid over her shoulder. "He does?"

And here she'd thought he cast all the blame upon Bertram.

"He does," Maeve replied, closing the ointment jar and wiping her hands clean on her apron. "He and Niall ... they take care of her in hopes she'll find her way back to them someday."

As the woman had begun pulling her hair into a single braid, Daphne had stared into the vanity mirror, studying the reflection of the maid. Her eyes had been downcast, her hands trembling as she worked Daphne's damp hair.

"Who is she to him?" she'd prodded, hoping the maid would pity her enough to tell her something ... anything. "He told me he loved her."

"We all love her," Maeve had whispered, her voice low and hoarse as if she fought back tears.

Then, glancing up to meet her reflection in the mirror, she had paused, her hands tangled in Daphne's hair.

"Please, ask me no more," she'd pleaded. "I've already said too much. The Master will not be pleased to know I've spoken of her to you at all."

Nodding in understanding, Daphne had let the matter drop, not wanting to invite Adam's wrath onto the innocent maid. Recognition niggled the back of her mind every time she thought of the mysterious Livvie, and she felt certain if she thought on it long enough, she might remember where she'd seen her before. Things had happened so suddenly last night, she'd hardly gotten a good look at the woman's face.

She stared silently at her reflection while Maeve finished her hair, the picture that confronted her one she hardly recognized. Her skin had gone pale, causing her eyes to look larger and darker and the red lines from where she'd been scratched to appear meaner. Turning her head slightly, she cringed at the evidence of Adam's sensual assault, purple bruises beginning to form along her throat where he'd suckled and bitten. Maeve had changed her into a new nightgown— this one an apricot silk with a low-cut bodice that displayed more of the marks along her collarbone and the swell of one breast.

Her cunt contracted, the liquid heat of desire combining with soreness to make her head spin and her stomach lurch. How could seeing the evidence of what had just transpired in the music room affect her this way? She should be sobbing with regret over her lost maidenhead, over the painful invasion that had stolen her innocence, the callous words he'd spewed at her once he'd finished with her. Instead, she found herself clenching her thighs together to stifle the feeling, to smother the longing opening in the pit of her womb.

She'd lain in bed for countless minutes trying to forget, closing her eyes and searching for the sleep that had eluded her the night before. Exhaustion had finally dragged her under, and she'd slept deeply for hours—though her rest had hardly been peaceful. Adam haunted her dreams; the feral glint of his eyes, the flash of white teeth, the sting of his bite, and the searing burn of his cock entering her for the first time.

She came awake gasping and panting, her nightgown clinging to her body, her limbs trembling uncontrollably.

Easing herself from the bed, she opted to freshen up on her own, not wanting to ring for Maeve and have the maid see her in such a state. Approaching the washstand, she peeled the damp nightgown from her body and quickly dipped a scrap of linen into the bowl of fresh rosewater that had been left there. It had long gone cold, but it brought her relief as she bathed the sweat from her skin. She winced when the cloth touched her mons, the tender flesh still swollen and aching. There was no more blood, however, so she supposed she ought to be grateful for that. Despite having bathed the bloodstains from her thighs, she scrubbed them again, certain she might never feel completely clean, as if those stains had sunk in deep, becoming a part of her, a permanent scar that would brand itself indelibly upon her soul.

Crossing to the armoire where her clothing had been hung, she caught a glimpse of herself in the vanity mirror. Her throat looked worse now—the purple stains already beginning to take on a yellowish hue. Tearing her gaze away, she swiftly selected a simple white muslin morning gown, a pair of stockings, and garters. As she slid her feet into a pair of slippers, her stomach growled, hunger beginning to gnaw upon her insides.

She left the room and headed straight for the dining room, knowing an afternoon meal would be available on the sideboard this time of day. Relieved to find the corridors empty save for a few chambermaids dusting the wall sconces, she ducked into the large, airy room, happy to find an array of cold foods that appeared to have been recently laid out. Filling a plate and taking a seat, she thanked the footman who appeared at her elbow with a glass of lemonade.

As she ate, staring out at the picturesque view framed by the dining room's parted drapes, she could almost pretend to be somewhere else. A beautiful, tranquil place far removed from London, her family, and the other things she would rather outrun than confront.

For instance, the truth that Adam had unearthed concerning the reason for her state of spinsterhood, of the countless marriage offers she had refused. She had wanted love, she'd told herself, and would not settle for anything less.

Yet, she'd loved the boy from the estate neighboring her family's, had dreamed of becoming his wife more times than she could count. She'd almost surrendered her virtue to him and had come close to letting him compromise her the last time they'd seen each other. At the time, she'd told herself fear had driven her to refuse him, to pull her skirts down over her legs and run from him, whispering a tortured 'I'm so sorry' before retreating. She'd been young, afraid, inexperienced. At least, this was what she had told herself.

Could the truth be something far more unpalatable? That she had been waiting for someone who did not handle her like a delicate porcelain doll? Someone who challenged her, frightened her, excited her?

Shaking her head, she clenched her jaw, setting her fork onto her half-empty plate with a loud 'clang'. No ... he was wrong about her, had been from the moment they'd met. She was not some fragile thing he could easily break, nor was she the whore he had accused her of being, just because he'd managed to coax her body to climax with his rough handling. She was a woman who had fallen down on her luck for the time being and had found a way to set it all right. When her time had ended here, she would return home thirty thousand pounds richer ... and perhaps wiser for having learned the truth about her family.

That decided, she took up her napkin and folded it, laying it beside her plate before quitting the room. She had grown far too restless to return to her chamber or to practice the harp. Nor did she believe she would find Adam in the gallery so they could spar together. So, she set off on a walk, hoping to explore parts of the castle she had not yet seen.

Adam had never told her she could not explore it on her own—only that she was forbidden to tread into the corridor adjacent to the one her room sat in. Of course, she realized it was because that wing of the palace was where Livvie had been ensconced. Now that she had made her presence known to Daphne, would Adam still want her to stay away?

Deciding to err on the side of caution, she went in the opposite direction. Passing Adam's study, the library, music room, and other sitting rooms she had already seen, she moved deeper into the third arm of the quadrangle. In it, she found more sitting rooms, and several sets of double doors which led into a massive ballroom. She entered the space, finding it dusty and shuttered, meager light streaming through stained glass windows. The colorful beams illumi-nated white pillars and large, iron chandeliers which would give the room a gothic yet ethereal feel once lowered and lit. Smooth, veined tiles lined the floors, and a raised dais for an orchestra was flanked by more of the statuesque pillars.

Had soirées ever been hosted at Dunnottar? She would imagine that if this manor had a lady, she would throw open these doors and host extravagant balls. She would be able to see the potential in the cavernous space, perhaps even hosting gothic masquerades or Grecian-themed balls. A sudden image of herself seated in the center of the dais, draped in white silk and strumming the harp before a captive audience, sprung forth in her mind. Uncertain where such a thought had come from, she turned away from the ballroom, swiftly closing the doors she had thrown open to access the room. It had been a preposterous thought, one with no basis in reality. This place was her prison and would continue to be for another twenty days. No matter how beautiful, it would always be the lair of a monster.

Continuing to the end of the corridor, she found stairs winding up a tower that would give her access to the second level. She climbed them and entered another corridor, this one seemingly lined with more bedrooms. She opened the doors to discover her assumption had been right. The rooms were as beautifully decorated as her own, filled with heavy, old furniture that had been remarkably preserved, as well as modern finishes that blended in seamlessly.

The fifth room on the right struck her as being different from the others. Instead of heavy drapes, sheer white curtains covered the windows, allowing in far more light than the other chambers. A large canopy bed flaunted more of the same curtains, though these had been embroidered with delicate pink rosettes. A matching bedspread of pink damask was etched with white flowers while a bench resting at the foot of the bed had been upholstered in a matching fabric. An oak writing desk faced one of the windows, covered in scraps of paper that appeared to have been written on. As she drew closer, she realized they were actually charcoal drawings—of flowers, birds, people. They were quite good, better than anything she'd ever attempted.

"Livvie," she whispered, reaching out to touch a drawing of a hummingbird drinking from the pistil of a flower.

Some instinct told Daphne this room belonged to her, that she had once filled this chamber with warmth, laughter, and creativity. An artist ... and likely the person who had so loved the garden Adam had taken her to.

Glancing up from the drawing, she spotted a large shape in the corner, covered with a white sheet. She looked over her shoulder to ensure no one might be coming who would see her, then approached it. Dropping to her knees on the thick rug, she reached out to move the sheet aside—revealing the large object to be a cluster of paintings that had been stacked together against the wall.

The first one took her breath away—an incredible likeness of Adam. The gilded frame contained a portrait depicting him in sporty riding attire, a crop held over one shoulder. Though he did not smile, humor curved his lips and alit his eyes—which the painter had captured as being mostly green. If she did not know better, she might have thought it must be someone else—someone younger, and happier. Yet, the artist had gotten his hair right, and the slope of his brow and the ridge of his nose, the soft pillow of his mouth. Even the stubble that grew along his jaw had been perfectly translated to the canvas, adding a dangerous allure to the powerful body encased in an athlete's riding wear.

She stared at the portrait for a long while, wondering what the younger, happier Adam had been like. A charmer, who the women of Scotland and London tripped over themselves trying to impress? A humorous fellow who could have rooms full of men in stitches with nothing but a well-timed joke? It was difficult to imagine; yet, the portrait proved a truth she could not deny. Adam had been irrevocably changed by the circumstances entangling her family with his.

Moving the heavy painting aside, she studied the next one—the image of a man who must surely be Adam's father. The resemblance was really quite striking. The two men possessed the same dark hair and peculiar eyes. He wore an expression similar to the one she typically found upon Adam's face—hard and implacable. An undeniable severity solidified his jaw and pinched his mouth into a tight line. Clearly a man of constant ill humor.

She pushed that one aside to reveal a woman, with golden hair and cheer dancing in her blue eyes. A beautiful young lady she did not recognize. Based upon the style of the portrait, it must be decades old—perhaps a likeness of Adam's mother in her youth. Adam possessed none of her features, having inherited the whole of his aspect from his sire.

Daphne moved the painting aside, unveiling one that sent her heart spiraling up into her throat. The woman staring back at her possessed a flawless alabaster complexion, complemented by glossy black hair and innocent, brown doe eyes. She recognized the pert nose, lightly freckled cheeks, and rosebud mouth. Dressed in finery and portraying the flawless image of a young debutante, she called to mind a girl Daphne had met several Seasons ago.

"Lady Olivia Goodall," she whispered, reaching out to touch the painting.

"Aye," said Adam's voice from the behind her, frightening her half out of her wits.

She gasped, leaping to her feet and spinning to find him lingering in the doorway, arms folded over his chest. His expression indicated neither anger nor disapproval; yet, she shivered beneath his stare all the same. Her skin prickled as if recalling what it felt like to be touched by him, her pulse racing as she fought the urge to run.

"She is a member of your family?" she asked, her mind spinning as she tried to recall what little she knew of the lady.

Daphne had been introduced to her at Almack's—which she had attended on the arm of a man. A cousin, perhaps. The man had been forgettable ... certainly not Adam.

"My sister," he confirmed, nodding toward the painting. "Well ... stepsister, to be precise."

That would explain why the two shared no resemblance. It began to make sense—why Adam had taken Olivia's ruination so personally, what Maeve had meant when she'd claimed all the residents of Dunnottar loved her.

"I remember her," she whispered, the things she had forgotten now coming back to her in a rush. "We were introduced at Almack's ... she was a lovely young lady. All the men wanted to dance with her. Her dance card had been filled within an hour of arriving."

"I know," he replied, leaning one shoulder against the doorframe. "She wrote me countless letters detailing the events of her first Season. After having spent all her life here in Scotland, she found London to be quite exciting."

Why had Adam remained behind while his young sister went off to enjoy the Season? One would think he'd chaperone her instead of a cousin. Where had their father been?

"I was away on the Continent," he continued, as if having read her mind. "For my Grand Tour. My father thought it a frivolous waste of time. He thought anything not directly related to the earldom a waste of time. You see, he insisted the Callahan named carried with it bad luck. Countesses who die young, Earls who languish in their absence ... a family line dwindled to almost nothing. After my mother's death, he married Lady Edith, a young widow with a daughter just out of nappies. His second wife did not last half as long as my mother did, and before long, he found himself a widower saddled with two children."

"I am so sorry," she whispered, uncertain what else to say.

Adam snorted. "So was I … for Olivia's sake, at least. I often think he was cold as a way to guard his heart from any more pain or loss. No matter what Livvie or I did, it was never enough to make him smile … never enough to make him love us."

"Which was why your cousin chaperoned her for her first Season," she supplied.

"Her cousin … he was a relative of Edith," he amended. "But yes, that is why. He could hardly be bothered with her, so he sent her off to London in the company of her cousin and his wife, who would sponsor her coming out and see to it she made a good match."

"Then, she met Bertram."

"Aye, little dove," he replied, inclining his head at her. "Then, she met Bertram."

She lowered her gaze to the rug, her shoulders sagging as she recalled an evening soirée, watching Bertram bow over the girl's hand and brush a kiss across the knuckles. Bertram dancing with her twice in one night. Bertram leading her toward the terrace for air, not returning with Lady Olivia for near an hour. Bertram leaning a bit too close as he whispered in her ear.

Wrapping her arms around herself, Daphne held on tight, feeling as if she might fall apart. The evidence had been in front of her the entire time, and she'd never realized it, never understood what Bertram had been up to. Or, perhaps a part of her had realized? Could she be as fragile as Adam had claimed, looking away so she did not have to acknowledge the truth?

"I saw them together," she admitted. "Bertram and Olivia. But, I never knew …"

"No one did," Adam said when she trailed off.

She glanced up at him, wondering if that could be pity she detected in his tone. Pity for her. As if he felt sorry for her, knowing she had been misled for so long, going about ignorant to the truth.

"Your brother is very good at what he does," he added with a sneer, all the compassion melting from his tone. "How do you think he's gone this long without being outed?"

Thinking over the things he had revealed to her just now, she understood where he was leading her. "My father. There is no way Bertram could have ruined so many without an angry papa or two turning up on our doorstep. I can only assume my father did what was necessary to bury the secrets and avoid scandal."

Adam grunted in response, his expression hardening. Her eyes widened in realization, her stomach lurching as the various threads he had fed her began to intertwine, creating a tapestry of deceit and pain that clearly displayed her brother's guilt.

"He turned her away," she whispered, bringing a hand up to her roiling stomach. "When she came to him to tell him what Bertram had done ... my father turned her away."

His jaw ticked with fury barely held in check, his voice coming out strained and clipped when he answered her. "Does that shock you?"

Thinking of her father—of the staunch viscount with the white hair and haughty demeanor—she shook her head. It would have felt like betrayal ten days ago ... when she'd thought him above reproach. Perhaps a bit snobby, but not a malicious person. Now, she was beginning to realize nothing was what she'd thought.

"No, actually," she replied. "He was not a cruel man, not to me, but he was a bit ... cold. Much like your father, I suppose. He never took much of an interest in me, though he was quite invested in Bertram's future. He would become the viscount someday, and the Fairchild bloodline is an old one."

"One of the bluest in all of England," he agreed. "Which was why Fairchild did not wish to sully it by marrying his precious heir off to a Scottish chit whose mother had come from new money."

Reaching up to press her fingers against her throbbing temples, she shook her head. "If I had known—"

She quickly clamped her lips together, recalling his words that morning as he'd dumped her into her bed. He did not want her apologies or platitudes. Yet, she could not help but think of what she might have done if she'd known about Olivia. Take Bertram to task, and demand he do the right thing. Yet, what would it have accomplished? Lady Olivia had simply been one in a string of conquests, all of whom Bertram had cast aside.

"When did you find out?" she asked, remembering he'd been on the Continent, and Maeve's claim that he blamed himself.

Perhaps much of his anger lay with himself for being in another country while his little sister was being preyed upon by her brother.

"Not until it was too late," he declared, before turning to leave the room.

Despite the sense of self-preservation telling her not to follow, her feet moved of their own accord, and she chased him out into the corridor, watching as his long legs carried him toward the stairs.

"Adam," she called out, halting him in his tracks.

Why did she call out to him? What did she want?

To console him? To seek comfort from the man who had been tormenting her from the moment she'd first laid eyes upon him?

He paused at the top of the stairs, his shoulders tensing as his hands clenched into fists. However, he did not turn back to gaze at her when he responded.

"Where was your father during all of this?"

Adam scowled. "Dying. Some disease of the heart, the physicians said. The Callahan misfortune claimed him, as he always knew it would."

Silence passed between them for another long moment, during which Daphne fiddled with the lace edging her gown.

"Have a care, little dove," he warned suddenly. "I might have been drunk last night, but that does not mean I was not well aware of what I was doing or who I was doing it to. I hardly think you would relish being thrown on your hands and knees on this staircase and ravaged. Or ... perhaps you would. Provoke me, and perhaps I will forget your body needs a reprieve and put that to the test."

Swallowing past the lump in her throat, she backed away from him, clasping her skirts in shaking hands. Fear lanced through her at the image he conjured, and she could practically feel the cold, hard steps digging into her knees and the palms of her hands as he took her from behind as mindlessly and brutally as he had when taking her maidenhead.

Yet, her core clenched in longing, the tips of her breasts pebbling and insides melting into molten fire. God help her, he had awakened something she was not certain she could ever put back to sleep. Some filthy thing in the depths of her soul that craved depravity ... sex ... oblivion.

She wanted to test him, to take a step toward him and see what it earned her, see what challenging him would result in. Instead, she retreated a few paces, which seemed to free him from the thrall. He disappeared swiftly down the staircase, leaving her in the hollow corridor alone.

ANOTHER SLEEPLESS NIGHT drove Daphne back to the music room, where she hovered in the doorway, staring listlessly at the pianoforte. Her heart sank when she entered to find it empty, though she did not know why she cared. It should be a relief to return to this place she'd begun to think of as a haven and find solitude. She most certainly did not care that Adam did not occupy the space, or that the evocative composition he'd played in the early hours before dawn no longer reverberated from these walls.

She approached the harp, reaching out to caress its strings, stroke her fingers over the golden angels. As she sank onto the low stool, her gaze flitted to the spot on the floor where Adam had ravaged her. Despite the rug remaining pristine, she imagined it carried a mark from their encounter, a stain that could never be washed clean. It confronted her accusingly, reminding her of the dark things that had happened here, of the twisted desires he had pulled from deep inside her, forcing her to confront and accept them.

Closing her eyes, she embraced the harp, seeking succor in the music. Louis Sphor's *Fantasia in C Minor* flew from her fingers without a second thought, despite it having been years since she'd laid eyes upon the sheet music. She didn't need it to remember each note, to let them carry her away. She kept her eyes closed and ignored the invisible stain upon the rug and the ache it caused in her chest. Her mind became lighter than air, and she floated away with the music.

She moved into another composition, one she had long forgotten the name of. It had been one of her first, though, and she played it as effortlessly as she had *Fantasia*. It was not until she neared the end that she realized she was not alone, that her music was no longer the only sound filling the confined space.

Opening her eyes, she found Adam seated at the pianoforte, his shirtsleeves rolled up to his elbows to reveal his strong forearms. The muscles stretched with fluid grace as his hands moved over the keys, playing in accompaniment to her composition. The two sounds melded and became one—strings and keys intertwining into harmonious notes flitting about on the air around them.

He sat with his profile presented to her, his gaze cast someplace she could not see. So, she openly watched him, traced the angle of his sharp, stubble-roughened jaw, roamed the undulating strands of his hair, soaked in the bunch and roll of his shoulders beneath the pristine white shirt.

Like last night, his expression had melted into one of stillness and peace as he played, the cares of the day washing away until he existed as one with the music ... and, in a way, with her. They played together naturally, Adam guiding her wordlessly into another composition, then another. After what felt like hours, they finally finished, reaching the end of their fifth composition without him flowing into another.

Daphne rested her instrument on the carpet, releasing a deep sigh as her body began registering the strain of playing for so long. Her fingers had grown tired, her shoulders and back aching from sitting so perfectly erect.

Adam had hunched on the bench, hands in his lap as he stared down at his keys. From where she sat, he appeared despondent ... grieved. She wondered if he had just come from Livvie, if the young woman had suffered another episode. Pity she did not wish to feel settled in her gut, causing her heart to twist violently in her chest. Without the anger he wore like a mantle, he appeared a pitiful creature ... a lion licking at the thorn in his paw. If she thought he would not maul her to death for drawing too close, she might have wished to help him remove it, to soothe the ache that obviously plagued him.

Folding her hands in her lap, she cleared her throat. "Where did you learn to play?"

He did not spare her a glance, reaching up to press his first finger to one of the keys. The long note rang out, quickly fading away without another on its heels to lend it strength.

"My mother," he replied, his voice low as if he were as loath to disturb the peace they had found together as she was. "Not a pastime typically taught to sons, but I was all she had. This was her instrument ... an extravagant wedding gift from my father. I spent hours in here sitting on this bench beside her, watching her play, matching the notes to the keys she struck. One day, I snuck in here alone and played an entire composition on my own. I was only five years of age."

She gasped, awed by the revelation that Adam was a bit of a musical savant. She'd heard of such people, but had never met one in person.

"You do not read sheet music," she observed aloud.

He shook his head. "I never needed to. There was something in me that seemed to understand the music without it. My father did not like it, but Mother saw what I had and nurtured it. While I am also adequate with the violin, harp, and cello, I never excelled at any instrument like I did the pianoforte."

She smiled at the thought of a young Adam sharing the piano bench with his mother, his little legs swinging inches off the floor, his hair tousled by affectionate hands.

"What of Olivia? Did you teach her the pianoforte?"

At last, he turned to gaze at her, the troubled expression on his face deepening and causing her chest to tighten painfully.

"No," he replied. "Olivia loved the harp and played it better than anyone I'd ever heard ... until you. It is why I took to calling her butterfly, for the way her hands would flit over those strings, so light and swift."

Staring at the golden instrument resting in front of her, she sighed, sadness slumping her shoulders. The beautiful harp had belonged to Livvie, no doubt—yet another thing Bertram had stolen from her, ensuring she could never enjoy it again.

"I purchased that harp for her on her birthday," he added. "When she reached seven and ten ... just before setting off on my Grand Tour. She loved the bloody thing. When I returned from the Continent to assume my place as the earl, I purchased Dunnottar and created this music room. I thought playing again might heal her ... make her feel more like herself."

He did not have to say the words that hung on the air between them—did not have to tell her he could hardly get her to look at the harp now, let alone touch her fingers to the strings.

She parted her lips, but then snapped them shut. She had been on the verge of apologizing, of uttering the words she knew would only infuriate him. Because her apologies meant nothing ... because expressing her regret would not give him his sister back or assuage her guilt.

"Come here."

His words turned her blood to ice water in her veins, a shiver of dread rolling down her spine. He did not look at her, did not seem impatient for her to obey his command. Perhaps because he knew she would obey, if for no other reason than to make it easy on herself.

Clenching and opening her hands, she slowly rose from the stool and forced her limbs into motion. She became aware of her cunt, still aching from their first joining, and her breasts, her nipples which had turned into hard points at just the sound of his voice and what his command suggested. Would he use her again, tear her clothes from her body and throw her to the floor?

He reached for her when she came near, his hold on her wrist so alarmingly gentle that she hardly knew what to make of it. Shifting back on the bench, he slammed the pianoforte shut, covering the keys before hauling her toward him. He pulled her down onto his knee, wedging her between it and the instrument.

Before she could blink, he had the bodice of her nightgown torn down, freeing her breasts. He released a heavy sigh before latching onto one like a starving man, suckling at her as if he'd never tasted anything sweeter than her nipple. She cried out, the pleasure of his lips and lashing tongue spiraling straight between her legs. Squirming in his lap, she ground her cunt against his hard thigh, seeking pressure and friction, relief from the desperation he'd created in her with nothing more than the touch of his mouth to her breast.

He released one and moved on to the other, cupping both orbs in his large hands and kneading them, squeezing and caressing as he tasted his fill of her.

Gazing up at her, he teased each nipple with little flicks of his thumbs, smirking when he drew a sharp gasp from her, then a yearning moan. He dragged his tongue slowly over one while pinching the other, and she gritted her teeth, hissing at the muddle the dual sensations made of her senses.

"Such a bonny little thing," he remarked, still steadily stroking her nipples with the pads of his thumbs. "Especially with my finger-prints all over your skin. Those other men who coveted you ... they valued you in your state of pristine goodness ... your white muslin and frills, your smooth hair, and your perfect posture. But not me, little dove. I much prefer you like this ... your hair mussed, your neck bruised from my lips, your back arched to its breaking point as I wrap my hands in your hair and pull."

She gasped when he scraped a fingernail over the tight bud of one breast, easing the sharp sting by drawing it into his mouth.

"No one else has seen you like this, have they?" he demanded, staring back up at her with fire in his eyes, turning the inner prisms into molten gold. "Have they, Daphne?"

She shook her head, and he reached around to grab one of her buttocks, giving it a tight squeeze and then a slap. It stung through the layers of her robe and nightgown, its warmth radiating at her core and further inflaming her.

"Answer me," he growled, nuzzling her breasts and treating them to little nibbles and soft, teasing bites. "Who has seen you like this?"

"N-no one," she gasped. "Only you."

"That's right," he crooned before taking one of her breasts deep into the cavern of his mouth, sinking his teeth into the soft flesh.

She groaned and thrashed in his lap, her channel pulsating with need, liquid heat gathering there and slicking the path into her body.

It did not matter if he hurt her when he entered her ... she would invite the pain just as she would the bliss that would follow, leading her to the rapture waiting for her on the other side.

"Say my name," he commanded, grasping her waist to lift her onto the pianoforte. "Tell me, who is the only man to see you like this, little dove?"

"Adam," she moaned when he swiftly parted her legs and hauled her down onto the enclosure over the keys, poising her at the perfect angle to enter her.

She grasped the edge of the instrument for purchase, her mouth practically watering as he began opening his fall, revealing the hard root of his cock. She whimpered when he stroked himself, pointing the thick tip toward her opening. Her inner thighs were smeared with the evidence of her need, but even as he slid his head into her cunt, she knew her wetness would not be enough. She was still so swollen, too tender from his first assault to accept him.

Yet, accept him she did, when he hooked his arms beneath her knees and yanked her to him while simultaneously thrusting his hips. She threw her head back and screamed at the invasion—equal parts ecstasy and agony. Her swollen channel gave way to let him in, sheathing him to the hilt, wrapping him in throbbing flesh.

"Again," he rasped, tightening his hold on her as he pulled back and prepared to drive into her once more. "Let me hear it again."

"Adam!"

He grunted as he impaled her over and over, sending waves of pleasure surging through her, resounding to the far reaches of her body. She chanted his name as he fucked her, mindless from the ecstasy, her body creating music at his hands as he played her as masterfully as he did the thing she lay upon.

"Adam ... Adam ... Adam!"

He took her slower than he had the night before, but his presence inside her had no less impact, driving her to climax so swiftly, she could hardly catch her breath before she went spiraling. She collapsed back onto the pianoforte, the edge biting into her back as he used its hardness for leverage and quickened his strokes, seeming to reach for his own end.

Pulling out of her with a rough groan, he spent, his liquid essence spilling over her belly and thighs, marking her, staining her. Her cheeks flushed while deep inside, a part of her practically purred with contentment. The part of her that craved Adam's depravity stretched and sighed happily, thrilled at being taken and sullied.

Closing her eyes, she fought to catch her breath, but also to avoid Adam's gaze. Her limited experience with him had prepared her for what would come next. If he did not spew his venom, punishing her with words, then he would leave her there, stunned and thrown off-balance, her body still throbbing from his invasion.

She was unprepared for the touch of linen against her skin. Opening her eyes, she found him cleaning her with his own handkerchief, the snowy white material soft against her thighs. The flush in her cheeks deepened, her face flaming hot as he took his time, painstakingly removing his seed from her stomach, then folding the cloth and using it between her legs. His face gave nothing away, his eyes shuttered and his lips a firm line as he completed his task and replaced the handkerchief in his coat pocket.

Then, he swiftly buttoned his fall before grasping her waist and putting her on her feet. Her nightgown and robe fell to cover her; yet, when he gazed into her eyes, she felt utterly exposed. He studied her in silence for a long moment before moving again, taking hold of her hand and pulling her along, leading her to the door.

She stumbled, her legs having not quite regained their strength. Grasping the hem of her robe, she followed him, uncertainty making her heart pound and her mouth go dry.

Where was he taking her ... and what would he do with her once they got there?

They reached her chamber a moment later, and he threw open

the door and pulled her inside. She found it empty, but prepared for her—a fire still blazing in the hearth, the bedclothes neatly turned down, a clean nightgown laid out beside the washstand where a fresh basin of rosewater sat waiting for her.

As if Maeve had known she would need to clean herself up when she returned. She wondered if the maid had waited up, somehow discerning Adam would use her again tonight. Or, perhaps Adam himself had ordered all this done.

He gave her a little push toward the washstand, which she took as a silent command to make use of it. Her hands shook as she walked to it, peering back at him over her shoulder. He had begun disrobing, his coat slung carelessly over the bench settled at the foot of her bed, his cravat thrown on top of it. She swiftly turned her back before he could remove his shirt, her throat constricting so tightly, she could hardly breathe.

Did he mean to have her again … in her bed this time?

She trembled with equal parts fear and anticipation as she removed her robe, then the nightgown—which had not survived the encounter in the music room unscathed. Droplets of Adam's seed had begun to dry on the fabric. Letting it slide off her shoulders, she took up the soap and scrap of linen waiting beside the washstand. She found the rosewater still warm, its scent mingling pleasantly with the floral-scented soap.

Making quick work of cleaning herself more thoroughly, she dried and then donned the clean nightgown. Like the other items Adam had ordered for her, this gown seemed more like something a courtesan would wear than a demure young lady, the black silk clinging to her breasts and waist, a high slit allowing easy access.

But, as she approached the bed, she supposed the title of 'courtesan' did not lay far from where she found herself.

Paid to be a man's plaything.

He stood on the other side of the bed in nothing but his breeches, his unbound hair falling down his back. His naked upper body was shown to its advantage, the moonlight illuminating the hard bulges and sinewy ridges. She idly wondered how he would feel if she pressed her hands against his chest. Would that part of him be hot to the touch, much like the velvety skin blanketing his cock? Would the coarse hairs tickle her fingers ... would it be soft to the touch like the hair on his head?

"Get in," he snapped, his voice breaking her out of her reverie.

Despite the strain in his voice, he did not appear to be vexed with her ... merely a bit impatient. She scrambled into the bed, swiftly covering herself with the blankets. He followed suit, climbing in beside her and turning onto his side. One long arm came around her, dragging her across the space between them until she rested against him. A gasp burned in her throat, a visceral reaction to the hot, male body pressed against her. He gave off a heat that seemed to sink through her skin and settle as deep as her bones.

"Relax," he growled against her ear. "I am not going to take you again ... not right now. That isn't to say I might not want to later. I'd rather keep you within reach if I wake up and decide I want you than have to cross the palace to wake you in the middle of the night."

Nodding her understanding, she swallowed past the anxiety lodged in her throat. His words hardly eased her mind. In truth, she would rather have endured him again right away as opposed to being awakened when she least expected. While she was clearheaded, she could brace herself for whatever he might do to her. In a state of half-sleep, she would be defenseless.

She lay silently for a while, staring at the ceiling overhead. Her body slowly relaxed against his, fatigue beginning to drag her under. The change in his breathing told her he had fallen asleep, which served to ease her anxiety a bit more. She turned to look at him, finding him no less intimidating in sleep than when he was awake. Even with his eyes closed, his lips parted, his breathing deep and slow, he reminded her of a wild cat—the strength in his muscles and the threat of the large hand splayed over her lower belly putting her on edge.

Despite that, she eventually drifted off to sleep beneath the heavy —yet somehow pleasant—weight of his arm, his warm breath softly fanning the side of her neck.

11

When Daphne woke the next day, she found the bed beside her empty. The sun streaming through the windows stung her eyes, its brightness telling her it must be at least an hour past noon. Her sleep had been restful, though Adam had awakened her twice during what remained of the night. The first time, she had come to with his cock slipping into her, the hem of her nightgown snatched up to her waist. He had entered her while she laid upon her side, his large body curled around hers, one hand possessively holding her hip. She had splintered within seconds, muffling her screams in the pillow as he'd pounded her from behind, his pelvis colliding with her buttocks in a rhythm matching her beating heart. He'd pulled away from her and spent with a low groan, turning away from her to spill his seed upon the sheets.

The second time, she'd been roused by his tongue between her thighs and the orange glow of dawn appearing outside her window. She had opened her eyes to find him lying between her spread legs, hair spilling over his shoulders, eyes closed. He'd lapped at her with a slow thoroughness completely at odds with his earlier claiming. He'd taken his time exploring her with languid tongue strokes and soft pulls of his lips, thrusting his hands beneath her nightgown to find her breasts so he could toy with them. He'd made her spend more times than she could count, his gentleness eventually giving way to urgency until he'd devoured her as if starving, his breath racing against her wet, tender flesh.

Then, without preamble, he'd sat back on his haunches and flipped her onto her belly. She'd hardly found her breath before he'd been straddling her, plunging inside her to the hilt. The ministrations of his tongue had made her so wet, the sting of his invasion had only lasted a moment. As he'd fisted her hair in one strong hand and pulled, forcing her back into a deep arch, she had closed her eyes and surrendered. He would have her whether she allowed herself to enjoy it or not ... at least, this was what she'd told herself while screaming her pleasure, gripping the bedclothes in her fists as he'd hurtled her toward another powerful climax. It was what she'd told herself as he'd pulled free of her sheath and stained her back with his seed ... when she'd collapsed onto the bed so he could wipe her clean before pulling her back against his chest and urging her to sleep a bit longer.

Now, as she sat up in bed, an emptiness yawned inside of her, opening in the pit of her gut. She should be glad to find herself alone, to be free of him for even a short time. Yet, she was forced to confront the fact that she'd just gotten her most restful night of sleep since arriving at Dunnottar, despite being awakened twice to slake Adam's lust. Or, perhaps even because of it.

Groaning, she ran her fingers through her tousled hair and lowered her head. What the devil was wrong with her? She should not miss his presence, nor should she allow herself to feel anything toward him except antipathy. The man had treated her cruelly from the beginning, never ceasing to remind her she was no more than a means to an end.

But then, his haunted gaze flitted through her mind, reminding of her of the reason for it all. Why he hated her ... why she was nothing more than a channel through which he could hurt Bertram ... why he could never care about her in any way. The things he'd revealed to her in the darkest hours of the night—his pain, his grief—made her pity him as much as she abhorred him.

"Oh, my lady, you're awake!" Maeve exclaimed.

Daphne glanced up to find the maid approaching the bed, carrying a tray laden with food and tea.

"The Master wanted me to ensure you had a proper meal," she continued, waiting for Daphne to sit up straight so she could lay the tray in her lap. "He was called away on urgent business to Kincardineshire, but should return in a few days."

Taking up a triangle of buttered toast, she bit into it and nearly swooned with pleasure. She hadn't realized how ravenous she was until she'd tasted the first bite.

"Why should I care where he has gone or when he will return?" she retorted, annoyed with herself for the sinking feeling in her gut as she digested the news.

She told herself it was only because Adam's absence meant she would grow bored. Without someone to fence with, how was she to occupy herself each morning? As well, she could hardly ferret out the other answers to her questions concerning Bertram and Olivia if he was not here.

Maeve did not reply, simply casting her a smug, knowing look before going about her duties. While Daphne ate, she selected riding attire, suggesting an afternoon ride while the weather was still so fair, then prepared another basin of rosewater.

After she'd eaten her fill, the maid set the tray aside then began her toilette. Once she had been bathed with the rosewater and wore a simple white blouse and skirt for riding, Daphne sat to endure having her hair combed, brushed, and arranged into a simple chignon.

Her spirits lifted a bit as she stepped out onto the front steps of the palace, turning her face up to the sun. She had not spent nearly as much time out of doors as she was accustomed to, and with the Scottish countryside stretching out for miles before her, she became filled with the urge to ride as far and fast as her mount would allow.

A stable groom quickly prepared her horse, and before long, she descended the escarpment, putting Dunnottar behind her. She rode for what felt like hours, her face breaking out into a smile as the soft breeze stroked its fingers through her hair and the sun caressed her face. Even the lingering soreness between her legs could not steal her enjoyment of the ride, the exercise going a long way to ease the tension in her tight muscles.

Her good mood lasted for the rest of the afternoon, which she spent reading in the garden.

It was there that Olivia happened upon her, seeming to have wandered away from her wing of the house.

Daphne gasped at the sight of her, frozen in place upon the bench she occupied with an open tome in her lap. She held perfectly still, not wanting to startle the girl, but captivated by the sight of her.

She wore a demure morning gown of spring green muslin, her dark hair unbound and hanging down her back. She walked through the courtyard barefoot, her steps slow and fluid. She moved with the same grace Daphne had noticed in Adam, though with her slender form and dainty feet, the motions appeared more dreamlike—as if Olivia floated instead of walking.

Approaching a rosebush bursting with open blossoms, she smiled, reaching out to touch one. She must be the reason Adam kept the garden so well-maintained. The girl looked at home here—as much a part of the scenery as the flowers blooming around her.

She appeared far more peaceful than she had the night she had attacked Daphne. As Olivia plucked a blossom and turned to face her, she realized why. Her eyes glistened with an unfocused sheen that told her she had recently come out of the haze induced by laudanum. The effects still lingered, keeping her passive.

A soft smile curved Olivia's mouth when their gazes met, and she brought the rose up to her nostrils to inhale.

"Hello," she murmured, her voice soft and lyrical when not strained from screaming. It carried the same soft Scottish brogue as Adam's. "I do not believe we've met."

Daphne closed her book and set it aside, trying not to move too quickly lest she startle the girl.

"I am Daphne Fa-"

She paused, clearing her throat, realizing the error she'd almost committed. Telling Olivia her last name would only set her off again.

"Just Daphne," she amended. "I am here as a guest of your brother."

With a giggle, Olivia came closer, twirling the stem of the rose between her fingers. "Hart always did have good taste in women. You're absolutely beautiful."

Daphne's smile was genuine this time. "Thank you. I find you to be quite lovely, as well."

But Olivia paid no heed to her compliment. Instead, she kept the rose in one hand while reaching out to Daphne with the other.

She held as still as possible and let the girl touch her hair, pulling the long rope of her braid from over one shoulder to trail it between her slender fingers. They were the hands of a harpist—dainty and feminine, with long, slender fingers she imagined would glide over the strings with ease.

"Such a lovely shade of red," Olivia murmured. "Just like—"

"Livvie!" a man's voice boomed from across the courtyard.

Both women turned to find Niall approaching them from the door leading to the main hall. His black coat strained at the seams, his shoulders and arms rippling with power as he clenched his hands into fists at his sides. He did not appear pleased, his dark eyes narrowing when they landed on Daphne, his mouth turning down.

Yet, Olivia seemed unaware of his displeasure, giggling as she shot to her feet and dashed toward him. "Niall!"

The butler turned his attention to the young woman, his expression softening considerably when their gazes met. Daphne looked on in shock as the girl threw herself at him, laughing as he caught her up against his body. He wrapped his arms around her and held her tight, bringing her up to meet his gaze. Her diminutive size made her feet dangle off the ground, her small hand cupping his face.

"Such a grumpy thing you are," she teased. "Careful, Niall ... so much frowning brings wrinkles."

He grunted as she began kissing him, her lips brushing his forehead and the bridge of his nose, then his lips. "Ye'll give me wrinkles on yer own, wanderin' off like that. And with no shoes, to boot. Hart'll kill me if ye injure yerself."

Daphne's mouth fell open at the clear evidence of affection between them. Despite Olivia not being in her right state of mind, there existed a familiarity here that could not be denied. She cared for Niall, and by the way the large butler handled her, he obviously returned the sentiment. Daphne would never have thought him capable of such gentleness; yet, he held Olivia as if she were made of glass, as if she were more precious to him than a handful of priceless gems.

"Come on, then," he murmured, turning to walk back toward the open door with her still in his arms. "Let's get ye back to yer room and into a pair of slippers."

Olivia clung to him, her arms wrapped tight around his neck as he carried her away.

"Good-bye, Daphne," she called out cheerily. "It was lovely to have met you!"

As if he'd forgotten about her presence, Niall turned to glare at her over his shoulder. "You ... stay there. We'll speak when I return."

She watched them go with a slack jaw. Niall had seemed like a different person in Olivia's presence, his careful handling of the girl baffling. Especially considering the man looked fit to kill her anytime she was in the room with him.

She sat quietly in the garden and waited—not because Niall had all but ordered her to, but because she needed to connect another thread in this convoluted tapestry. She needed to know what else Adam was keeping from her. It would seem there was more than met the eye ... so many facets of this situation she remained ignorant to.

When the butler returned, he once again wore his disdainful expression, his dark eyes searing her like burning, hot coals. Daphne stood to face him, placing her book upon the bench and clasping her hands demurely before her.

"Niall, I—"

"Lady Olivia is not well," he interjected, fury lending a shaky quality to his voice. "Days like this one—when she's more like her normal self—are rare. I won't have ye ruinin' that."

She reared back as if he'd struck her, taken aback by the venom in his words. "Ruin it? I did not even know she was here. In fact, I had no idea she was Adam's stepsister until after she had attacked me. He told me what happened to her ... what my brother did."

"Then you ken why even the sight of ye is enough to send her spiralin' into madness again," he retorted. "Keep yer distance, or I'll make the rest of yer stay at Dunnottar a livin' hell. The Master might have become obsessed with your cunt, but I haven't forgotten who ye are and what ye Fairchilds did to her."

Her mouth fell open, and she struggled to find words to defend herself, to remind him she'd had nothing to do with Olivia's condition, and the Fairchild name did not mark her as a monster.

Before she could, he was gone, spinning on his heel and striding away with his hands balled into fists at his sides. Snapping her mouth shut, she thought better of it. The sight of her near Olivia had been enough to rile him, and she did not wish to provoke him further.

As she sank back onto the bench, her book forgotten, she stared off across the garden with unseeing eyes. There were many things she still had yet to discover, but one thing had been made exceedingly clear ... Niall was in love with Olivia. Whether she returned the sentiment or not, the butler cared for her in a way that went beyond the relationship of a servant and the lady of the house. She had read the devotion in his eyes when he'd gazed upon her, had heard the tenderness in his voice when he'd spoken to her.

Knowing this only made her guilt increase, the number of people her brother had affected with his poor decision-making growing by the day. Olivia. Adam. Niall. All three of them irreparably damaged by the Fairchild family.

"Bertram, you fool," she whispered. "What have you done?"

ADAM REMAINED AWAY from Dunnottar for several more days, during which Daphne nearly went mad from boredom. Her days continued with the same monotony as before, with morning rides and after-noons spent in the music room, library, or garden. She kept her distance from Niall and did not encounter Olivia again. Perhaps the butler had become more vigilant in keeping her out of sight in Adam's absence, determined to keep her away from Daphne. Maeve continued to treat her with kindness, though went back to being tight-lipped when it came to the subject of Adam or Olivia.

Daphne did not want to admit to herself that she missed Adam's imposing presence in the castle—that without the fear he inspired, she was bored to tears, that her body remained in a state of height-ened arousal, craving his touch. Most of all, she bemoaned the loss of the music he could create, the haunting notes of the pianoforte filling the music room and tugging on something nestled deep inside of her. She found herself visiting the music room for no other reason than to sit before the pianoforte, her fingers lightly stroking over the keys, the pads of her fingers tracing the same places his had been. That inevitably led to remembering the times he'd taken her in this room —on the rug, on top of the piano.

There must be something terribly wrong with her—some defect making her crave depravity. How else could one explain that Adam had been right about her all along—that she longed for brute force and pleasure with pain, complete oblivion over simple gratification? She would never give him the satisfaction of admitting it aloud, but she could no longer fool herself. She had always known there was something setting her apart, a reason no man had ever seemed like the right one.

Lord Hartmoor is the furthest thing from being the right man as could be, she told herself, appalled she might even consider such a notion.

While his cruelty toward her might be justified in light of Bertram's transgressions, it did not negate the fact that he possessed the capacity for destruction. Despite her body seeming to want him with a madness that could not be explained, her logical mind real-ized how bad for her this man truly was. If she let him, he would devour her, then use her bones to pick his teeth. That could never happen. She must endure what remained of her time here with her heart and soul intact. And when she left, she would not give in to the urge to look back.

On the fourth day of Adam's absence, Daphne decided to explore more of the castle on her own, having grown bored of the garden and music room. The mystery and gothic beauty of Dunnottar held her entranced as winding stairways led to various wings she had yet to discover. She found doors leading out into small courtyards—some planted with flowers or arranged with furniture for lounging, others crumbling and overrun with climbing vines and foliage. She liked these places best and loved running her hands over thick vines and ancient stone, wondering what sorts of assignations might have taken place there.

But it was the discovery of secret passageways that truly enthralled her. Pushing aside the fear that she might lose herself in the dark tunnels built into the walls, she had gone in search of a lamp and entered the labyrinth. Swallowed by darkness, she entered in one place and emerged somewhere else, only to discover another passage, another secret, another hidden route from one wing to another.

Before long, she pushed aside a large panel and found herself confronted with a tapestry. Frowning at the heavy thing, she inclined her head, the sound of feminine voices coming at her through the curtain. One of them sounded familiar, even muffled by the thick fabric separating her from whoever stood on the other side. The other was low and sweet, high-pitched.

A child.

Her breath caught in her throat, her lungs burning as she reached one hand out to touch the tapestry. The surface of her skin prickled, gooseflesh rippling over her arms, a tingle traveling down her spine. Not once had she come across any evidence indicating the presence of a child in Dunnottar. Yet, the cheerful giggle carrying through the tapestry was clearly not that of a servant, or even Olivia. There was a distinctive, childlike warmth to it … a lightness unburdened by the cares of someone who had reached maturity.

Her hands shook, the light in her lamp flickering and beginning to sputter out. She'd wandered for so long, the wick had nearly burnt to ash. Some part of her warned that no good could come from entering the room, her instincts telling her to turn back, to go the way she'd come and forget she'd heard the sound of a child's laughter. Yet, another part of her would not allow her to turn away without investigating the sound, without seeing for herself the final secret Adam had withheld from her.

She slowly peeled the tapestry aside, her throat growing tight as it revealed what appeared to be a nursery. Cheery yellow paper adorned the walls while an ornate chandelier overhead flooded the chamber with light. It had clearly been decorated for a girl—with white lace etching the curtains and pink and white damask upholstery covering miniature pieces of furniture. Skipping ropes, dolls, and other children's toys littered the carpet while a white rocking horse rested in one corner. A massive doll's house took up an entire corner of the room, its insides filled with opulent replicas of Chippendale and Hepplewhite furniture. The room was fit for a princess, as opulent a nursery as any that existed in London.

Movement in the center of the room drew her eye, and she found Olivia sitting on a small, child's chair, her back turned to the open passageway. Daphne recognized the tumble of dark, lustrous hair, as well as the voice speaking in cheerful tones to a person she could not see. A low, round table sat laden with what appeared to be a tea set, and when Olivia fell silent, the child's voice came again. The girl sat on the other side of the table, blocked from her view by Olivia, who laughed at something the child said. Daphne did not discern a word, the pounding of her heart filling her ears and blotting out all sound.

Her feet moved of their own accord, drawing her deeper into the room, closer to the table. If she ventured close enough, she could lay eyes upon the child. She could see for herself that things could not be as they seemed.

Olivia remained oblivious to Daphne's presence, lifting a child-sized teapot and pretending to pour tea into a matching cup. However, the child seated across from her glanced up just when Daphne drew close enough to see her over Olivia's shoulder.

Her footsteps faltered, and the lamp fell from her hand with a thud, the meager flame sputtering out, the odor of kerosene stinging her nostrils as it spread a stain upon the carpet. It became forgotten as she brought that shaking hand over her mouth, choking on a gasp as she stared into the eyes of a child who could not be older than five years of age.

She had the face of an angel, with a tiny button nose, a sweet moue of a mouth, and soft, round cheeks. Her eyes, wide and round, were the same velvety brown as Olivia's, innocent, and full of mischief. But it was her hair that commanded Daphne's attention. Long, fat spirals tied back from her face with a pink ribbon ... gleaming auburn in the light of the chandelier. The glossy strands bore the unmistakable mark of Fairchild lineage, the decadent red shining with faint gold highlights that would shimmer in the sun.

Daphne drank the girl in, marking off every bit of evidence portraying a truth too shocking to bear. The freckles on the bridge of her nose, the bowed upper lip, the tiny beauty spot just beneath one eye, the evidence of high cheekbones that would become more apparent as she grew older.

That face was her face.

No, not her face ... *Bertram's* face.

"Hello," the girl said with a wary smile, breaking Daphne out of her reverie.

Olivia turned to gaze at her over one shoulder, the gleam in her eyes putting Daphne at ease a bit. She seemed to have been recently dosed with laudanum, her cheeks flushed and a light sheen of sweat dampening her brow. However, she remained docile, unlikely to attack.

"Good evening," Daphne croaked, her voice hoarse from the lump lodged in her throat.

She could hardly make sense of what she was seeing, though she faintly registered that she stared at a child of her own family ... Bertram's child. There could be no denying the resemblance.

"I am Lady Serena Grace Goodall," the little girl said when the room fell silent again.

Her heart warmed at the polite severity of the girl's tone, as if she'd been taught how to introduce herself and the importance of including 'lady' before her name.

"It is lovely to meet you, Lady Serena," she managed, coming closer to the little table and kneeling to the left of the table. "I am Daphne."

"I have never met another person with hair like mine," Serena declared.

Your father's family is overrun with redheads, she thought.

"It is unusual," she replied aloud. "But you carry it quite nicely. What a pretty girl you are, Serena. How many years are you?"

"Four," the child replied. "But it is nearly my birthday. Mama says I may have a puppy when I have turned five ... but only if Uncle Adam allows it."

"He frowns and argues when we try to browbeat him," Olivia chimed in with a girlish giggle. "But he will come around. He dotes on Serena ... gives her anything her little heart desires."

"How wonderful," Daphne murmured, for lack of anything better to say.

She'd grown dizzy, her stomach roiling as she attempted to digest this final revelation, the evidence of Bertram's sins sitting right before her.

Before she could part her lips to form more words, a dark shadow fell over her, making her blood run cold. Her entire body stiffened, her spine tensing and her mouth going dry. Serena came to her feet, her expression one of pure joy.

"Uncle Adam!" she squealed, dashing around Daphne and disappearing from sight.

A man's deep laugh sent a cold stone of dread hurtling into her gut, the heavy weight making her feel as if she would be violently ill. She remained where she sat, head lowered, breath coming in short, panicked spurts as she tried to remain composed while Olivia rose to greet the man who had entered the room. From the corner of her eye, she spied the nursery door, which stood on the side of the room opposite the passage she had come through.

"What have we here? Who is this bonny lass throwing herself into my arms?"

Adam's deep voice resounded through the room, carrying with it a tenderness Daphne had only witnessed when he spoke to Olivia.

Serena giggled. "It's me, silly! Serena."

"Truly?" he said with an exaggerated gasp. "My, how you've grown in my absence. You're practically a young woman!"

The little girl laughed again, the sound turning into the exuberant glee that almost always accompanied being tickled. Daphne dared a glance over her shoulder to find him holding her beneath one arm, his fingers teasing her ribs while she kicked and flailed, screaming with delight.

He had eyes only for Serena, his affection for the girl clear as he lifted her upright and ceased his assault in order to embrace her. The girl wrapped her tiny arms around his neck and held fast, closing her eyes and sighing happily.

"I missed you," he murmured, his eyes closed as he nuzzled the top of her head. "Have you been a good girl in my absence?"

"Did you bring me a present?" she countered, sitting up to look him in the eye.

Adam chuckled. "That all depends on whether you have behaved yourself."

"Oh, I have," the girl declared. "Haven't I, Mama?"

Olivia smiled and nodded, her words a bit slurred from laudanum when she spoke. "She's been an angel."

Adam nodded as if satisfied, then set the girl on her feet. Daphne twisted her fingers together, hands shaking in her lap as she waited for him to look at her, to acknowledge her presence in the room and act accordingly. She knew without being told that she was not welcome here.

"Very well," he replied, reaching out to ruffle Serena's neat curls. "Nanny is looking for you. Go find her, and I will come give you your present shortly."

"Can Daphne come?" the girl asked, oblivious to the tension tightening her uncle's jaw and darkening his eyes. "She has red hair, just like me!"

"Aye. That, she does," Adam said, his tone becoming harsh and biting as he swiveled his gaze in her direction. "But Lady Daphne will be going now. Her visit at Dunnottar has now come to an end. You will not be seeing her again."

Serena looked as if she wanted to protest, but Olivia stepped in, taking the child's hand.

"Come along," she urged her daughter. "I shall try to talk Niall into bringing us a pot of chocolate from the kitchen. Would that not be lovely?"

The girl forgot Daphne at the news of hot chocolate and skipped from the room beside her mother.

She watched them go, desperation making her heart pound. It lay on the tip of her tongue to call out to them, to beg them not to leave her alone in the room with Adam. But her tongue had turned into some unwieldy, useless thing taking up space inside her mouth. Words failed her. She could only sit there, locked in Adam's gaze and shaking like a tree battered by a raging storm.

His face hardened once they were alone, nostrils flaring and eyes blazing with green and gold tongues of fire. His hair had been pulled back, but a few strands hung around his travel-weary face. Dust clung to his boots, his clothes wrinkled. He must have just arrived home, coming straight to the nursery to greet his niece.

Her chin trembled, the realization of what would happen next slamming into her with all the force of a battering ram.

"Adam," she squeaked, managing to find her voice. "I can explain ..."

"Get up," he growled, narrowing his eyes at her.

Her limbs moved on their own accord, as if responding to his command. She shot to her feet, her legs tingling as blood rushed back into them, her head spinning from the sudden movement.

His arm shot out through the space between them, his hand clenching around her upper arm in a bruising grip. Without a word, he was hauling her toward the door, not bothering to shorten his long strides for her. She stumbled along, forced to practically run to keep up due to his bruising grip on her arm. The limb throbbed, her fingers tingling and going numb from lack of blood. Turning down a bend in the hallway, they now traversed the one leading to the front of the palace ... the one holding her guest chamber.

The concealed nursery had sat in the corridor Adam had forbidden her to go into. Her heart dropped into the pit of her gut and remained there, his intent clear as he continued dragging her, blowing past the open door of her chamber.

"Adam, wait," she pleaded, digging her heels into the floor to try to impede their progress. "Please ..."

He merely tightened his grip and kept walking, ignoring the wide-eyed stares of servants who ventured past them, some pausing in their tasks to look on with slack jaws. Maeve appeared, trotting toward them with horror written on her features.

"Master—"

"Gather the clothing Lady Daphne arrived with," he barked without so much as a glance in her direction. "She is leaving."

Tears sprung to Daphne's eyes as she tore at the hand wrapped around her arm, desperate to explain, to free herself from his hold.

"Please, I beg you," she tried again. "It was an accident, Adam. I did not mean—"

Her words broke off on a cry when he abruptly stopped, swinging her around to face him. The wrath contorting his features frightened her to her core, the bite of his fingers around her arm nothing compared to the heat of his searing glare.

"I warned you," he ground out, his voice shaking with barely contained fury. "I believe I was quite clear about what would happen if you disobeyed my directive."

"Then you never intended to tell me about her? A child born of my family ... my own blood?" she accused.

Taking her other arm in his free hand, he shook her as if she weighed no more than a rag doll. "Serena might look like a Fairchild, but she is a Callahan. You have no claim to her, and now that you are leaving, will never have contact with her again."

"Do you think you need to protect her from *me*?" she sobbed, hot tears splashing her face. "She is my niece ... I would never—"

"No," he spat, his upper lip curling in disgust. "You will *never* ... because you are leaving this instant. Our agreement became null and void the second you stepped foot inside the nursery."

The sound of footsteps drew Daphne's gaze to Maeve, who had come dashing down the corridor, a rough burlap sack slung over her shoulder. She handed the sack reluctantly to Adam, who released one of Daphne's arms to take it.

"Master, perhaps you should—"

"Finish that sentence, and I will throw you out beside her," he roared, leveling a heated glare at the maid.

She shrank away from them, casting an apologetic glance at Daphne before turning to walk away.

"Do not do this," she begged, turning her tear-filled eyes to Adam. "I will be good ... I will do whatever you want ... Let you do whatever you want to me. I cannot return to London with nothing."

"Why not?" he taunted with a rough, humorless chuckle. "You came with nothing."

That was not true. She'd come with her virtue ... the one thing she'd had to barter with. Now, she would leave without it, possessing nothing else with which to bargain.

Before she could attempt begging again, he had dragged her to the front doors. A footman rushed to pull one of them open, and without preamble, Adam hurled her over the threshold, tossing the sack out behind her. Stumbling onto the landing of the front steps, she whirled to face him, tremors rocking her from head to toe as she struggled for composure. Tears soaked her flushed face, her heart thundered wildly, and hot, bitter bile rose up in the back of her throat.

"Go to the stables to retrieve your horse," Adam commanded, one hand braced upon the open door. "Go home."

The heavy panel slammed shut between them. Seconds later, she heard the ominous sound of the bolt being slid into place, barring her from the inside. She rushed toward the imposing oak door on shaking legs and fell against it. Pounding her fists against it, she sobbed, raising her voice to be heard through the wood.

"Let me in! Adam, please ... I'll be good. I promise! I'll do anything!"

She pounded the door until pain reverberated up her arms, her knuckles scraped and bleeding. She screamed and called out to him, desperation driving her mad, stealing away every ounce of her pride. He could not send her away—not without the thirty thousand pounds she had sold her body for. Without it, she would ride back down the mountain penniless as well as in disgrace. Her family home would be lost, and she could not even be certain where her next meal might come from.

Dunnottar and the lord who lived inside might prove intimidating and downright frightening, but nothing terrified her like a future without the thirty-thousand pounds she'd stood to gain. Her entire outlook rested upon securing those funds. She shuddered to think what she'd be reduced to without them.

"Please," she whispered hoarsely, sinking to her knees and leaning her weary body against the door. "I'll do anything."

Yet, no answer came from the other side of the door. He did not hear her soft whispers any more than he had her shrill cries. She did not doubt he'd put her out of his mind as he easily as he had his home.

This could not be the end. There must be some way to earn her way back into his good graces. With such a short time left of the agreed-upon thirty days, she could not face what going back to London empty-handed might mean.

Determined to wait him out, to force him to confront her, she curled up against the door. Drawing her knees to her chest and holding fast, she lowered her head. Dusk had arrived, bringing with it a chill in the air. Before long, night would fall, causing it to become downright frigid.

Reaching for her sack, she found the coat she'd worn while traveling from London. It would only offer so much warmth when she wore a thin day gown without undergarments. However, it would be better than nothing and might keep her from catching her death.

She did not intend to leave until Adam decided to come out and carry her down the escarpment himself. As she fished her hat from among her other belongings and pulled it down over her ears, she steeled herself for the cold night ahead.

12

D aphne passed the night and a good portion of the following day on the front steps of the palace. As night had fallen, she'd huddled in the doorway and hugged her knees to her chest. Shivering and clenching her teeth to keep them from chattering, she had almost given up. She'd been so cold, her breath turning into mist on the night air, the tips of her fingers going as pale as the moon.

A groom had come from the stable, attempting to coerce her into leaving. He'd told her that her horse had been prepared and 'the Master' would expect her to be gone by morning. She had waved him off, declaring she would not leave of her own accord. The groom had seemed flabbergasted, unable to believe his ears. Yet, she had merely turned her head and ignored him, determination winning out against her need to find someplace to warm herself.

She'd slept fitfully, awakening when powerful shudders wracked her body, her teeth clattering so hard, she was afraid they might shatter.

Morning seemed to take ages to arrive, the overcast sky allowing only a bit of the sun's warmth. The door had swung open sometime later to reveal Maeve, who'd looked at her as if she were a dog who had been kicked.

"The Master doesn't know I've come," she murmured before setting a tray on the ground beside her. "You must hurry and finish before he rises and discovers I've been here. If it means anything to you, he spent most of the night pacing in his study. He even came back to the door after night had fallen, but seemed to think better of opening it."

Reaching out to grab the warm china cup filled with tea, she gave the maid a grateful smile. "Thank you."

She did not wish to acknowledge Maeve's claims concerning Adam ... did not want to let herself believe he might care about her in the slightest. The maid was simply trying to make her feel better. If Adam gave a bloody damn about her freezing to death on his front steps, he would come outside himself to retrieve her.

As she gulped the hot tea, heedless to the way it burned her tongue, Daphne told herself the feeling was mutual. She did not care for him any more than he cared for her. She merely needed him to let her back inside so she could earn her thirty thousand pounds. If she could convince him to allow her to finish out her time here, she would return to London with what remained of her dignity.

She'd made quick work of her breakfast, scarfing down the cakes Maeve had brought her and polishing off the tea. The maid had returned to take her empty tray, then disappeared quickly into the large house. Daphne had huddled inside her coat as best she could, shivering and counting the minutes. She realized most of the day had passed her by once her stomach began rumbling again, hunger gnawing upon her insides.

Relief flooded her in a euphoric rush when the door swung open to reveal Niall. His staunch, emotionless expression became the most welcome sight in the world as he reached out to extend a hand to her. She placed hers in his, releasing a sigh of relief when he hauled her to her feet. Though, he did quickly release her, as if touching her had burned him.

"Come along, then," he said wearily.

She studied him as they entered the palace, searching his face for any hint of what she might expect. They moved in the direction of Adam's study, so she assumed he had decided to speak with her. Niall gave nothing away, though the tightness of his mouth and flash of his eyes told her he likely disapproved of his master's decision. She couldn't help a smug smirk as he opened the door of the study and inclined his head to indicate she should go in.

"Thank you, Niall," she said imperiously before sweeping through the opening with her head held high.

He grunted something in response, then slammed the panel behind her, enclosing her in the cavernous room. The warmth of the large hearths reached out to her, bringing the feeling back to her fingers and toes. Her numb face began to thaw, the heat of the fire almost painful after her skin had been so thoroughly drained of warmth.

She found Adam seated behind his desk, his appearance not at all what she expected. He looked haggard, his hair tousled as if he'd raked his fingers through it a hundred times. He wore no coat or waistcoat, and the buttons of his wrinkled shirt hung open. But his face shocked her most of all—the dark circles beneath his eyes, the downward curve of his lips. He looked as ghastly as she supposed she did.

"Thank you for seeing me," she murmured once she'd come to rest just before his desk.

Casting her gaze downward, she felt the weight of his stare, the way his gaze seemed to trace every visible inch of her. She shivered, feeling as if he'd peeled the clothing from her body with his eyes.

"I did not wish to, but you are as stubborn as you are reckless, little dove," he replied. "I had thought to come out there myself, throw you over my shoulder and carry you to the stable, then throw you into the saddle of your horse. But then ..."

She glanced up at him and wrinkled her brow when he fell silent. "Then?"

He met her stare boldly, a smirk curving his lips. The expression lacked all humor, the catlike motion more akin to a predator that had cornered its next meal. She swallowed past the lump in her throat and resisted the urge to run. He had allowed her back into the palace, and now, she must do whatever it took to get back into his good graces.

"Then I decided to let you convince me," he said, inclining his head.

The lump in her throat expanded, the realization of what he was saying making it difficult to breathe. "H-how am I to do that?"

He made a little sound—a short huff of laughter—as if her ignorance amused him. Bracing his large hands against the edge of the desk, he pushed his chair away from it. Then, leaning back casually, he braced his hands behind his head and raised his eyebrows at her.

"Please me, and I will let you stay," he declared.

She sucked in a sharp breath, her gut clenching at what his words implied. Please him? In almost every sexual encounter they'd shared, he had been the one in control. She had been a vessel for his use, and he had done with her what he pleased. Only once had she acted of her own volition. That day in the garden, when she'd knelt and taken him into her mouth.

Raising her chin, she reminded herself of the power she'd felt in that moment. Despite being upon her knees, she had drawn the sounds of pleasure from the back of his throat, had made him weak with nothing more than the touch of her lips. If she could do that, then she could certainly do this. Her livelihood depended upon it.

"I am waiting," he added when she did not reply or move.

The impatience edging his tone was not encouraging. He was already in a dudgeon and angry with her for disobeying his commands. This would be an uphill battle.

Clenching and then releasing her hands, she began moving toward him. Forcing her hands to work, she reached up to begin unbuttoning her coat while rounding the desk. Still regaining their feeling, her digits were clumsy and unwieldy as she worked to remove the garment. He stared up at her with a blank expression, his eyes a deep, dark brown that betrayed nothing as she edged into the space between him and the desk.

He slouched and spread his legs, inclining his head and watching her expectantly. Taking another fortifying breath, she sank to her knees on the carpet. Reaching up with both hands, she braced them on the strong thighs trapping her between them, smoothing her palms over the fabric. He was hot to the touch, as always, his hard body humming with barely concealed power. She stroked up toward his pelvis, edging her way to the noticeable ridge pressing against his fall. He was at least half-hard, the imprint of his cock through the fabric making her mouth water.

She reveled in the sensations caused by looking at him like this, not bothering to fight the lust he inspired. Now was not the time for maidenly reticence or resistance. She needed to please him, and while he claimed to like it when she fought him, just now, it would not be enough. With him sitting passively, watching her every move, she must act like the whore he'd often accused her of being.

Laying one hand over the bulge, she tested him, skimming her hand over him from base to tip, then back down again. She fondled him through his breeches, squeezing with light pressure now and then. With each squeeze of her fingers, his cock surged, growing and filling with blood in response to her touch. By the time she began unbuttoning him, it had become fully engorged. It fell free of the confining garment as if it had fought its way out, straining toward her with a mind of its own.

Wrapping her fingers around him, she gave him another stroke, using her thumb to caress his tip. He remained silent, staring blankly down at her while she worked him, smearing him in the wetness she coaxed from his slit. His stillness unnerved her, so unlike the other times they'd been together. She had become accustomed to his roughness—his hands fisting her hair, the brute force of his body relentlessly battering her.

Determination drove her closer, emboldening her to take him

into her mouth. She detected the slight hitch of his breath as she took him in as far as she could, sucking her way back up to his tip. His cock twitched in her mouth, the thick vein running along the bottom pulsating against her tongue. The primal scent of his musk flooded her senses, making her cunt clench and the tips of her breasts tingle. Squeezing her thighs together, she took him in again, then again, fucking him with her mouth.

She grew bolder, flicking her tongue against his head with each pass, lightly scraping him with her teeth, joining her mouth with a hand to pump him. Before long, he began to move, his hips undulating beneath her, his hands gripping the arms of his chair. His breath quickened, becoming noisier and harsher the longer she sucked him. He seemed determined to fight her, to make it difficult for her, but she fought back, giving him everything she had. She took him in her fist and stroked him, lapping at his head and dipping her tongue into his slit. She gave him both her hands, still using one to stroke him, the other gently kneading the heavy sac below the thick root of his cock. After a while, he began bucking his hips at her, creating more friction between her hands and his cock. She relaxed her jaw, opening her mouth to take his tip in with each stroke.

Before long, she glanced up to find him watching her from beneath heavy eyelids, his lips parted as he sucked in ragged breaths, his chest heaving. The urge to take him into her body overwhelmed her, the pulsations of her inner channel having now become painful. Her face flushed at the licentious images flitting through her mind, fantasies of sitting upon his cock making her feel like the most wanton creature who ever lived. But, he was paying her to be a wanton, to act like a whore.

She ignored the rough sound of annoyance he made when she released his cock, gripping the arms of his chair and coming to her feet. His entire body had gone tense, his fists curled on the chair arms, fairly trembling as if he held himself in check. Yet, he remained as still as ever while she snatched up her skirts, then climbed onto him. Wedging her knees into the spaces between his body and the arms of the chair, she positioned herself so her naked quim rested just over his cock. She shuddered at the feel of him against her, his flared head brushing her inner folds. Rotating her hips, she enveloped his head just within her opening, then let her skirts fall.

His eyes burned green and gold, the prisms of his irises flickering with lust and depravity in equal measure. She held his gaze, her mouth falling open on a soft sigh of relief as she lowered herself onto his lap. Gasping, she let her head fall back as he filled her, her channel giving way to let him in, stretching and then clenching to hold him deep. She braced her hands against his chest and tested the motion of her hips. She rocked against him first, then swiveled her hips in a slow circle, one direction and then the other. Each movement sent a burst of pleasure through her, the grinding of her clit against his pelvis hurtling her toward her own end so quickly, it left her breathless.

Holding on to his shoulders, she found a rhythm she liked, her soft pants turning into moans that echoed from the room's high ceiling. Beneath her, he was moving again, his hips matching her rhythm, his hands leaving the arms of the chair to touch her. He palmed her hips, squeezing and kneading her buttocks through the fabric of her gown before moving upward to cup her breasts.

"God, yes," she cried, arching her back to fit herself into his palms, her nipples growing even harder in response to his touch.

He snatched down her bodice and plucked at them with his fingers, sending lightning strikes of pure ecstasy into her core. Her movements became wilder, less precise, and she rode him toward climax. Forgetting about pleasing him, she focused on what she wanted for a change, gritting her teeth and straining toward an explosive ending.

Swifter than she could prepare for, his hand came up to her throat. His palm covered her, his fingers digging into the veins supplying her pulse. Fear gripped her when he tightened his hold, his gaze burning hotly while he went on bucking up beneath her, drilling his cock into her while cutting off her air supply. Her blood roared in her ears, and the fear in her gut melted into liquid heat, making her even wetter, her cunt clenching around him in the beginnings of a climax.

She made a choked sound and closed her eyes, surrendering to his hold. Would he strangle the life out of her now, as he'd threatened to before? Was this how she would die—with his cock inside her and his hand wrapped around her throat?

"Breathe," he commanded.

The pressure eased, and precious air filled her lungs, the blood rushing swiftly back to her head. She splintered, her lips parting on a silent cry as a powerful climax tore through her, exacerbated by the sensation of flying that washed over her at the exact moment he released her throat. The orgasm slammed into her with the force of a hailstorm, twisting her insides violently, then releasing in a heavy rush that stole the strength from her limbs.

She fell against him, too weak to do anything but ride the raging tide of her rapture while he stroked in her a few more times before following. Taking her waist into his hands, he swiftly lifted her off him just before he spent, the hot spurts of his seed staining them both. The warm, sticky liquid spewed against her belly, staining her gown, a gush of it splashing against her bodice.

Resting on his thighs, she found her limbs too weak to support her. She fell against him, cringing at the feel of her wet clothes clinging to her skin, but unable to do anything about it. Adam sat beneath her for a moment in silence, his ragged breaths harmonizing with her soft pants.

After a while, he shifted beneath her, pushing her to sit up. Her face flushed as she gazed down at the mess staining his shirt and her gown, the reality of her position once again making itself apparent. She must look like a Haymarket strumpet—legs spread over his thighs, gown bunched up around her hips, hair mussed, and her bodice pulled down to expose her breasts.

Yet, the heat in his stare made triumph rise in her chest. He did not need to speak the words aloud for her to know she had won.

· · ·

HALF AN HOUR LATER, Daphne sat immersed in a large tub in the washroom off Adam's bedchamber, her mind still reeling from all that had happened since the day before.

After they had gathered their bearings following the explosive encounter in his study, Adam had risen to his feet and taken her hand, swiftly propelling her from the room. She'd hardly had time to think about the mess staining the front of her gown or the weakened state of her limbs as she'd struggled to keep up with him.

"Where are we going?" she'd huffed, out of breath by the time they'd reached the top of a winding staircase.

It had not taken her long to realize they stood in the same corridor where she'd discovered Olivia's bedchamber. Or rather, what had once been Olivia's bedchamber. Now, she was hidden away in the forbidden corridor along with her daughter. Daphne's niece.

"My bedroom," he'd said, his tone still brusque and clipped despite the fact that she'd just made him spend.

He'd seemed as tense as ever, his shoulders squared, back erect, steps ringing out a swift cadence on the tiles.

"Henceforth, you will go wherever I go," he'd added, pausing before a closed door and reaching for the nob. "I do not trust you out of my sight."

Her heart had sunk at his declaration, but she had not protested. He had not thrown her back out on her arse, so she had no reason to complain. Besides, she had less than a fortnight left; she could endure being under his thumb for such a short time.

He had ushered her into a room as dark and masculine as the man who dwelt there, summoning servants to order a fire stoked in the hearth as well as a bath. While they had waited, she'd studied the room with unabashed curiosity, drinking in the black and gold decor. Dark wood panels covered the walls, polished until they gleamed. Black damask curtains had been pulled away from large windows, allowing in the light of the afternoon and framing the Scottish countryside beyond. The heavy furniture was ornate and well made—antique like most of the house's other rooms. A black and gold counterpane lay flat upon the mattress, several pillows arranged neatly against the headboard.

The scents she had begun to associate with Adam proved even stronger here, flooding her senses with cedar, cigar smoke, and a pure masculine aroma that seemed uniquely his own.

An open door led the way into a washroom equipped with the latest in plumbing technology. Metal pipes descended from the ceiling, pulling cool water in from the cistern to mix with the piping hot water the footmen toted from the kitchen. A contraption Adam referred to as a 'shower bath' sat in another corner of the room—appearing like a large basin with wooden rods reaching upward, holding a curtain which enclosed its inside. While undressing and preparing to get into her own bath, she'd watched Adam undress, then open the curtain, revealing that the big basin had what looked like a pump built into its side. The wooden poles held an upper basin, which would hang over Adam's head once he stepped inside.

Peering over the edge of the massive copper tub, the heat of the water soothing her body, she had watched Adam continue disrobing. Unable to look away, she had drunk in every detail, having realized that he never fully undressed when they were intimate. Her mouth had gone dry at the sight of him, rippling with power and strength— bulky cords of muscle flexing and bunching beneath supple skin. Dark coils of mahogany brown hair covered his chest, then trailed down his abdomen, turning into the coarse nest at his groin. He was chiseled like a statue, deep grooves carved out between the bulges, his legs all taut sinews. His hair hung down his back in soft waves, past his shoulder blades in length. In London, that hair might be considered indecent, the mark of an ill-bred man, not a titled earl. Yet, it suited him, made him seem so much a part of the wild and untamed lands surrounding his castle.

He met her gaze, but said nothing, seeming unruffled by her unguarded perusal of his nude body. Leaving his clothes in a pile on the floor, he approached the shower bath and stepped into the basin, his height forcing him to hunch a bit to keep from hitting his head.

Bending down to grasp the pump, he worked it with one hand, the slender pipes attached to the wooden poles rattling a bit.

"How does it work?" she'd asked, wrinkling her brow.

She had been too curious to worry that he might not wish her to speak at the moment.

"The footmen fill it with water, and I use the pump to move it up these pipes and into the upper basin," he said as he straightened. "Then, I simply pull this cord."

She watched as he reached up to pull a rope attached to the upper basin. The action produced a shower of water from overhead, which doused him from head to toe. Then, he took up a cake of soap and used it to lather himself, scrubbing his skin, then his hair before working the pump again to refill the upper basin. Pulling the cord once more, he drenched himself with more water, rinsing clean.

It was a marvelous invention, one she had heard very little about. She felt certain these were being installed in the homes of the peerage who were not as financially bankrupt as her family.

He'd left the room then, wrapping a length of linen around his waist, his hair curling and dripping water all over the tiles.

Maids had come into the room to clean up behind him, ignoring her altogether. Not long after they'd left, Adam returned, dressed in breeches and a shirt, his feet bare and his damp hair pulled back from his face. Seeing him this way proved oddly intimate—his shirt hanging open and his feet bare as they sat in his private washroom. He dragged a footstool toward the tub and sank onto it.

Producing a hairbrush, he took hold of her hair, which she'd let hang over the lip of the tub after washing it, so it could dry. Without a word, be began dragging the bristles over her hair, his grip surprisingly light, his ministrations gentle. Closing her eyes, she sighed, surrendering to the warmth of the water and the soothing glide of the brush over her hair.

He did not allow her peace to last for long ... though he did continue brushing her hair while he spoke.

"I will tell you the rest now," he stated. "Everything you need to know about Serena. But, I warn you, Daphne ... after this day, you will not ask me about her again. You will not try to interfere in her life, and you will never again attempt to go into her wing of the house."

She opened her mouth to protest, to remind him that Serena was her niece, and he had no right to separate them. She wanted to insist that her stumbling upon the nursery had been an accident, not a purposeful defiance of his orders.

Instead, she merely nodded her acquiescence.

"As I told you before, your father turned Olivia away when she tried to inform him of Bertram's indiscretion," he continued, his voice eerily calm as he wove the rest of his tale. "She tried to contact both of them several times throughout the rest of the Season, insisting Bertram do the right thing. Her greatest fear had become having a man offer for her and eventually needing to explain her lack of virginity. She was ignored ... until she realized she had become pregnant. Olivia tried once more to approach Bertram, thinking he would surely do the right thing now that a child had been sired. Your brother insisted the child surely could not be his ... he accused her of trying to trap him into marriage and insisted she must have lain with other men after being with him, and he had no way of knowing who had actually fathered the child."

Anger burned the surface of her skin, her eyes filling with tears that she dashed away with a shaking hand. Damn Bertram, he had turned out to be the worst sort of cur. She could not even find the words to defend him, having seen the child for herself and witnessing Olivia's horror at being in the presence of a Fairchild.

"So, because Bertram and your father could not be counted upon, she went to the only other man in London who might take pity upon her," Adam said.

"Uncle William," she whispered, closing her eyes. "What did he do to her?"

"He went to your father, of course, who brought him into the fold," Adam spat, his hand stilling with the brush as his voice quivered with fury. "Together, the two decided Olivia must be dealt with before she could bring public shame upon the Fairchild family. She could not simply be bought off the way the other ladies had been, that much was clear. William took the lead, insisting he had things well in hand. He called upon Olivia and told her Bertram was young and foolish and might need some time to come to his senses. In the meantime, her condition would need to be hidden from the public. He told her he would send for her ... have her taken to some estate owned by your family where she could hide in peace and await Bertram's arrival. William insisted he would bring your brother to heel, and all would be well. Olivia has always been a gentle soul, and far too trusting. She believed him."

Daphne gripped the edge of the tub so tight, her fingers began to ache. She didn't dare move, or speak, or even breathe, needing to hear what her mind had already guessed at ... needing him to say it aloud.

"He tricked her," Adam whispered, his voice lowered and raspy with rage. "He met her and spirited her away under the cover of darkness ... but it was no estate he took her to. Instead, he drove her clear across England to an asylum for unwed mothers."

The acrid taste of vomit lingered in the back of her throat, and she feared she would become violently ill. Asylums for unwed mothers were little more than prisons run by old crones who spent more time chastising the poor women for being wantons than they did actually caring for them. Some of them were known for conditions little better than Newgate, with many of the women wasting away while waiting to give birth, or dying while in labor. The children then became orphans, handed off to the woman's family or placed in orphanages or convents. To think of Olivia—a sweet young lady who had loved flowers and music—in such a place made her want to wretch.

"Oh, Adam ..."

He did not reply, but continued with his tale, the words coming faster now, as if he needed to get them out.

"I did not discover her location for several months. Her cousin wrote to tell me she had disappeared, assuming she'd run off with Bertram, whose company she'd been seen in several times. I immediately traveled to London and sought Bertram out. He insisted he had not seen her in quite some time and had no idea where she'd gone. It wasn't until I discovered her in that asylum, where she had already given birth to Serena—and nearly died in the process—that I realized that he'd lied to me. The child resembled him too strongly for anyone else to have sired her."

She craned her neck to look at him, which was made difficult with his hand fisting her hair. He had tightened his grip, causing her scalp to sting as she tried to look at him, to see the emotion he hid beneath a flat tone. Just as they had that night in the music room, his eyes appeared haunted, swirling with pain and grief.

"I cannot imagine what she went through," she whispered, the only words she could say as Adam would have scoffed at any apology she offered.

"A cold room with no hearth," he growled, lifting his gaze to meet hers. "Meager food, and hours of chores forced upon her ... a penance for her sin, they said. The midwives who cared for her ... they told her the pain was her burden to bear. They did nothing to help her, even when she nearly bled to death. God was judging her ... she must suffer his wrath. And if she lived, it meant she had atoned and He had accepted her repentance."

She sniffled and choked back a sob, unable to stifle her tears any longer. Her heart ached for Olivia, who had done nothing to deserve her fate. Just as Daphne had done nothing to deserve hers ... and yet, an overwhelming guilt caused her to question her own innocence. How could she have walked about so oblivious to all of this? It had happened under her nose, but she'd been so self-absorbed and concerned with her own affairs, she hadn't recognized the plight of another woman. A woman she might have helped if she'd known.

"I brought her home and called for the best doctor in Kincardineshire ... put her in her bedroom just down the corridor from this one and hoped being surrounded by her own things would cheer her up. Niall ... damn the fool ... he'd been in love with her since we were children and he was a mere stable boy. He'd been her first kiss, he'd taught her to ride, he ... he thought perhaps he could help. But it was too late. Her mind had fractured from the distress ... she went mad. In the midst of all her rambling and ranting, we discerned that the midwives had mentioned sending for William to come retrieve the child."

She gasped, remembering the first time she'd ever encountered Olivia. She had screamed and clawed at Daphne, declaring she would not take 'her' away. The 'her' had been Serena, she felt certain. Olivia had feared a Fairchild would come and take away her daughter. As the pieces of this crumbled mosaic began to form a clear picture, Daphne despised what she saw ... disdain welled up deep in her gut for the man who had raised her and the brother who had fooled her into believing him the good sort. The best man there was, she'd often called him. It made her ill to realize he was the complete opposite of everything she'd ever believed.

"You accused Uncle William of murder," she reminded him.

He shook his head. "You assumed that, but I never actually said he murdered her ... I said he paid for her life with his. You saw her, Daphne ... she did not die, but she is trapped inside her fractured mind. It is as if all the things that made her who she was died. Sometimes, I believe she wishes she had."

"You must know, I would never ..." she trailed off with a hiccup, trying to rein in her turbulent emotions. "I would never try to hurt Serena, or take her away from her family."

"No," he agreed, releasing her hair and cupping her face. "I do not believe you would, little dove. But Bertram or your father might, if they knew she had survived. As far as they are concerned, she died at birth ... and that is how it will remain."

She nodded, flinching when he gripped her jaw, his fingers tightening almost painfully. "I promise ... I will say nothing."

"I do not think you want to know what the consequences will be if you forget yourself and let it slip," he murmured, a clear threat in his lowered voice. "I think we understand each other, Daphne. Do we not?"

She took a shaky breath and nodded again, fear ramping up her pulse and making her cunt clench with longing. How could this man make her respond to fear and degradation with lust? Just now, she found herself wishing he'd lower his hand, tighten his fingers around her throat again and give her more of the oblivion he had subjected her to in his study. She wanted him to blot out the entire world, where only the two of them remained in sharp focus, and claim her body in a way no one else had. She doubted anyone else ever would.

"And you understand now why you must pay," he added, inclining his head and studying her pensively. "Why the only way to truly ruin Bertram is to ruin you?"

Again, she nodded. Because she understood better than he imagined ... she even agreed with him that it must be her. Bertram would not care about anyone else, but his sister ... he would take her ruination as a personal affront.

"I understand," she whispered, lowering her eyes. "Do what you must, Adam. Whatever you think you need to do to me ... I can endure it."

Nodding slowly, he stroked his thumb over her lips. "Aye, I know you can. Perhaps that is why I've enjoyed this far more than I ought to ... because you endure and submit so beautifully. If you were not who you were, and I was not who I am ..."

Her breath hitched when he fell silent, her gaze searching his as he looked away and shook his head.

What? She wanted to ask him. *What would happen if I was someone else—if you were someone else?*

But he did not continue. He simply shook his head and released her, rising from the stool.

"Bathe, dress, and join me in the bedroom. We will take dinner here."

With that, he turned and left the washroom, closing the door behind her.

Heaving a sigh, she laid her head against the edge of the tub and tried to make sense of the things he had not said.

Another tear slid down her cheek, this one for Adam. For a man who seemed emotionless, but who felt things far more deeply than she'd realized. She did not want to endure the things he'd made her feel, nor did she want to pity him. Yet, she did. He made her want to soothe him, to make right everything her father, William, and Bertram had done.

How she would go about that, she was not sure. All she had to offer him was her body, and while he seemed to take pleasure in it, she realized it did not account for much. In truth, she had nothing, and when this had all ended, she would *be* nothing ... no more than a tool he had used to exact his final revenge.

13

For the next sennight, Daphne spent her every hour—both waking and sleeping—with Adam. She slept in his bed and ate her meals at the little table near a window overlooking the countryside. She joined him in the gallery each morning to watch him and Niall practice their fencing, after which he always engaged her in a few bouts. Those times proved enjoyable, learning more about her opponent, and besting him more easily than she had when she'd lost their wager. It became more like a dance between them than a duel, each knowing the moves of the other with an uncanny foresight. After that, they would take their morning ride. They would gallop for hours, across the meadows and through the trees ringing his property.

Then, he was all business, bringing her into his study while he attended to his day's work. The first few days, he had forced her to sit upon the floor at his feet—a position that had made her spine bristle with indignation. Yet, she grew accustomed to it, indulging in reading or drawing—even though she was abominable at it. He often gazed down at her from where he sat, his face inscrutable, but his eyes swirling with good humor and amusement. Did he enjoy seeing her like this—docile at his feet?

On the third day, she had come into the study to find the harp sitting in the midst of the room, the low stool resting before it. When she'd raised her eyebrows at him in surprise, he'd simply told her to play for him. And play, she had. She'd played for hours, losing herself in the music while he worked, practicing every concerto she knew by memory, then asking for sheet music so she could learn new ones.

In the evening, there was dinner, and often time spent in the music room where Adam would play. Not for her ... as he seemed barely cognizant of her presence once he began. He played for himself, seeming to pour all of his anger and grief onto the keys. She heard it in every note, felt it in the energy that permeated the air as he unleashed it in the only way he seemed capable.

And, of course, he made use of her body frequently and in just about every way he could imagine. He threw her up on his desk and fucked her from behind; he threw her to the gallery floor and fucked her after fencing; he lifted her skirts on the floor of the music room. Their mating was frenzied, desperate ... crude. He pulled her hair hard enough to make her eyes water, but it only made her moan louder. He squeezed her throat until her vision grew hazy, but that only made her climaxes stronger. He pounded her mercilessly, leaving the insides of her thighs sore in the following hours, but she urged him on, wrapping her legs around him and compelling him to take her harder, faster. He did other things she enjoyed—things that made her question her own sanity. Like tying her legs to opposite bed posts to open her wide and expose her secret flesh. Or spanking her while fucking her from behind, until she could not separate the pain from pleasure. Or leaving his fingerprints and bite marks in places no one could see, but that she felt for days after his claiming. She liked to touch the sore spots, press down on them and close her eyes, remembering the blissful torment of being claimed by him.

In truth, he was supposed to be about her ruination, but it began to feel as if he had set about her liberation. The more he used her, teaching her what her body was capable of and subjecting her to the sort of pleasure that ought to bring her shame, the more she reveled in her own wantonness, in the power that came with being desired and inspiring lust. She had grown accustomed to going without undergarments, prepared to be taken at any moment, in any place. Her days held a sort of excitement she had never known, a thrill she could not get from riding hell for leather or sneaking an erotic novel.

She rarely encountered anyone aside from Adam, Niall maintaining his distance and doing a better job of keeping both Olivia and Serena out of her sight. While she wished to inquire about them, she refrained, not wanting to provoke Adam. He might not let her back in if she tempted him to toss her out again. She forced herself to accept that Adam did not want his sister or niece to have anything to do with Daphne or her family. After all the Fairchilds had done to them, she felt obligated to respect his wishes.

On the seventh day, she became acutely aware of preparations being made for a party. It began with the dressmaker, who arrived to take her measurements. Shop girls helped drape her in navy blue satin, rolling out spools of decadent black lace and gasping over how the colors made her hair appear redder and her eyes a more vibrant shade of blue.

Then, she noticed maids coming and going throughout the castle with freshly laundered tablecloths, polished silver candelabras, and fine china. Remembering the invitations she had seen when rifling through Adam's desk, she realized he had invited guests to Dunnottar ... guests he would parade her in front of. In the days that passed with several more fittings and talk amongst servants of the rich cuisine being prepared for the event, Daphne grew more anxious over the inevitable humiliation.

It would be Adam's coup de grace ... the final blow to her reputation, and by proxy, that of her family. They'd never be able to show their faces in public again without receiving the cut direct.

The party would take place on her last evening at Dunnottar, ending her stay in the same way it had begun—with humiliation.

On the night before the party, she sat on the edge of Adam's bed, picking at a loose thread on her dressing gown and waiting for him to emerge from the washroom. She'd bathed and donned the robe with nothing underneath—fully expecting him to strip it from her when he entered the room.

Instead, he halted at the foot of the bed and studied her with a furrowed brow. "Is something wrong?"

Shaking her head, she stood and untied the belt of her robe. "Of course not. I am ready."

He approached, eyeing the bare skin she revealed with her open robe. She held her breath as he reached toward her, bracing herself for the first touch. It never failed to send her blood rushing through her veins and goose bumps rippling over her skin.

However, he did not touch her except to close the open sides of the robe and tie the belt loosely at her waist. "Do not lie to me, little dove. I don't relish taking a sulking woman to bed. Tell me what is bothering you."

Sighing, she shrugged one shoulder and tried not to show him how terrified the impending party made her. "Tomorrow. I have an idea of what will happen, but knowing hardly eases my mind."

He folded his arms over his chest. "It is only a dinner party, little dove ... hardly anything to distress yourself over. Besides, I have not even told you who our guests will be."

She snorted. "Does it matter? You would not invite anyone unimportant. Whoever comes will see me here unchaperoned and know ... they will know ..."

"That I've fucked you," he offered with an amused smirk. "Aye. They'll know we fucked and will likely see that you enjoyed it. They'll see you dressed in finery I provided, and think—"

"They will think me a whore."

He raised his eyebrows. "What do you care if they do? In fact, why do you care what they think of you at all? As you've recently learned, most people are not what they seem. The people who would condemn you for what you've done have their share of secrets."

"Yes, but their secrets will not be exposed to the entire *ton*," she countered. "And I ... I *don't* care what they think of me."

He gave her a knowing glance. "Tell yourself what you must, but I can see the fear in your eyes ... fear of judgment and scorn. Fear that someone might see you as what you truly are."

"A whore?" she spat, avoiding his gaze, shame burning her cheeks.

Even now, saying the word called to mind the night he'd taken her maidenhead—when he'd lain on top of her and whispered the word in her ear before tearing into her with his cock.

He reached out to tip her chin up with his fingers, shaking his head once she'd met his gaze.

"A woman more beautiful and daring than any of them could hope to be. Do you not understand why those stuffy old windbags and withered-up crones hate ladies like you? It is because they secretly wish they could display their talents with something more than bland watercolors or insipid needlepoint. It is because they want to be the sort of woman a man would swim across oceans and crawl over deserts to claim. Because they wish they were like you ... they wish to *be* you. They might turn their noses up to find you here with me ... but they will go home green with envy that no man would pay a ha'penny for *their* bodies, let alone a grand fortune like thirty thousand pounds."

Her mouth fell open, the impact of his words leaving her breathless. Was that truly what he thought of her? His words proved the kindest he'd ever spoken to her, even when she considered that he was only fattening her up for the slaughter ... preparing her to be flaunted as his lover in a public setting.

"When you walk into that dinner party tomorrow night, you will do so with your head held high," he told her, his tone leaving no room for argument. "You will let them see how little you care for their opinions. And you will leave the next morning a very wealthy woman."

Closing her mouth, she nodded, acquiescing as she knew she must. One more day. She could endure it ... she had lived through the twenty-nine before it.

Without another word, Adam re-opened the sash of her robe, tearing the garment from her shoulders and tossing it aside. Then, he swept her off her feet and tumbled her onto the bed, where he joined her and proceeded to make her forget about her troubles, offering her comfort in the form of pleasure.

DAPHNE'S final day at Dunnottar began innocently enough. After breakfast with Adam, she was informed the dressmaker had come to deliver her gown and its accoutrements. The woman insisted on a final fitting to ensure the fit was exact. Satisfied, she had left after collecting a generous reward from Adam for having turned out an elegant evening gown in three short days.

After their morning fencing bout, however, the day took an unexpected turn. Instead of going on their morning ride, they adjourned to the study, where Adam mentioned having some affairs that could not wait until later. The unexpected break in their routine hardly ruffled her. She sat before the harp and played while he worked, taking comfort in the familiar, playing all her favorite pieces on the beautiful instrument. After today, she would never get to touch it again.

Around the time they typically took the afternoon meal, Adam stood and declared his work to be complete. Then, studying the clock standing near one of the hearths, he gestured for her to stand.

"Everything should be arranged now," he declared, rounding the desk to approach her. "Come."

Confusion furrowed her brow, but she trailed him, now accustomed to following his commands swiftly and without question. He led her to the main hall of the palace, where Maeve stood waiting for them with a large basket held in one hand. But it was the sight of the person standing beside her that made Daphne's steps falter. She choked on a gasp and blinked several times, certain her eyes must surely be deceiving her.

Yet, Serena stood before her, looking quite adorable in a walking dress of white muslin, her auburn ringlets tied back with a matching ribbon.

Gaping at her, then at Adam, Daphne tried to wrap her mind

around what she was seeing—because, surely, he had not arranged for her to spend time in Serena's company.

Yet, as the little girl rushed forward and leapt into Adam's arms, it became clear this was exactly what was happening.

"Are you ready for our walk, Princess?" he asked, the warmth in his voice when he spoke to the child nearly bringing tears to Daphne's eyes.

He might hate the Fairchild family, but there could be no denying his love for Serena.

"Oh, yes," the girl replied with a wide smile. "Do you think Cook packed jam tartlets in our basket?"

With a chuckle, he gave one of Serena's curls a gentle tug. "Perhaps. We shall have to wait and see. If we open the basket now, that would ruin the surprise."

Setting the girl back on her feet, he took her hand, then extended the other one to Maeve. The maid beamed while handing the basket over, then executed a swift curtsy and disappeared down the corridor.

Daphne lowered her gaze and fumbled with the skirts of her gown, feeling like an intruder. The two of them were part of a family to which she did not belong. That Serena was of her own blood made no difference when the child did not know her.

"Come, little dove," Adam said, drawing her gaze up from the floor. "Serena is quite looking forward to spending the afternoon with us."

Furrowing her brow, she darted a glance at the little girl, who was watching her with open curiosity while clinging to her uncle's hand.

"You ... you wish me to come with you?"

Leaning in close and lowering his voice so only she could hear him, he murmured in her ear. "I have already secured your promise to keep her existence a secret. So, what is the harm in allowing you a few hours with her?"

Her eyes stung as gratitude over the simple gesture overwhelmed her. While he had done small things that might be considered kind during her time here, they were as beneficial to him as they were to her. Purchasing her garments meant she always looked her best for him. Letting her play the harp entertained him. The gown he'd had made for her would be worn to a party designed to achieve his own aims. Even allowing her to return after throwing her out benefited him, as it meant she went on warming his bed.

But this ... allowing her to spend time with Serena did nothing to benefit him. Which meant he had decided to do it for her ... and perhaps, in a way, for the child, as well.

"Thank you," she whispered hoarsely, fighting the urge to weep.

She did not want to upset Serena, who would have no idea why Daphne stood there blubbering like a fool.

Bending the arm holding the basket, he offered it to her with a smirk. She took it, the fit of her hand in the crook of his elbow surprising her in its rightness. If things between their families had not happened the way they did, she might pretend things were different. That the little girl who looked so much like her was her own child, and Adam ...

No. She could not think that way. It would be dangerous to allow herself to fall into the trap of delusion. The only thing between her and Adam was a thirty-thousand-pound agreement and weeks of carnal pleasure. That hardly meant he cared about her, and in truth, he had given her no reason at all to care for him.

She would accept this gift as her due—her right as an aunt. Even if she might leave Dunnottar in the morning, never to see Serena again. She would always remember the short time she'd been privileged to know her. Never would she blame Adam for his decision to keep her a secret. That rested upon the heads of her brother and father, who had ensured Serena would never be a part of the Fairchild family.

Leaving the palace, they traversed the large courtyard toward the gatehouse, where the keeper raised the portcullis for them. Instead of taking horses, they walked, Adam insisting they make their way down the northern face of the escarpment, to where the sea lapped at the shore. Daphne's spirits lifted at the prospect of being able to walk along the beach—something she had not done during her stay at

Dunnottar. The weather proved pleasant—mild with just a bit of a crisp breeze.

As they walked down the sloping path, Serena chattered excitedly in the way children were wont to do. Daphne hung on every word, engaging the girl in conversation about the things she liked. Dolls. Seashells. Horses. Ribbon. She clung to those tidbits, storing them in her mind along with other details she picked up. The way Serena's hair shimmered with golden highlights in the sun, just like hers. How her little nose crinkled when she grinned, and the pitch of her sweet voice.

How had something so precious been born out of such darkness?

It was nothing short of a miracle.

When they reached the sand, Serena released Adam's hand and dashed off ahead of them, squealing with delight as the wind whipped through her hair. Daphne felt Adam watching her as she observed Serena, and her face warmed, his perusal putting her on edge.

"She is a beautiful child," she said, for lack of anything better to say.

"Aye," he agreed. "That, she is."

Serena had removed her shoes and stockings and now inched toward the edge of the water, giggling in anticipation of the sea washing over her feet.

"She seems so ... happy," she added.

"Niall, Maeve, and I ..."

She glanced up at him when he fell silent, her chest squeezing painfully at the sadness turning his eyes into dark pools. He turned to gaze at Serena, his expression softening as if seeing her so happy put him at ease.

"Olivia is in no condition to care for her," he continued. "Even on days when she is lucid and calm, she thinks of Serena as a playmate. It is almost as if she's become a child herself. So, Niall, Maeve, and I ..."

"You do what you can to care for her," she supplied. "It seems you are doing a good job of it."

Shrugging one shoulder, he swiveled his stare back to her. "It never feels like quite enough. She knows she is loved, but I am only her uncle, and Maeve and Niall are only servants. The girl has no mother."

Joining her hand with the other upon his arm, she clung to him, leaning close. "That is not true. She does have a mother ... and even if she realizes Olivia is not perfect, I am certain Serena knows that she loves her. That sort of bond is not easily broken."

Slowly nodding, he seemed to digest that for a moment before speaking again. "Aye ... I suppose you are right."

They stood that way for a time—Daphne hanging on to his arm, her head rested upon his shoulder while they watched Serena play in the surf.

"Go on," he chided after some time had passed. "This is your chance to get to know her. Do not waste it."

Taking his advice, she dropped his arm and kicked off her slippers. After peeling off her stockings, she set off across the sand toward Serena. The girl waved her over, delighted to show her the shells that had washed ashore.

For hours, they splashed and played in the water, dug in the sand for shells, all under Adam's watchful eye. He kept his distance, seated in the sand beside their picnic basket, his posture and bearing more relaxed than she'd ever seen them.

Finally, they trudged back toward him, the hems of their gowns soaked and speckled with sand, their hair hopelessly tousled by the wind.

"You look like a couple of sea sprites, the pair of you," Adam quipped as they knelt in the sand before him.

"Are sea sprites magic?" Serena asked, her eyes wide with expectation.

Chuckling, he reached out to swipe a bit of sand from her cheek. "Aye, little one ... they are the most beautiful sort of magic."

The girl smiled up at Daphne, nestling close against her side as Adam opened the basket and began producing its contents.

"Did you hear, Daphne? Uncle Adam says we're magic."

She could not help a smile, raising her hand to lay it upon Serena's head. "Yes, sweetling, I heard."

"You must be," Adam replied with a smirk, retrieving a dish from inside the basket and pulling back the cloth covering to reveal an array of jam tartlets. "Because I believe you wished these into existence."

Daphne giggled at Serena's squeal of excitement. The girl was on her feet in a moment, reaching out for a handful of the little tarts. Within seconds, she'd devoured three, staining her lips, cheeks, and fingers with jam.

Adam urged her to slow down so she did not make herself ill, and the three settled in the sand to enjoy the array of foods Dunnottar's cook had sent along for them. She gorged herself on meat pies and fruit, and joined Adam at swigging a crisp white wine straight from the bottle.

By the end of the meal, Serena had found her way into Daphne's lap, where she curled up and promptly fell asleep. She clung to the girl, not caring about the jam-stained fingers clutching at her bodice or the heavy weight in her lap. Arranging the girl more comfortably, she glanced up to find Adam watching them, a pensive expression upon his face.

"I had not realized how strong the resemblance was until I saw you with her," he remarked. "It is quite uncanny."

She wanted to smile at that, but was not altogether certain he considered her resemblance to Serena a good thing.

"She seems to like you," he added. "The only other woman she is ever so happy with is her mother."

He looked away then, falling silent, and Daphne did not need him to utter the rest aloud for her to understand what he did not say. Olivia could only make Serena happy when she was in a lucid state of mind.

Adam sat staring out over the sea in silence, long tendrils of his hair whipped against his neck by the breeze. An unexpected surge of tenderness swept over her, and before she could think about what she was doing, she had reached out to him. Her hand found his face, her fingers smoothing over the coarse stubble sprouting along his jaw.

He turned to look at her, his jaw hardening against her hand as if the gesture displeased him. Yet, his eyes melted into a warm pool of molten gold at the center as he nestled closer to her touch, rubbing his jaw against her palm as if seeking succor.

"I once called you a villain," she whispered, still steadily stroking his jaw. "But now that I have come to see why you were forced to become this ... knowing what drove you to these lengths ... I think that cannot be true at all."

His eyes burned into hers as he held her gaze, green flames erupting through the gold and disrupting the tranquility of his stare.

"You place too much hope in my goodness, little dove," he replied. "I am not your hero."

She shook her head, stroking her thumb over his lower lip. "Not my hero ... Serena's. Olivia's."

He did not respond, intently watching her while Serena slept in her arms and the sea rolled and crashed against the shore. Finally, he closed the distance between them and pressed his mouth to hers, surprising her with his tenderness. Resting one large hand over hers, he kept her touch against his jaw and drank from her mouth. She opened to him, no longer foolish enough to think she could fight him. He had stripped her bare, taking away all of her defenses and maidenly sensibilities, revealing the core of her—a part of her no one else had seen.

She gave in and kissed him, knowing it was foolish to wish it would never end ... but wishing it, anyway.

AFTER RETURNING FROM THE SHORE, Adam placed a sleeping Serena in Maeve's waiting arms and handed the picnic basket off to Niall. Then, taking her hand, he led her up to his chambers, where their attire for the dinner party had been laid out upon the bed. Butterflies began fluttering in her stomach as she waited for Maeve to arrive and see to her toilette, transforming her from sand-speckled siren to an ornamental fixture. It was a role she played well, having been used as a tool for gaining position and power by her father for years. Since her coming out, it had pleased him to dangle her before prospective suitors—men he knew she'd never choose, but whose notice might open the right doors for the Fairchild family.

If there was one thing Daphne knew how to do, it was endure being the center of attention. For the first time, however, the attention would prove her ruination ... her social destruction. As she submitted to Maeve's ministrations, allowing the maid to bathe and dress her before arranging her hair, she thought of Olivia. She thought of the devastation that had been made of the young lady's life and knew she must go through with this. She must endure this final act of penance for the things Bertram had done. Because it could be far worse. She might not have been allowed to escape Dunnottar with her sanity, something that might elude Olivia for the rest of her life.

She had no idea who might attend this dinner party, but like everything else Adam did, she did not doubt they had been selected with care. They would be influential people ... people who had the social standing to see her shunned by the London *ton*. Then, the ruination of the Fairchilds would be complete.

"All done, my lady," Maeve declared after pinning a final lock of hair into place. "My, but you are lovely. Doesn't she look ravishing, Master?"

Daphne turned to glance at Adam over her shoulder from where she sat in a chair near the window to have her hair dressed. With no vanity in his chamber, she did not sit before a mirror, and so could not see for herself what Maeve had done to her hair or the light cosmetics she had used upon her face. However, Adam's reaction to her appearance told her everything she needed to know.

His eyes widened, and his nostrils flared, as if he drew in her scent from across the room. His jaw ticked, and one hand curled into a fist—the motion making her scalp tingle. He often did that just before reaching out to grasp handfuls of her hair, so she wondered if he imagined doing it now.

"Aye, Maeve," he replied, though he did not spare a glance. "She is a vision. You may go now."

"Enjoy your evening," the maid chirped before dipping into a curtsy and turning to obey Adam's command.

Daphne remained in her chair, frozen in his stare as he approached. He looked quite dapper himself—as elegant as she'd ever seen him, in fact. Black evening attire clung to his large frame, expertly tailored and fitting with the latest fashion. A silver watch fob showed against a black and navy blue embroidered waistcoat, his matching blue cravat affixed with a diamond tiepin. His hair had been tamed and tied at the back of his head, emphasizing the chiseled lines of his face. As he moved toward her, the bulges of his muscles rippled beneath the fabric like rolls of the tide, reminding her of the power concealed beneath his finery.

He stood over her, his gaze tracing her from the top of her head to the gloved hands resting in her lap, before looking back up at her face again. Placing two fingers beneath her chin, he lifted it, keeping a gentle hold on her face.

"Are you ready?"

She nodded, though her stomach continued to twist and roil at the thought of going downstairs to face his guests. Offering her his free hand, he waited for her to accept his assistance before pulling her to her feet. He took her hand and pulled her along, guiding her toward the full-length mirror in one corner of the room. He stood behind her, bracing his hands upon her bare shoulders as she confronted her reflection.

The dark blue satin bodice clung to her breasts before falling away from the gown's high waist, the fabric flowing like water over her waist, hips, and legs. Its off-the-shoulder neckline revealed quite a bit more skin than she'd ever shown in public, along with a generous amount of bosom. White gloves covered her hands and arms to above the elbows. Maeve had pinned her hair back in a whimsical coiffure, with navy blue bands adorning her crown and a cluster of flowers at one ear. Tiny ringlets framed her face, which Maeve had enhanced with just a hint of rouge at her cheeks and lips and kohl around her eyes. As always, a ribbon matching her gown had been tied around her neck, a flirtatious bow resting against her collarbone.

He stroked one cheek while studying her reflection, his fingers trailing down the side of her neck. "Remember what I told you, little dove. What they say, what they think ... none of it truly matters."

She nodded as if in agreement, but could not help but wonder whether he might truly believe that. If he thought none of it mattered, then he would not use them to make a spectacle of her. Of course it mattered. Still, she kept her chin high as he tucked her hand into the crook of his arm and guided her from the room.

The low hum of voices reached out to them as they descended the staircase—Niall's rough brogue mingling with the cultured tones of their guests. Her grip on Adam's arm tightened, her legs growing weak as they reached the ground floor. From down the corridor, she spotted several people gathered within the foyer, handing their wraps and capes off to a small army of waiting footmen.

Seeming to sense her discomfiture, he gently patted her hand, laying his over where it rested in the bend of his arm. He kept it there, lending her his quiet strength. She raised her chin a tick, adopting the mask of apathy she liked to wear in social settings. The one that hid her boredom and annoyance ... the one that covered all her secrets.

"Ah, there our host is now," boomed one of the waiting guests, spotting Adam and coming forward to greet them. "It is good to see you again, Hart. It has been too long."

"Indeed, it has," Adam replied, removing his hand from atop hers so he could extend it to his guest. "Loring, may I present Lady Daphne Fairchild, who has been a guest of Dunnottar recently. Lady Daphne, this is Lord Eugene Loring."

Forcing a smile, she released Adam's arm to make her curtsy to Lord Loring—a viscount, if she recalled correctly. They had never been formally introduced, but his wife held a reputation as one of London's biggest gossips.

Said wife pushed her way past the others to gape at her, a hand pressed against her heavy bosom as if in shock.

"Lady Daphne? Lord Fairchild's daughter?"

She forced a smile and inclined her head at the woman. "Yes, my lady. It is an honor to meet you ..."

She raised her eyebrows to remind the woman she had so rudely begun launching questions at Daphne before even introducing herself.

"Lady Loring," the old busybody replied imperiously.

Raising her nose and sniffing disdainfully, she moved away from Daphne as if a noxious odor wafted from her.

As if she could smell the sinful nature radiating from her like a cloud of fog. Ignoring the woman, she suffered through the rest of the introductions, pretending not to notice the way Adam's guests watched her. Portraying various degrees of curiosity or shock, they all seemed to wrestle with themselves over whether to greet her politely or turn their noses up at her. An unmarried woman, a guest of a man in a remote castle in the most far-flung corner of Scotland? Surely, fodder for the gossip mills. Now, not only would they chatter about how the Fairchild family had become paupers, they would also spread the word of her fall from grace.

A knock upon the door drew her eye to Niall, who had been standing nearby like a silent sentry, waiting for the introductions to end so he could see them into the dining room. Now, he moved to answer it, ushering in what she assumed to be the last of Adam's guests.

An exchange of voices made her blood run cold, the low, deep resonance of the person greeting Niall sending her insides into a frenzy. Her palms began to sweat, and her heart sank into the pit of her gut.

Her feet propelled her backward, horror overwhelming her as the top of a man's blond head appeared from behind the door. It did not matter that those gathered around her blocked the view of his face ... she'd know his voice anywhere. She had run her fingers through that hair while lying on soft patches of grass with her skirts pulled up around her hips and his questing fingers slipping into her drawers. Squeezing her eyes shut, she found her mind's eye flooded with visions of him hovering over her, the sun gleaming off his golden hair like a halo, his eyes twinkling as he lowered his head for their first kiss.

"No," she whispered.

He could not be here ... not now. She could tolerate being the object of ridicule and scorn for just about anyone ... but not him.

Before she realized what she was doing, she had spun on her heels and begun to flee. Adam made a grab for her, but missed, his hand closing around open air as she began retreating down the corridor.

"Daphne?"

His voice froze her in her tracks, and she halted, tears filling her eyes. It was too late ... he had recognized her. Blast and damn her hair, which would always give her away in a crowd.

Clenching her skirts in her damp hands, she took a deep breath. There could be no escaping it. Things would only go worse for her if she fell apart in front of these people. Then, not only would they report to the *ton* that she'd become a fallen woman, they would also make mention of her unspeakable manners.

Blinking back the tears, she put her mask back in place and turned. He had followed her, standing far closer than she'd realized. His sweet, handsome face filled her vision, his earnest blue eyes boring into hers, the light of the chandelier overhead making his hair gleam like precious gold.

He smiled, though his wrinkled brow and incredulous gaze belied the expression.

"Daphne," he repeated, as if assuring himself it was truly her. "My God, I thought I was seeing things, but ... it truly is you."

Inclining her head, she forced a girlish smile and forced herself to speak. To greet the man she had hoped would someday become her husband.

"Robert," she murmured. "It has been an age."

"Six years, at least," he replied quickly.

Too quickly. As if he had counted each passing year following her departure to London for her first Season.

"What are you doing here?" he asked, glancing over his shoulder as if to assure they would not be overheard.

No such luck. Adam approached, his expression as inscrutable as ever. Moving to stand between them, he took hold of Daphne's hand and placed it back in the crook of his arm.

"Daphne is my guest," he stated, emphasizing her name as if wanting Robert to be aware that he'd heard the way he'd addressed her so informally. "She has enjoyed the hospitality of Dunnottar for several weeks ... have you not, little dove?"

The intimacy of Adam's pet name put a flush upon her cheeks, and she lowered her eyes just as Robert fixed her with a questioning stare. Tension stretched through the air between the three of them, and she silently prayed the tiles would open up and swallow her.

Niall materialized nearby, clearing his throat to capture Adam's attention. "Dinner is served, Master."

She had never been more grateful for the man than she was just then.

"Shall we adjourn to the dining room?" Adam murmured before steering her past Robert without waiting for a response.

Plastering a smile upon her face, she let him lead her, mortified by the way he skirted propriety by escorting her. As the host, he should accompany the highest-ranking woman in the room ... which most certainly was not her.

"You invited him on purpose, didn't you?" she hissed, trying to keep her voice down as the others filed behind them.

He gave her one of his predatory smiles, though it did not quite reach his eyes. "Who ... Mr. Robert Stanley?"

When her only response came as a withering glare, he chuckled.

"Aye, little dove," He confirmed. "Though, I was not entirely certain he was your past amour. I simply looked into the estates neighboring yours in Suffolk ... those with sons who would be of an age with you. I ventured a guess, but was not sure—at least, not until you just confirmed it."

Snapping her mouth shut, she clenched her jaw, certain she might embarrass herself even more if she spoke. It had just become more difficult for her to endure this night; however, it was not impossible. Robert had always been the genial sort. He would cause her to feel more embarrassed than she already did, and for that, she supposed she must be grateful.

However, it hardly brought her comfort once her next thought thrust to the forefront of her mind.

By inviting Robert here, Adam had just torn the last bit of her innocence to shreds.

14

D aphne slowly spooned small portions of a vegetable soup into her mouth, trying to still her shaking hands so she did not stain the pristine white tablecloth. Keeping her eyes lowered, she murmured a few times here and there in response to the conversation taking place at the table around her. Otherwise, she remained silent, her tongue a heavy, cumbersome thing in her mouth. Each spoonful of soup tasted like ash, her stomach rebelling against every swallow. She remained constantly aware of the constant scrutiny ... of the disdainful and questioning gazes being tossed her way.

While Adam proved the consummate host—regaling his guests with tales of Dunnottar's history and promising a tour after they had concluded their meal—she seemed to be the main attraction. At the far end of the table, Lady Loring had already engaged in her favorite pastime, whispering to the ladies closest to her while casting disdainful glances at Daphne from the corner of her eye. Near Daphne sat a woman she had not noticed in her shock over Robert's arrival—Lady Stanley, Robert's mother. Her wrinkled face held a heavy measure of censure as she gazed at Daphne from across the table, and every so often, she could be found shaking her head and murmuring under her breath ... words such as 'shameful' and 'despicable.'

The woman had seemed to want to balk at the way the seating had been arranged, with Adam at the head of the table and Daphne seated to his left, and Robert wedged on her left. Seated across from them, she had a clear view of her son beside a harlot and the man who had paid to possess her body.

"Time has certainly done little to change you," Robert said suddenly, drawing her attention away from the soup.

When she raised her eyebrows in question, he cleared his throat and flushed. The endearing trait had always given away his embarrassment, turning his cheeks and the tips of his ears scarlet.

"That is to say ... you are as lovely as ever," he added. "And I daresay as spirited."

"Oh, yes," Adam muttered between bites of soup, his droll tone unmistakable. "Lady Daphne possesses quite a bit of *spirit*."

Across from her, Lady Stanley issued a soft gasp, dropping her spoon to clatter to the saucer beneath her bowl. Robert seemed oblivious to Adam's ribbing and carried on.

"Do you remember what great fun we used to have—you, Bertie, and me?" he asked, his eyes twinkling with good humor as he leaned toward her, his soup forgotten. "Riding, running about in the woods between our lands. Our governesses had quite the devil of a time keeping up with us, that is for certain. And you, as wild and untamed as any boy your age."

Despite her position at the moment, the memories he conjured made her smile. They called to mind simpler times, when the world had not been so complicated. When she'd only been a girl who loved to run and play with the boys, wearing her brother's old breeches and leaving her slippers behind to traipse about barefoot. In the country, a girl could get away with such behavior, surrounded by trees and covered by the sky, her deeds going unseen by the judgmental eyes of the London *ton*.

"You paint the picture of quite a little harridan," Adam mused as the servants came forward to remove the soup and prepare to serve the main course.

Robert chuckled, leaning back in his chair and glancing past her at Adam. "She was quite endearing, my lord. Imagine my surprise when I returned home from Harrow one summer to find she had transformed into a young lady."

"As girls are wont to do," Adam murmured dryly.

Daphne busied herself by taking a sip of wine, needing to cool her face due to the images Robert's recollections brought to mind. Of them wading in a shallow stream in the woods—without Bertram for company, for a change. Of him eying her exposed calves as she held her gown aloft and licking his lips hungrily. Of him lifting her into his arms after she'd stepped on a stone and cut her foot ... using his own cravat to stifle the bleeding ... leaning over her for a kiss.

He had taught her a woman's pleasure, plucking her tender, budding breasts, and causing her to realize how massaging the little bud of her womanhood could cause stars to explode behind her closed eyelids.

"Yes, well, some things never change," Robert said, filling the awkward silence. "Lady Daphne has always been a unique sort of lady, sharing many of the same interests as Bertram and I. Quite rare to find in a woman, I must say."

"Oh, I think our friend Bertie has developed quite a few *new* interests over the years," Adam muttered.

Daphne sputtered, nearly choking on a mouthful of Madeira. Setting her glass down, she broke into a coughing fit, her throat burning as she struggled to breathe through the wine she had nearly inhaled in response to Adam's jibe. Of course, it would seem innocent to anyone who was ignorant to Bertram's misdeeds.

Thankfully, the servants had just finished laying out the main course, and conversation faded to a minimum as the men served themselves and the women seated at their side. Adam filled her plate from the dishes closest to them, seeming to remember her preferences. During an intimate meal, where they dined alone, she might have found it endearing. However, she could feel the probing eyes of

Robert and his mother upon them, seeming to catalog their interac-
tions—their *familiarity*.

"Quite a shame, the trouble that has recently befallen your family
as of late, Lady Daphne," Lady Stanley spoke up while using her
knife to cut a portion of lamb.

Daphne paused with her fork halfway to her lips and frowned.
She could not be certain exactly what the woman referred to given
the events of the past five years.

"Thank you, my lady," she replied, grasping at the first thing that
came to mind. "The loss of Uncle William was quite a devastating
blow."

"Hmph," the woman mumbled between bites of her lamb. "I am
certain. Being forced to abandon Fairchild House in London must
have only added to the strain."

This time, it was Daphne who dropped her utensil, the shock of
the woman's words lodging in her gut like a dagger. Had her parents
been forced to sell their townhome in London? Her grandfather had
purchased that house in Grosvenor Square, one of the loftiest
addresses in Mayfair. Did that mean they had returned to their estate
in Suffolk? Circumstances there were even direr than in London—
the lands producing just enough to cover the necessary expenses, and
even some of those would soon be neglected. In the coming years, it
might become a ruin ... a relic of a long-forgotten family fallen into
the gutter.

"I .... I ..."

She fumbled for words, uncertain of how to respond when Lady
Stanley had blindsided her. The woman gave her a knowing look ...
as if she had known Daphne to be ignorant of this development. Of
course she was ignorant; she'd been acting as Adam's whore for the
past four weeks.

"Many families have faced ruin due to the actions of their patri-
archs," Adam cut in, his tone icy enough to lower the temperature in
the room tremendously. "As we all know, young unmarried ladies are
hardly to blame for the fates that befall them."

Daphne swiveled her gaze to Adam, who might have reduced

Lady Stanley to ash if looks could kill. The woman's face reddened, but she simply returned her attention to her lamb.

Adam met her gaze and gave her a curt nod, as if to reassure her. But why? He had created this situation to gain his own ends. She was not stupid enough to believe he cared about the loss of Fairchild House. It had to have been just another step in his plan to ruin them.

Had he spoken up to protect her from Lady Stanley's humiliation? No, he could not possibly care about that, either. This entire farce was about humiliating her.

Whatever the cause, she was grateful for the temporary reprieve. Though, she was hardly surprised by Lady Stanley's behavior. The woman had never liked her, thinking her beneath her precious son— even though she was the daughter of a viscount, and Robert the son of a baron. Daphne was too wild, too unconventional to wed Robert, and the old biddy had made her thoughts on the subject known quite frequently.

The rest of dinner continued without another embarrassing incident, the conversation turning to small talk. Adam engaged Robert over fencing—an interest they shared, while Daphne sulked in silence, moving the food about on her plate to make it look as if she'd eaten. All the while, Robert watched her pensively. She shuddered to think what he might find if he looked too closely. Like the evidence of what Adam's touch had turned her into, and how much she'd enjoyed it.

After the dessert course, Adam announced he would lead them on a tour. This, his guests seemed excited over, as many had only heard rumors of the old ruin of a castle the Earl of Hartmoor had turned into his own personal palace.

He kept a hand at the small of her back while leading the party down the winding halls of the castle, flaunting the music room and sun rooms, as well as the library. He impressed them all with his knowledge of the castle's history, right down to the various builders who had influenced its aesthetic over the past few centuries. Even she found herself enthralled by the tales he weaved, some of the information being things he had not yet told her.

"I have heard rumors of secret passages and caverns," said one of the gentlemen. "As well as an escape tunnel leading out to the shore?"

"Aye, there are many passages one could get lost in," Adam confirmed. "The cave you refer to was used for escape in many of the battles that took place here. It leads through a postern gate and down the side of the escarpment on the north face. Would you like to see it?"

The entire group agreed collectively, even Lady Stanley seeming excited over being able to see this cavern for herself. Even Daphne could not help that her curiosity had been stoked, the cavern being one of the few places she had never seen.

They set off with Adam in the lead. He made a stop along the way to retrieve a large candelabra, using it to light their way as they moved toward darker parts of Dunnottar ... the parts that had not yet been renovated. She found the darkened corridors beautiful in their starkness, the shadows clinging to various corners lending it all a gothic feel.

After a while, he led them into a long, dark corridor paved with stones. Adam chuckled when a few of the women gasped and whimpered in distress, moving closer to the men who had accompanied them.

"Never fear, ladies," he quipped. "I am certain the brave men in our company would protect you from anything that might come rushing through this tunnel."

The light he carried moved on, and they followed, the others walking past Daphne faster than she could keep up, eventually putting her toward the back of the procession. After a while, the stone gave way to earthen walls, and the ground beneath them began to slope sharply. The smell of earth mingled with that of the ocean as they drew nearer to the shore. Adam continued his tale of the battles that had been won and lost here, of the men who had only survived because of the tunnel they stood in. Her attention became stolen away by the hand brushing hers in the dark. A man's hand.

"Daphne," Robert whispered near her ear, his familiar scent flooding her nostrils as she leaned close. "Daphne, we must talk."

Her gaze flitted to Adam's shadow, large and ominous at the front of their group. He seemed oblivious to them, attending to the entertainment of his guests.

"Robert, please ..."

His hand enclosed around hers, squeezing tight. "Just tell me if he's hurt you, Daphne. Should I call him out?"

She snatched her hand away as if he'd burned her, uncertain why allowing him the liberty felt so wrong after all they'd shared together. It felt like betrayal of Adam.

"Ask me no more, I beg you," she hissed. "You will only make matters worse."

She tried to move past him, but she felt his presence near her constantly. He stood at her back during the rest of their walk through the cavern, then beside her once Adam had guided them to the moonlit shore.

After what felt like an eternity, Adam turned to lead their party back toward the tunnel. Turning to fall in line with the others, Daphne lifted her skirts and trudged over the sand. Just before the mouth of the cave could swallow her up, a hand closed around her arm, and she was brought up short.

Robert.

She stifled a sound of alarm as he pulled her into his arms and propelled her toward the outside edge of the cave. Pressing her against the hard rock, he covered her mouth with his hand and kept it there until the voices of the others had faded down the tunnel.

Then, removing his hand, he replaced it with his mouth. His kiss muffled her protest, his hands insistent as they swept over her shoulders, her neck, moving up into her hair. He kissed her hungrily, lapping at her with his tongue and cupping the back of her head the way he knew she liked.

The way she used to like.

Now, she could not help but compare his kiss to another's and find it lacking. His body was too sinewy against hers, lacking the hardness of Adam's. He held her too gently, as if she were some fragile thing he was afraid to break. She almost wished he would tighten his hold on her hair, thrust his hips at her, bite her lip ... something to show her that he realized she was no longer the innocent maiden he had kissed and touched in hidden meadows six years ago.

When he finally pulled away, she sighed, the sound one of disappointment. He hardly seemed to notice, pressing his forehead against hers and stroking her cheek. He pressed little kisses against her nose, her cheeks, her neck.

After a while, she placed her hands against his chest and pushed. She did not know why she'd allowed it to go on this long. Perhaps she had sought some of that lost innocence. Maybe, her disappointment was not with him, but in her own self and the depths she had sunk to.

"Robert, we cannot do this," she insisted. "Adam ... he will not like it."

"So, it is *Adam*, is it?" he scoffed.

The moonlight illuminated his face, showing his clear annoyance. She had never noticed how petulant he looked when angry.

"I'm sorry," he said quickly, running a hand through his hair. "The rumors of your family's desperate situation have reached Suffolk. I cannot blame you for whatever situation you've found yourself in, but ... dash it all, Daff! Why did you not come to me?"

Indignation bristled her spine, annoyance heating her face. "You? The man who refused to offer for me after I came of age? The man who let me go off to London for my first Season and did not even possess the bollocks to come after me?"

He grasped her shoulders again, holding on tight, his eyes wide and wild as he drew her back to him. "I have so many regrets, Daphne ... you have no idea. I was young, and thought perhaps there might be more for me to learn before I could marry you."

She scoffed, rolling her eyes. "More like you thought there might be more *cunt* for you to chase!"

He reared back as if she'd struck him, and she reveled in the satisfaction it caused her. He needed to understand she was not the girl he'd once known.

"You are right," he replied, lowering his head. "I was a fool, and after I had finished chasing the things I came to realize were meaningless ... there was only you. The woman I love. The woman I—"

"It is too late," she interjected, knowing she could not bear to hear him confess to wanting to marry her.

"Of course it isn't," he declared, giving her a shake. "Do you not realize I've loved you since I was a boy? Nothing will change that."

"I cannot be what you want me to be, Robert," she argued, trying to dislodge herself from his hold and failing. "I am ruined."

He grew stronger in his desperation, his fingers biting painfully into her arms. Finally, a display of strength from him ... and she did not find it the least bit appealing.

"Do you think I care that he's had you?" he demanded. "I don't... not when I know he must have coerced you or forced you ... God, Daphne, tell me he forced you, and I will call him out. The bastard ... sitting there flaunting you like some bloody mistress! Baiting me with those sly remarks. Say the word, and I will give him what for."

She stifled a laugh at the thought of Robert attempting to engage Adam in a duel. The man who had so effortlessly bent her to his will was no weakling. She could imagine him wrapping one massive hand around Robert's throat the same way he had her ... only this time, he would squeeze and squeeze until Robert ceased to draw breath.

"Things are different now," she said. "Please ... leave me be."

She tried to brush him off, but he pursued her, grasping her wrist and attempting to pull her back against him. Despite knowing she had no need to fear him, she struggled in his hold.

"Robert ... unhand me this instant ... let ... let go!"

"Just wait a moment ... please!"

A dark shadow fell over them both, blotting out the moon. She went still, the shiver running down her spine putting her at ease instead of frightening her. Robert, fool that he was, only tightened his grip, narrowing his eyes at the intruder.

Adam's voice washed over them like a frigid tide, turning her blood to ice in her veins. "Is there a problem here?"

"See here, Hartmoor—"

Daphne wrenched her arm from Robert's hold and rushed toward Adam, seeing in his eyes what the fool behind her could not. Murder glimmered in the depths, turning his irises into cold, hard emeralds. He clenched and unclenched his hands at his sides, pulsing them as if imagining strangling the life from Robert.

"Everything is fine," she said, hoping the softness of her tone would convince him. "Adam ... we are fine. Robert simply wished to have a word with me in private."

She pressed a hand to his chest, flinching when he growled, moving as if to take a step toward Robert. The hard muscles flexed and hardened against her palm, but her touched stilled him, though he never took his gaze away from Robert.

"If you are quite finished now, perhaps the two of you might come inside," he snapped. "Mr. Stanley, I do believe your mother is wondering where you've gotten off to."

Robert's gaze burned into her back, and Daphne felt it sliding over her, watching the way she interacted with Adam ... the way she touched him.

After a long moment of silence between the two men, she felt movement at her back.

"Of course," Robert replied, his voice clipped and strained. "I shall go to her directly. I am certain we will depart shortly. We've a house party to attend not far from here. Daphne, it was lovely seeing you again."

She avoided meeting his gaze as he brushed past them, storming back toward the cave and disappearing inside.

Lifting her eyes to meet Adam's stare, she choked on a gasp, her breath hitching at the expression she found upon his face. Moonlight slashed across his features, illuminating the pure rage burning in his eyes. His mouth contorted into a sneer as he leaned down toward her, one hand shooting out to grasp her jaw.

Her pulse ramped up at his touch, the familiar fear curling low in her belly and spreading warmth between her legs.

"Did he touch you?" he growled, his fingers biting into her jaw. "Did you *let him* put his hands on you?"

Knowing he had clearly seen her struggling in his hold, she knew not to lie to him. However, telling him Robert had kissed her would be a mistake.

"J-just when he grabbed my arm," she managed between rushed breaths. "That is all."

He narrowed his eyes at her, but then nodded as if accepting her word. "Then you aren't hurt?"

She shook her head. "Of course not. Robert would never—"

"Come," he snapped, taking hold of her arm and pulling her along the way Robert had gone.

The darkness swallowed them without the benefit of his candelabra, but he walked confidently, allowing her to relax at his side. For some reason, her heart thundered in her chest, her mind hardly put at ease by his easy acceptance of what he'd just seen.

The tension in Adam's body did not abate, only seeming to increase as they drew closer to the castle, his long strides forcing her to trot to keep up with him.

She shivered at the silent promise his tight hold upon her arm made. He was angry, and she was sure to suffer his wrath once his guests had departed.

The insides of her thighs became smeared with arousal as she wondered just what he might do to her.

She almost laughed again at the absurdity of it all. When she'd told Robert she had been ruined, she had not meant it in the way he'd thought. Losing her maidenhead had not ruined her ... *Adam* had ruined her. He had made her want things she should not, things no proper lady should desire. And now, she could not stop craving him or the things he'd taught her body to enjoy.

She was ruined ... perhaps even beyond repair.

· · ·

An hour later, with the party guests gone, Daphne followed Adam into his bedchamber. The tension that had been present during the encounter on the shore had not left his body. In fact, it had seemed to grow worse with each passing minute, his scathing glares settling on Robert several times throughout what had remained of the evening. Then, he would settle that stare upon her, his eyes promising retribution.

The guilt and fear she had experienced upon being caught alone with Robert melted away, indignation taking its place. He had no right to be angry with her when he had orchestrated this entire evening. She had gone along with it all, smiling and putting on a brave face just as he'd told her to. Was it not enough that he had destroyed what remained of her reputation? Had he not been satisfied with her performance, even after all the insults and slights she'd suffered throughout the evening?

By the time the last of the guests departed, she had begun returning his angry glares with a few of her own. The long evening had frazzled her nerves, and she was short on patience, as well as exhausted.

So, when she pushed the bedroom door closed behind her, it was with the intent to undress and fall immediately into bed.

Adam, it would seem, had other ideas.

He kept his predatory gaze upon her while he disrobed, each movement of his hands clearly showing his agitation. It showed in the way he jerked at his cravat, tossing it carelessly onto the bed, and the way he tore at the buttons of his waistcoat, sending one of them skittering across the floor in his haste.

Once he had stripped to the waist, he raised an eyebrow at her. "You are still dressed."

Scoffing, she rolled her eyes and folded her arms over her chest. "So it would seem."

He moved toward her, the firelight emanating from the hearth playing over the muscles moving fluidly beneath his skin.

"Do not play games with me, Daphne," he growled.

Not in the mood to cower away from him after being browbeaten all evening, she jabbed one finger at the center of his chest.

"Why not?" she challenged. "*You* certainly seem to enjoy playing them! Is that not why you purposely invited Robert and Lady Stanley here without warning me?"

Reaching out to grasp her wrist, he hauled her closer—until their bodies collided. The heat of his skin burned through the satin of her gown, searing her to the bone.

"You precious *Robert* is fortunate I did not tear him limb from limb for daring to lay a hand upon what is mine," he snarled.

She fought his hold, but he only tightened his grip on her wrist. When she swung her opposite hand at him, he snatched it out of the air, too, holding both her arms between their bodies and refusing to let her go.

"I do not belong to you," she spat, unable to help the spark of defiance causing her to go against him.

She'd spent her entire night being as quiet and demure as possible, biting her tongue to keep from retorting to every rude remark that fell from Lady Stanley's lips. She refused to cower anymore.

His smile chilled her to the core, sending a tremor of dread down her spine.

"But you are. You agreed to thirty days and nights, and until the sun rises at dawn, you still belong to me, little dove. Which is why I am going to make you pay for letting that simpering mama's boy touch you. I am going to make you pay for letting him touch you, and lying to me about it."

Her boldness began to melt away as he spun her around and pushed her toward the bed, throwing her facedown upon the coverlet. She tried to stand, but he was on top of her in an instant, his fingers fisting in her hair and wrenching upward. Her back arched, and her scalp tingled, his breath tickling her ear as he pressed his mouth against it.

"You were about to lie to me again," he murmured. "So allow me to save you the trouble. I *know* he had his hands on you ... that he kissed you ... tried to help himself to what belongs to me. I can smell him on you. The little milksop is more perfumed than you are."

She closed her eyes and released a sigh of regret, cursing herself for a fool. Of course he had known.

"I tried to fight him," she whispered hoarsely, tears springing to her eyes. "But he would not take no for an answer."

Adam chuckled, the low rumble vibrating through her entire body. "Of course he wouldn't. The idiot still thinks you're his ... that you are the same little girl he petted and kissed all those years ago."

She gasped when he released her hair, swiftly taking hold of the back of her gown and tearing it. It rent as if it were made of paper instead of satin, baring her naked back to him.

"Did you like it when he kissed you, little dove?" he taunted, yanking her dress down her body to reveal her buttocks and stocking-clad legs. "Were his lips more pleasing than mine? Softer ... gentler?"

She gasped when he thrust a finger into her, not bothering to be gentle. But then, she did not need him to be, her cunt wet and ready for him. Squirming beneath him, she clenched the counterpane in both hands and held on, gritting her teeth to hold back a moan. His thick digit caressed her inner walls, slowly moving back and forth inside her.

"Answer me," he ground out, adding a second finger. "And do not lie to me again. Did you like it?"

Her back arched, and her knees pulled beneath her body, raising her arse into the air and inviting him in deeper. She shamelessly rocked against his hand, seeking her pleasure, wordlessly begging for more.

"N-No," she whimpered, turning her head to rest it upon the bed, closing her eyes and surrendering to the moment.

There was no use fighting him. She had long since learned that he would only work harder to break her if she did ... and he would not be gentle about it.

"I did not like it," she added.

"Why not?" he prodded, sliding his thumb between her lower lips and seeking out her clit while still steadily pumping three fingers in and out of her channel. "Why didn't you like it?"

She gasped, spreading her legs wider and undulating her hips, so close to spending, she could taste it.

"He ... he was *too* soft ... too ... gentle."

Adam growled, the sound low and ominous. She could not tell if it were a sound of approval or one of anger.

"And you do not want soft or gentle, do you, little dove?" he urged, deepening his reach inside her, slamming his knuckles against her with each thrust.

"No," she replied, no longer caring what it meant for her to admit to that ... what a wanton it made her.

All she cared about was reaching the climax Adam held just out of reach, finding the sort of glorious ending only he could give her.

"Is this what you want?"

His question was her only warning before he withdrew his fingers from inside her, then cracked the palm of his opposite hand against one of her buttocks. Her skin stung at the point of impact, the strength of the blow knocking the wind from her. Parting her lips on a silent cry, she tightened her hold on the bedclothes.

"Is it?" he urged, spanking her again, this time slapping her opposite cheek.

This blow forced the air from her lungs, and it came out on a low moan. Her legs trembled beneath her, her inner channel clenching greedily with the echoes of her desperation.

"Yes!" she screamed when he hit her again, harder this time ... so hard, she toppled onto her stomach.

He took hold of her hips and yanked her back into position.

"I warned you my next punishment would not be so merciful, did I not?" he rasped, before smacking her three more times in rapid succession, these blows more powerful than the ones before them. "But you do not want me merciful, do you? You want me punishing, and cruel, because that is the sort of insatiable little tart you are, isn't it? *Answer me!*"

"Yes!" she cried breathlessly between blows. "Yes, yes, yes!"

The pain in her buttocks dissipated into something else the more he struck her, the fire he lit upon her arse melting to combine with the heat of her desire.

"He does not know you ... he never can," he panted out between ragged breaths, pausing in the midst of his punishment. "He would never appreciate you like this, little dove, at your most beautiful and vulnerable. That is why you ran off to London without marrying him ... why you arrived at the age of four and twenty still a maiden. Isn't it?"

She nodded, the coverlet beneath her cheek damp from her tears. A sob tore from her chest as the truth came crashing down upon her, so heavy she could hardly breathe beneath its weight.

"Yes," she whimpered. "Yes ... it's true."

She closed her eyes and wept into the counterpane as he went back to spanking her. Sinking into the darkness, into a haze where only this feeling existed. She needed to escape her own thoughts— the truth that despite her accusations, *she* was the reason Robert was not her husband. She could have returned to Suffolk at any time, and he would have offered for her. She'd always known that. Instead, she'd hidden from him in London, knowing he could never give her the things she truly desired ... the cravings she hid in the darkest corners of her heart and mind.

When she spiraled back up out of the haze, he was positioning himself at her entrance, hands holding tight to her hips. She threw her head back and cried out when he entered her, the first brutal thrust triggering her climax. Her core clenched and spasmed around him, the echoes of it so powerful, she felt them as deep as her womb. Her lungs burned from the breath she held, unable to release it while he pounded into her, his pelvis smacking against her sore arse and his cock drilling into her relentlessly.

Glancing at him over her shoulder, she found him lost in his own desire—eyes squeezed closed, lips parted as guttural groans spilled from within, the muscles in his abdomen bunching and flexing with each movement. His hair had come loose from its binding, falling over his shoulders and draping him in beautiful sable waves.

Just as suddenly as he'd begun, he pulled out of her abruptly, wrenching a cry of dismay from her. He laughed, the sound both cruel and mocking as he strummed a finger down her spine.

"Do not worry, little dove ... I am far from being finished with you."

She gasped when his finger delved back into her channel before pulling out again. Then, he was probing her rear entrance, sending a fresh rush of heat and shame through her. He had never done this to her before ... never violated this forbidden part of her by delving the tip of his finger inside.

"Adam," she whimpered, struggling against the need to protest and the desire to know where this would lead. "Wait."

"Mine," he rasped, thrusting the finger wet with her juices in and out of her rear passage. "Every part of you, Daphne ... all of it is mine."

She choked on a protest when he pulled his finger free, grasping her buttocks with both hands and spreading her wide.

"Wait," she gasped when the head of his cock touched her there, his tip seeming impossibly large against the little opening. "Adam ... please ..."

He shifted against her with a groan, his cock nudging against the tight hole, sending lightning strikes of sensation through her entire being.

"You know how I love it when you beg, little dove," he moaned, pushing against her again, gaining an inch into her this time.

The new sensation gave way to burning pain as he forced his way inside of her inch by slow inch, groaning and panting with each surge of his hips. She sobbed and clawed at the coverlet, clenching her teeth to try to muffle the sounds.

"I can't ... it hurts ... please," she moaned, her words contradicting her body. Her knees spread wider, her back arching deeper as if to take him farther in, to take every inch of him.

"You can," he replied, his voice rough and tortured, as if he hovered on the same line between bliss and agony that she did. "Touch yourself, Daphne ... breathe ... relax."

She released a shaky breath while working a hand beneath her body, searching for her clit. When her fingers found it, she gasped, in reaction to both the pleasure it caused and the evidence of her own desire. She was absolutely drenched, her cunt wetter than she'd ever experienced.

"Yes, that's it," he urged, slowly withdrawing a few inches and then plunging into her arse, his grip on her buttocks tight enough to leave fingerprints. "Let yourself feel ... do not fight it."

She released another sob, this one combined with a sound of pleasure as she circled her fingers over her clit. Adam gave her more of his cock with each thrust, the burning sensation at odds with the pleasure exploding from where she touched her little bud of pleasure. Then, his pelvis came to rest against her arse, his entire cock lodged inside of her. She continued to breathe slowly, in and out, urging her body to unwind and accept him instead of fighting him.

When he moved again, circling his hips against her, it sent a ripple of bliss to the tips of her fingers and toes, tearing a surprised moan from deep in her throat. He did it again and again, teaching her body a new pleasure, one that seemed ten times as intense as what she felt when he thrust inside her cunt.

"Aye, little dove ... that's it ... slip your fingers into your cunt ... fuck yourself with them."

She did as he commanded, heightening the ecstasy to near unbearable limits. Yet, she persevered, steadily pumping two fingers in and out of her sheath while Adam fucked her arse, moving faster and faster with each stroke.

"Goddamn it," he groaned, his entire body trembling against hers. "Jesus-fucking-Christ ... Daphne ... Daphne ..."

His name on her lips, rough and ground out from between clenched teeth, sent her over the edge, and she shattered again, her screams reverberating off the walls. Her vision went black as her channel pulsated around her fingers, her body wracked with spasms so violent, she could not control them. She collapsed onto her stomach and Adam followed, his chest resting against her back as he pumped into her arse a few more times before spending with a tortured groan.

He fell limp on top of her, resting there for a moment and panting in her ear. His hair fell around them, blanketing her in a cocoon of sable silk. She closed her eyes and surrendered to the oblivion, allowing her body to float in the blackness that filled her mind. It enveloped her like a warm blanket, dragging her into unconsciousness.

She was not certain how long she remained that way, but when she came to, Adam was carrying her into the washroom. The candelabra resting on the washstand illuminated the shower bath, which he carried her to with long, sure strides.

How could he stand after what they'd just shared? She felt as if she were half dead, let alone capable of standing on her own two feet.

She tried to mumble something to that effect, but it came out unintelligible, slurred as if she were drunk.

"I've got you," he murmured, keeping his arms right around her as he rested her feet on the wooden bottom of the lower basin. "Hold on to me, little dove."

She wrapped her weak arms around him, resting her head against his chest. A moment later, water washed over them in a warm deluge, startling her back to full wakefulness. She gasped, raising her head as the water doused her head, the droplets splattering her face. It rinsed her clean, washing away Adam's touch and his seed. His hands moved over her without lingering in any place overlong, helping the liquid remove the traces of him that could be washed away. The soap followed, a masculine-scented cake that reminded her of him. He used it on them both, somehow managing to get them both clean before rinsing them.

Then, he was carrying her again. Laying her on the counterpane and toweling her off with clean linens. After that, he maneuvered her so he could remove the coverlet and rest her on the cool, dry sheets. Fanning her damp hair out on the pillow, he then laid his body over hers, gently parting her legs and lowering his hips between them.

Despite having just had him, her body roared to life when his head kissed her entrance, his cock having surged back to life. She arched her back, clawing at his shoulders as he thrust into her, so slowly and gently that tears sprung to her eyes again. He wrapped his arms around her, burying his face against her shoulder as he took her slowly. The throbbing soreness in her arse mingling blissfully with the pleasure he created in her sheath, his pelvis at the perfect angle to stimulate her clit with every stroke.

"Ah, little dove," he whispered, nibbling her ear and kissing her neck as if he were her lover instead of her tormentor. "If things were different ... if you were someone else ..."

She moaned in response, unable to say with words that she knew what he meant ... that she heard the things he did not say.

"In the morning, I will let you go," he groaned. "But not now ... not tonight."

No ... tonight, he was still the monster who had dragged her into his cave. And she was his little dove—ripped from her cage and clenched in the jaws of a beast.

As climax swept over her once again, Daphne had no choice but to admit to herself she was exactly where she wished to be.

15

"Well, then ... here we are."

Daphne pulled aside one of the carriage window curtains and stared at the unassuming stone facade of the building looming over her. Across the conveyance from her sat Niall, who had been tasked with returning her to London.

Adam, apparently, could not have been bothered to even see her off.

She had awakened in his bed alone, with no more than the lingering soreness in her buttocks and the scent of him clinging to her skin to offer proof of what had transpired the night before. Maeve had entered the room with a breakfast tray and a carriage dress draped over her arm ... along with a chemise and corset.

With the sunrise, Adam's restriction against undergarments had been done away with. While she had eaten, draped in his shirt from the evening before, servants had come in and out of the washroom to fill the bathtub for her. Maeve had insisted upon a long soak to relax her for the journey back to London. She'd wondered if the maid somehow knew what Adam had done with her the night before. It almost felt as if it had been emblazoned across her face for the world to see.

She had enjoyed the bath, soaking away the stiffness in her muscles—though Adam's spanking and penetration of her arse could not be washed away with a single bath. She would likely feel the effects of that for at least another day.

She had waited for him to appear while Maeve dressed and groomed her, turning her head at every sound, hoping for even a glimpse of him. With each passing minute, it had become more and more apparent she would not see him ... perhaps not ever again.

That had stung, knowing the words he'd uttered in the heat of the moment had meant nothing.

If you were someone else ...

But she was not someone else. She was Lady Daphne Fairchild, and he had made sure to remind her that, in the harsh light of day, she meant nothing to him other than a means to an end. He had achieved his revenge, and now, he was done with her.

When Maeve had escorted her to the foyer of the palace, she had gazed mournfully into the music room, where the harp had been returned. She would miss the beautiful instrument most of all.

They'd found the door to Adam's study closed as they'd passed it, though the warm, red glow showing beneath the crack had told her he occupied the room. Tearing her gaze away from the imposing double doors, she had followed the maid to the front doors ... where Niall had stood waiting for them, dressed for travel.

"The Master has entrusted me with seein' ye safely home," he had said while reaching into his coat pocket. "And he has instructed me to give you this."

He'd retrieved an envelope stamped with the Hartmoor seal and thrust it toward her. She'd broken through the red wax and peeled open the envelope, hoping to find a note inside ... a letter ... some form of a good-bye.

She'd found only a bank draft made out to her for the grand sum of thirty thousand pounds.

The only thing he had ever promised her, delivered promptly before her departure.

Lifting her chin, she had tucked the draft into the envelope, then slid it into the pocket of her carriage dress. She had not uttered so much as a word to the butler who seemed to hate her as much as Adam did. Not even a 'thank you.'

Niall had not seemed to mind, muttering a simple 'let's go,' at her before exiting the palace. Maeve, however, had pulled her into a warm embrace.

"I am going to miss you, my lady," she had said, her voice heavy as if she fought back tears. "I had hoped ... oh, well, it does not matter what I hoped. Do not mind me. Safe journey back to London."

Daphne had given the maid a sad smile, but said nothing else. She had not wanted to let on that she had hoped, too.

The trip to London went by uneventfully, with not a word passing between her and Niall. What else was there to say? She had come to Dunnottar and served her purpose. Now, she would return home.

But, where was home? She supposed she must discover where her brother, father, and mother lived now that they'd had to part with Fairchild House.

Returning to the present, she glanced back to Niall with a frown. "Where are we?"

Inclining his head, he gestured toward the buildings surrounding them. "These buildings are flats rented by those who cannae afford townhouses, or do not wish to shoulder the expense of rentin' one durin' the Season."

Turning back to study the windows facing the street, she found candlelight burning through several of them. Shadows moved around inside—people going about their lives, oblivious to all else.

"This is where my family lives now."

"Aye," Niall confirmed. "The Master supposed ye'd wish to return to them."

Why would Adam assume such? Did he not realize she was disgusted with what they had done?

But then, he must know until she could deposit her bank draft, she would not have the funds to find a room at an inn. As well, he would surely realize she would wish to confront them about what she knew ... what they'd hidden from her.

"Well, then," she said, parroting the butler. "Do you happen to know which flat?"

"Third level," he replied. "Second door on the left."

"Thank you."

With that, she left the carriage, carrying only a sack filled with the clothing she had worn to Dunnottar. Her horse, she'd left behind upon realizing she would have no place to keep him in London. She could only hope Adam would see him cared for.

Daphne did not look back to watch the carriage drive away with Niall, focusing upon the entrance to the unimposing building. It did not strike her as being a den of poverty, and while it was not the loftiest of addresses, nor was it situated in London's slums. Still, it was a far cry from the opulent townhome she had resided in since coming to the city for her first Season.

Due to the late hour, she found the corridors of the place empty, for which she was grateful. Making her way to the third level, she located the flat Niall had spoken of and rapped upon the door. Voices and movement came from the other side, and a moment later, she found herself confronted with the familiar face of Ruthers, her father's valet.

These days, he seemed to work as a servant in many capacities, which included answering the door.

"Lady Daphne!" he exclaimed, his eyes wide as he took her in from head to toe.

She realized she must look quite inappropriate—showing up in the dark of night without an escort. Her ensemble did not even include a proper hat.

Nevertheless, she did not have the patience to explain her sudden appearance, nor did she feel the need to give an accounting to a man who worked for her father.

"Are you going to let me in?" she blustered, raising her chin imperiously.

The servant blinked, seeming to shake off the shock that had settled over him. Moving away from the opening, he pulled the door open wider.

"Of course ... do forgive me. Come right in."

She swept into a small vestibule that opened into a set of two rooms with large doorways that allowed her to see straight into the back of the flat. This room she stood in must be the main parlor, with what appeared to be a study beyond it. A corridor curved left and right, leading deeper into the flat—toward bedchambers, she assumed.

A flurry of movement caught her eye, and she turned just as Bertram descended upon her with open arms.

"Daff!" he exclaimed. "By Jove, it is good to see you."

She held her hands up to ward him off, backpedaling before he could wrap her in his embrace. Just the thought of him touching her made her skin crawl, the black stains of his sins sure to rub off on her.

His face fell as he regarded her, seeming hurt by her rebuff. He looked like hell—the auburn of his hair having lost his luster while dark circles had begun to form beneath his eyes. His skin was sallow and pale, though a flush to his cheeks told her he must be in his cups.

"It would seem you do not return the sentiment," he muttered, scraping his fingers through his locks, tousling them even more.

"Where is Father?" she snapped, gazing about the little parlor. It held none of the furnishings from Fairchild House, which led her to believe they, too, had been sold off.

"Right here, dearest."

She glanced up to find him coming toward her from an open door to the left—the kitchen, she realized. A woman bustled about inside, who Daphne recognized as a maid from Fairchild House. Perhaps she acted as their housekeeper.

So, they were not completely destitute, after all. Obviously, her father had managed to secure the funds to retain a two-person household staff.

He paused before her with a tray held in one hand, his whitened hair standing on end. Lord Gilliam Fairchild looked older than she remembered, his cheeks drooping and his face etched with deep lines.

"Bertram and I were just about to sit down for dinner," he said, giving her a smile.

It seemed almost tentative ... shy. As if he were afraid of her.

"I am certain Cora made enough. Would you like some?"

Clearing her throat, she lowered her gaze. Knowing what he had done, she could hardly stand to look at him. And she certainly could not stomach a single bite of food with the way her stomach roiled and pitched.

"No, thank you," she replied as politely as she was able.

She was a perfect little dove, just like Adam had said—remembering to smile prettily and mind her manners, even when in the company of a rapist and the scoundrel who had helped cover his tracks.

"It is good to see you," her father remarked, setting the tray upon a low table resting before a floral damask sofa. "You look ... well."

Her jaw tightened as she turned to face him. He settled onto the sofa while Bertram shuffled forward and took a nearby armchair, pulling up close to the table.

"Did you expect otherwise?" she snapped.

Bertram scowled, slumping in his chair. "Pheasant *again?*"

Her father narrowed his eyes at his son. "It is cheap, and one of few meals Cora knows how to prepare. You may eat it or go hungry."

Ignoring him, Bertram turned his gaze to her. "I know you might be angry with us, Daff. But we could not have come for you ... not unless we wanted him to hurt you."

She laughed, the sound rough and humorless. "And what makes you think he did not?"

Her father paused in the midst of buttering his bread, wincing as he glanced up to meet her gaze. "You do not look ... abused."

If only they knew. Yes, she had been abused ... but, oh, how she had enjoyed being in the clutches of her captor.

"You must understand," Bertram tried again, his eyes wide and pleading. "He had us over a barrel ... there was nothing more we could do if we wanted—"

"Bertram, for once in your life, keep your trap shut," their father snapped, his gaze flitting back and forth between the two of them.

Daphne narrowed her eyes, a niggling of suspicion beginning to trickle down her spine. "Why was there nothing you could do? What did he say to keep you from coming for me?"

It was the one thing she had never understood—just what Adam's letter had contained in order to keep her father and brother from coming to Scotland to retrieve her. Had he threatened her life ... *their* lives?

Her eyes widened as she realized she had seen neither hide nor hair of her mother. "Where's Mama?"

"Gone," her father sighed, running a hand over his haggard face. "She has taken up residence with her sister in Mayfair. She would not ..."

"She wouldn't descend into the gutter with us," Bertram said with a harsh, humorless chuckle. "Too good for the likes of us, she is."

"She is simply accustomed to a certain lifestyle," her father defended. "Soon, I will be able to give that to her. I will win her back ... you will see."

"Goddamn it, old man," Bertram seethed. "If you haven't the sense to realize she is never coming back—"

"The letter," she snapped, having had more than enough of the both of them. "The one Lord Hartmoor sent ... I want to see it."

She would get the answers she sought, and by morning, she would find herself a hotel to reside in. Not a permanent solution, but one that would buy her time until she could figure out what to do with the rest of her life.

"Daphne, dearest, no good can come of reading it," her father implored.

"Save your endearments," she retorted. "I am not the same oblivious chit who ran off to Scotland looking for answers, and I will not be put off by your diversion or your excuses. I wish to read Hartmoor's letter ... now!"

"Dash it all, let her read it," Bertram grumbled, rising from his chair and stumbling toward an escritoire in the corner. "She may as well know the truth."

"Bertie, don't!"

But it was too late. Either her brother was truly too stupid to realize what was happening, or over imbibing had made him reckless. Retrieving something from the desk drawer, he lumbered back toward her.

"Here," he muttered, thrusting an open envelope in her hand before returning to his chair.

He slouched there and watched as she studied the broken seal. The same one stamped onto the envelope thrust down into her dress pocket. Inside, she found a letter written in Adam's familiar hand.

Fairchild,

You may cease worrying for your daughter. She has made her way to Dunnottar, where she will remain as my guest for thirty days and nights. The things your despicable son did to my sister were child's play compared to all the ways I intend to use Lady Daphne. I warn you not to attempt any acts of chivalry that might put you within my reach, for I may not be charitable enough to allow you to leave my presence with your life.

While I feel this particular twist of fate to be your due for what befell my sister, I do understand the worth of one's only daughter. Enclosed, find compensation in the amount of ten thousand pounds. This is my payment for your daughter's maidenhead. Rest assured, I intend to exact every cent from her over the next thirty days.

Regards,

Hartmoor

The slip of paper fluttered to the floor, the tips of her fingers having gone numb by the time she'd gotten to Adam's hastily scribbled signature at the bottom. Her mouth had gone completely dry, and she had ceased feeling her legs. It was a wonder she did not sink to the floor.

"You see, we could not risk it," her father said, his voice low and soft, as if he worried speaking too loudly might set her off. "He might have—"

"Harmed you or Bertie?" She interjected with a scoff. "You stayed away to save your own necks."

"It wasn't exactly—"

"What did you do with it?" she whispered, her eyes filling with tears.

"Daphne, please ..."

Ignoring her father's pleading, she dashed away her tears.

"What did you do with the money?" she screamed, hands balling into fists at her sides. "The ten thousand pounds he paid you to bed me! Where is it? What have you done with it?"

"The bank draft only reached us a few days ago," Bertram said with a dismissive wave of his hand.

He acted as if selling her to Adam had meant no more to him than the turn of a card in a gaming hell.

"By then, we'd already been forced to sell Fairchild House to pay our debts," her father chimed in. "The money is all we have to live off of now."

A laugh bubbled in her throat, the sound deranged and shrill, even to her own ears. It began as a giggle, but swiftly grew into a cackle that nearly shook the rafters.

The bloody fools. They had fallen into Adam's trap, just as she had. He had dangled thirty thousand pounds in front of her, knowing full well by the time she'd earned it, her family would have lost everything. He'd known they'd be desperate and greedy enough to accept payment for the use of her body. How ironic, that the ten thousand pounds her father had taken in exchange for her was not even one third of what she herself had earned.

And to think, she had intended to come home with that money and turn it over to them. Daphne, the unexpected hero ... the salvation of the Fairchild family.

Her eyes began to water as the laughter increased, her sides beginning to ache with how hard it rocked her insides. The two men watched her as if she'd gone mad, and perhaps she had. Finally, she'd broken under the strain of it all.

It was so ridiculous, what could she do but laugh? She had

earned the money, only to discover her family was far beyond redemption.

Finally, she fell silent, straightening and swiping at her damp cheeks.

"You sold me," she said with another little chuckle. "The two of you kept that money knowing what he would do to me ... knowing ..."

Bertram was on his feet in a moment, reaching out to grasp her shoulders. "We did what needed to be done! And perhaps, for once in your life, you did what was required of you, as well."

Daphne shoved him so hard, he stumbled back onto the table, splintering the wood and sending china crashing to the floor. Her father leapt to his feet, crying out in dismay—whether in shock over her behavior or in reaction to his lost dinner, she was not certain.

"Do not ever touch me again," she growled, stepping forward to loom over him. "I did what was needed ... by ferreting out the truth about you. You, and Father, and Uncle William."

"I knew it," Bertram snarled, struggling to his knees and attempting to wipe the soup from his hair using his sleeve. "I knew he would poison you against me."

"Poison," she said with a scoff. "That is exactly what you are ... all of you! I know what you did to Olivia, Bertram. Father, I know about all the times you hid his secrets ... all the people you paid to keep silent while your son went about raping half the debutantes in London! 'Tis no wonder we were so easily beggared."

"Now, see here," Bertram blustered, finding his way to his feet.

"I know about how Father sent Uncle William to dispose of the evidence," she accused, jabbing his chest with her index finger. "To dispose of *your* child."

Her brother blanched, finally seeming to realize there was nothing he could say to convince her to believe his lies. She knew the truth, and he had been exposed for the lecher he was.

"I loved you," she whispered, another tear slipping down her cheek, and then another. "I loved you so much, I was willing to risk my reputation, my life, my *body*, to exonerate you. To set things right.

And you let me ... you let me put myself in that position, all the while knowing this was a mess of your making."

"Daff, listen to me," he said, softening his tone and trying to force a smile. "It was a simple indiscretion, that is all. At times, a gentleman misinterprets a lady's signals ... it was a simple misunderstanding. Surely, you must know—"

"No," she interjected. "I do not know you. I've now come to realize I never did."

Turning for the door, she put them behind her, now unable to even abide the sight of them. A part of her had hoped they could be redeemed ... yet, she knew now what a mistake that had been. They had not been worth her sacrifice—but, God help her, they would not reap the benefits of what she had earned. She would figure out a way to build a life for herself. She would put them all behind her—Bertram, her father ... Adam.

"Daphne! Daff ... wait!"

She paused halfway down the corridor, turning back to find Bertram rushing toward her, his eyes wide with desperation. Was that fear she saw? Had Adam been right all along? Had ruining her also ruined Bertram? She certainly hoped so.

"I saw her, Bertram," she murmured, shaking her head. "I saw Olivia with my own eyes and witnessed her fear. She looked at me and saw you ... and I've never seen a more terrified woman in my life. And you have the nerve to call it a mere *indiscretion*?"

He lowered his head, finally finding the grace to look ashamed of himself. "Things weren't supposed to happen this way, Daff. You have to believe me."

"No," she agreed. "I was not supposed to reach adulthood only to find that the people I love—the men I counted on to protect me—turned out to be the true villains."

Bertram sneered at her, issuing a derisive snort. "You would take Hartmoor's side over ours? The man who bought your cunt for ten thousand pounds?"

She almost laughed in his face, nearly revealing that she was now wealthier than he could ever hope to be with what Adam had paid her for access to her body.

"Yes," she declared. "Because for all his sins, Hartmoor never once lied to me. From the moment I met him, I was never mistaken about who he was or what he wanted from me. You, I have loved and trusted my entire life ... which has turned out to be a mistake. I will not commit the error of allowing you to engage me with more lies."

She put him behind her once again, marching back toward the stairwell. Balling one hand into a fist, she shoved the other into her pocket, finding comfort in the feel of the envelope hidden there. Inside it lay her future ... and now, she would put the past behind her.

Coming to the ground level, she swept through the vestibule. She hoped to find a hansom cab to take her to her aunt's home, where her mother had taken refuge. She could not stay forever, but a few nights would give her enough time to get her affairs in order.

So determined was she on her mission, she did not see the hulking shadow of Niall until he was upon her. She shrank away from him, too on edge to allow the hand reaching toward her to land.

"What in blazes do you want?" she snapped, glaring at the man who only reminded her of the one she was truly angry at.

The one who had ripped the veil from over her eyes and exposed the world for what it truly was. The one who had given her a taste of something that had made her feel alive before discarding her like refuse.

"I would rather be well on my way to Dunnottar, believe me," he retorted. "But my Master gave me strict orders not to return until I had sat here long enough to ensure you did not come back out."

Wrinkling her brow, she glanced up to find the carriage that had carried her to London coming back toward them up the lane. It had likely been circling the block since she'd gone inside, while Niall waited in the shadows.

"Why?" she murmured, her voice cracking as tears flooded her eyes once again. "Why would he do that? Why do any of this?"

Niall's expression remained hard and emotionless as he shrugged one big shoulder. "I cannae pretend to know his mind. I only know he suspected ye might leave shortly after arrivin', and he was most adamant that I ensure ye make yer way safely to yer final destination."

Swiping at her eyes once more, she sighed. At least, she would not need to ask her mother to pay for the cab.

"Very well," she relented. "You may take me to my aunt's address in Mayfair. Once you've deposited me there, I trust I won't be seeing you again?"

"I most certainly hope not," he countered, leading the way to the carriage.

He offered her a hand up, but she ignored him, pulling herself into the vehicle on her own. It occurred to her that she'd left her sack behind in the flat—the one containing the clothing she'd worn to Dunnottar.

No matter. She had no reason to go back.

Glancing back up at Niall, who now sat across from her, she smirked.

"When you see your Master again, thank him for me," she said, making herself more comfortable on the carriage seat.

"Whatever for?" he muttered.

The carriage began to move, and for the first time all day, Daphne smiled ... a true smile.

"For setting me free."

EPILOGUE

3 months later ...

Adam stomped through the open doors of Dunnottar, his hands clenched into fists at his sides. A footman closed one of the large double doors behind him, shutting out the bitter cold. Despite the hours he'd just spent riding hell for leather across the wilds of Scotland, he was in a state of heightened agitation. His body remained on edge, every muscle stretched taut, every vein pulsating with blood heated to its boiling point.

Niall appeared from seemingly out of nowhere, his ever-present scowl marring what might have been considered a handsome face.

"Enjoy yer ride, Master?" he asked, though he sounded as if he could not care less.

Niall—who was as much Adam's friend as he was his butler—was angry with him. He had been ever since the day he had relented and allowed Daphne back into the palace after throwing her out on the front steps. When it came to the Fairchilds, the only person who wished for their blood more than Adam might be Niall.

The man did not understand the nuances of warfare. He did not understand that a true general did not dash across the battlefield and stab his enemy in the heart. He drew out the death of his nemesis, strategically cutting pieces of him away bit by bit ... until there was nothing left.

He had spent five years methodically destroying Bertram Fairchild, as well as his father and uncle. That had proved far more satisfying than a fleeting duel or bout of fisticuffs.

"You know very well I did not, so sod off," he snapped, storming past Niall and down the corridor.

He did not have it in him to endure Niall's censure, or Maeve's moping about. One of them was angry for letting Daphne stay while the other would not stop glaring at him because he'd let her leave.

Bugger them both.

He wondered what either of them might say if they knew that though he had sent her away, she was not truly gone. She haunted him daily, traces of her seeming to linger in every nook and cranny of Dunnottar. He saw her in the meadow where he'd first revealed Bertram's true nature to her, her bonny face wet with tears, the sun glinting off her hair. He heard her in the music room, the heavenly sound of her fingers against harp strings soothing him like no amount of spirits or fucking could. He smelled her scent in that room, too, heard her cries of surrender as he'd taken her down to the rug and torn through her maidenhead. He even saw her in his study, kneeling quietly at his feet with a book in her lap, eyes demurely lowered.

The chit had no knowledge of how she'd enflamed him, the simple act of dropping to her knees on the floor enough to fill his cock with blood to near bursting. He'd had her in every way he had imagined, but now that she was gone, he found himself imagining more.

"It is over, you bloody moron," he groused at himself as he stormed into his bedchamber and slammed the door. "She served her purpose."

That was certainly true enough. He'd gotten what he wanted from her, striking out at Bertram through her. What else was there?

Forcing his gaze away from his bed, he gritted his teeth, a primal growl tearing through his chest. She even haunted him here, her cries reverberating from the walls and ceilings, the memory of spanking her until her buttocks glowed red before impaling her tight arse disturbing his dreams.

Bringing her into his private sanctuary had been a mistake … he realized that now. But, what else was he to have done after she'd stumbled upon Serena, disobeying his direct order?

As he entered the washroom, he told himself he only missed having an available cunt around whenever the mood to fuck struck him. That he'd merely been obsessed with the novelty of bedding Bertram's little sister … defiling her in every conceivable way.

However, even that did not calm him, his body as restless as ever, his cock hard as stone … despite that fact that he'd frigged himself upon waking this morning. As well as right before he'd gone to sleep. And the night before that … and the night before that.

"Fucking hell," he muttered, pacing toward the washstand and gilded mirror in the corner where he stood to shave.

Niall often referred to him as a barbarian for not hiring a valet, but he'd always preferred dressing and grooming himself.

Bracing his hands upon the washstand, he bowed his head. He closed his eyes and attempted to tear his wayward thoughts away from Daphne. Yet, closing his eyes only worsened the effect, the red swirls moving about on his eyelids reminding him of her hair. Clenching one hand into a fist, he imagined wrapping that hair around his hand and yanking until she cried out … until her eyes watered and she whimpered.

God, he'd never seen anything more beautiful than the sight of her surrender, of the moment fear left her eyes and submission to his will settled in. He had been right about her all along, having seen it in her eyes the first time he'd laid eyes upon her.

Daphne craved danger, the thrill of a threat, the promise of destruction. She danced upon the precipice, taunting the darkness, beating her pristine white wings as if to flaunt herself, to goad the beast lurking in the depths.

Come and get me, her every movement seemed to say.

He had enjoyed every moment of stalking, and eventually, overcoming her.

Opening his eyes with a strangled sound of frustration, he spied a little scrap of silk lying beside the basin a chambermaid had filled with clean water for him.

Taking it up, he smoothed his fingers over it, lifting it to his nostrils. It still held her scent ... though its strength faded more and more with each passing day.

It was one of the ribbons she'd worn around her neck—he'd found it in the guest chamber she had once occupied. He grinned at the memory of throwing her up on the dining room table after tearing off her gown—her body stripped of everything except for this length of ribbon.

With a grunt, he tore open his breeches, unable to abide this torment any longer. He could no longer fight what felt like a force of nature, a gust of wind blowing him in a certain direction.

With the ribbon still in his hand, he fisted his cock, wrapping himself in silk and a rough, calloused palm. His head already seeped with moisture, he was so wound up, and he stroked himself with a brutal desperation born of a need she had created. He jerked his cock while imagining holding her down and drilling her like a madman, one hand wrapped around her throat. He recalled the way her eyes had widened the first time he had compressed the vital veins in her neck, slowing the flow of blood. She'd been afraid, but that had only made his lust surge, and he had tightened his fingers, wanting to test her mettle.

As expected, she had performed beautifully, closing her eyes and allowing the sensation to heighten her climax, sucking in a mouthful of air just as she spiraled into oblivion.

He doubled over from the force of his own completion, grasping a scrap of linen just in time to catch his seed. He pumped his hips, wringing himself dry despite knowing it would never be enough. By evening, he would be right back where he'd started, wanting a woman who no longer lay within his reach.

But ... she had never been completely out of reach. He held the entire Fairchild family in the palm of his hand. With one closed fist, he could smite them into dust. She would never be completely free of him.

Glancing down at the scrap of ribbon stained with his seed, he came to a decision. His body unwound, his muscles relaxing.

Peace washed over him, and he found balance once again, the sort of calculating calm that typically ruled him.

The answer was simple.

He felt this way because they had unfinished business. She was not completely out of his blood, but this was a problem easily remedied.

Adam made quick work of cleaning himself up before leaving the washroom, stalking into his chamber and retrieving a large trunk from beneath the bed. He threw a few items inside before having a sudden thought.

He found the bell cord to ring for Niall and went back to work.

By the time his friend and butler had arrived, the trunk had been half-filled with the things he would need for his journey.

"What's this, then?" Niall asked, brow furrowed as he took in Adam's erratic packing method.

"Prepare a carriage for travel, Niall," he barked. "I am leaving immediately."

"Why? Where are you going?"

Ignoring his first question, Adam chuckled, the excitement of the hunt to come making the hairs on the back of his neck stand up. This time, when he got his hands on his little dove, he was going to exorcise every debauched fantasy of her he'd ever had. She would not escape him until he was well and truly ready to let her go.

"London, Niall," he declared with a feral grin. "*We* are going to London."

BOOK 2: THE DOVE

A quest for vengeance...
Lord Adam Callahan, Earl of Hartmoor has spent the past five years destroying the Fairchild family as recompense for the ruination of his sister. Yet, it never seemed like enough ... until the family's only daughter appeared on his doorstep searching for answers. In her, he found the perfect tool for his final revenge. His plan had been simple —coerce Lady Daphne Fairchild into an illicit affair and ruin her.
An unexpected obsession...

After thirty days and nights in his bed, Adam sends Daphne back to London a fallen woman, the final blow that will see the Fairchild family scorned by society. However, he is hard-pressed to forget the beauty of her submission, or the brief moments of peace and balance she brought his tortured existence. Despite the bad blood between their families, he is determined to possess her, to stake his claim on her beyond the thirty nights she gave him. She will fight him at every turn … which will only make the chase, and her inevitable surrender, all the better.

Printed in Dunstable, United Kingdom